1985

Melville's Humor

Melville's Humor
A Critical Study

Jane Mushabac

Archon Books

1981

First published 1981 as an Archon Book,
an imprint of The Shoe String Press, Inc.,
Hamden, Connecticut 06514
Printed in the United States of America

Library of Congress Cataloging in Publication Data

Mushabac, Jane.
Melville's humor.

Bibliography: p.
Includes index.
1. Melville, Herman, 1819-1891—Humor, satire, etc.
I. Title.
PS2388.S2M8   813'.3   81-10981
ISBN 0-208-01910-3   AACR2

to
Arthur Morgenroth

Contents

ACKNOWLEDGMENTS ix

ABBREVIATIONS xi

I INTRODUCTION 1

II EXTRACTS AND ETYMOLOGIES 5

Rabelais, de Bergerac, Bayle, *Lazarillo,*
Jonson, Burton, Johnson, Sterne, De Quincey,
Lamb, Irving, the almanacs

III EMBARKATIONS 37

Typee, Mardi, and *White-Jacket;*
Omoo, Redburn, and "Old Zack"

IV WHALES AND CONFIDENCE 79

Moby-Dick, "Bartleby," *Israel Potter,*
The Confidence-Man; "Benito Cereno"

V AGATHA 148

Problem works: *Pierre* and "Billy Budd";
Afterword

NOTES 162

BIBLIOGRAPHY 181

INDEX 192

Acknowledgments

I am grateful and indebted to many individuals and institutions, in addition to the scholars acknowledged in the notes. I was very fortunate to have Irving Howe's incisive and challenging suggestions on this study from its inception. Taylor Stoehr's cogent criticism of the book provided the stimulus for its completion. Morris Dickstein, Alfred Kazin, Mary Frosch, Robert M. Greenberg, Henry Mallard, Toni Levi, and Judith Layzer read the manuscript and suggested improvements. Coleman Parsons, Helaine Newstead, Allen Mandelbaum, and Roberta Thornton provided encouragement and help. Joyce Morgenroth and Janet Chalmers went over several chapters with painstaking care and invariably asked the right questions. Jeanne Ferris, my editor at Archon, was thoughtful and instructive.

The American Association of University Women's award of a fellowship allowed me a year devoted to research and writing. The New York Public Library Manuscript, Archives, and Rare Book Divisions; the City University of New York Graduate Center Library; Queens College's Paul Klapper Library; and the Baruch College Library provided books and in each case a gracious, helpful staff.

Finally, I wish to thank Lois Mergentime and Martha Gold Hollins, who typed the manuscript; Hazel Weill for providing a quiet work space near home; George Blecher, Phyllis Kantar, Michael Greenberg, Beverly Lieberman, Thomas Engelhardt, and Catherine Mallard for memorable conversations and help in many forms; and, above all, my parents, Estelle Mushabac and Victor Mushabac, for their boundless generosity and humor—and my husband, to whom the book is dedicated.

J. M.

Abbreviations

The abbreviations used in the text to indicate page references for quotations from Melville's fiction, and the editions cited, are as follows:

B   "Bartleby," in *Piazza Tales,* ed. Egbert Oliver (New York: Hendricks House, 1948).

BB   "Billy Budd," in *Billy Budd,* ed. Harrison Hayford and Merton M. Sealts, Jr. (Chicago: University of Chicago Press, 1962).

BC   "Benito Cereno," in *Piazza Tales.*

E   "The Encantadas," in *Piazza Tales.*

IP   *Israel Potter* (New York: Warner, 1974).

M   *Mardi,* The Northwestern-Newberry Edition of the Writings of Herman Melville, ed. Harrison Hayford, Hershel Parker, and G. Thomas Tanselle (Evanston: Northwestern University Press and the Newberry Library, 1970), vol. 3.

MD   *Moby-Dick,* ed. Harrison Hayford and Hershel Parker (New York: Norton, 1967).

O   *Omoo,* Northwestern-Newberry (1968), vol. 2.

P   *Pierre,* Northwestern-Newberry (1971), vol. 7.

Poor Man's   "Poor Man's Pudding," in *Selected Writings of Herman Melville* (New York: Random, 1952).

R   *Redburn,* Northwestern-Newberry (1969), vol. 4.

T   *Typee,* Northwestern-Newberry (1968), vol. 1.

Tartarus   "The Tartarus of Maids," in *Selected Writings of Herman Melville.*

TCM   *The Confidence-Man,* ed. Hershel Parker (New York: Norton, 1971).

WJ   *White-Jacket,* Northwestern-Newberry (1970), vol. 5.

I
Introduction

Over the past sixty years a great deal has been written about Melville's work. Unfortunately, much of the criticism has made Melville seem ponderous and anguished.

Melville's novels are profound and stark, but to miss their humor is to miss their charm and brilliance. Melville's fiction is full of sexual and heretical teasing, full of hoax and parody and spiel. His fiction plays with us, flirts with us, deliberately astounds us with confusion and a sense of miracles. Humor is his signature.

Melville's humor suggests man's failings, achievements, giddy illusions of achievement. Melville uses archaicisms for deadpan—then sings magnificently and ludicrously about the universe and man's great progress. We need to recall that Melville wrote during a moment of great optimism, in the first half of the nineteenth century. His fiction is steeped in the excitement of the Reform Movement, the opening of the frontier, transcendental and evangelical positivisms and ecstasies.

In *White-Jacket,* for example, the men cheer for Jack Chase the way mobs roared in wild exultation at Andrew Jackson's inauguration. The men in *White-Jacket* also "rob from one another, and rob back again, till, in the matter of small things a community of goods seems almost established; and at last, as a whole, they become relatively honest, by nearly every man becoming the reverse" (*WJ* 39). So, a utopia of thievery, a community of isolatoes. In the late twentieth century such wild exuberance and deflation across the board are no longer common. Nonetheless, that is what humor is about—grand camaraderie, grand ideals, and grand gestures: stealing victory out of the jaws of defeat; stealing defeat out of the jaws of victory.

In different novels, Melville gives us different styles. Sometimes, as in *Moby-Dick* and *Israel Potter,* he is on the upswing, freewheeling, expansive. Sometimes, as in *The Confidence-Man,* he is tart, wry, quiet. Sometimes he deliberately puts the two styles back to back, as in "Bartleby." But humor was not something Melville "did" for the public. From the first, humor was his métier and vision; from the first his humor was erotic, expansive—and grim. His development consisted of a growing confidence in his art over the years of his fiction writing, 1844‒56. The achievement of each of his novels and stories depends upon how well in each one he rallies his humor.

Melville's was not the first humor built on giddy dreams for humanity and the universe. His models of prose humor gave him direction as well as forms, styles, and motifs. There were three main veins of that prose: the Renaissance extravaganzas of Rabelais, Cyrano de Bergerac, Bayle, and Burton; the romantic and amiable humor of Sterne, Lamb, and De Quincey; and the American humor of, for instance, Washington Irving, Davy Crockett, and one Squire Varmifuge Vampose who "deposeth" on the "sea-sarpent."

I suggest Melville found a tradition of prose humor which, beginning in the Renaissance with the opening of the New World frontier, celebrated a new man, a man of infinite potentials. Singing this new man's praises as well as continually undercutting his glory, these works gave Melville a tone. They supplied him with forms: the extravaganza, the *jeu,* the anatomy, the novel of sensibility, the English cock-and-bull story, the twister, the tall tale— and others.

The prose humorists gave Melville an approach to characterization, in which characters are flat and protean, unbalanced and balanced again by their humors and vast enterprises. We should note that it was in the Renaissance, with the new emphasis on man's mind and genius, that the word humor developed. Originally, the word referred to any of those four bodily fluids seen as the keys to a man's temperament. Then it referred to a predominance of one of the fluids, making a man act oddly. By the seventeenth century, as we see in a popular travel narrative of 1682, humor had taken on a new, broader meaning: the amusement one man found in watching another man's odd behavior—or the capacity to be thus amused.[1]

The prose humorists borrowed from one another as Melville borrowed from them all. It is the measure of Melville's achievement that he both encompassed and enlarged the tradition he found in the prose he read.

In his own time Melville won a good part of his reputation as a humorist.[2] The Melville revival beginning in 1921 sought to play down that view of him. While his humor has been regularly acknowledged, in most criticism it has been relegated in one way or another to the periphery of his achievement.[3] It is easy for this view to slide into another, unfortunately one with much currency, in which he is read as anguished and with very little humor at all. This view is partly derived from Hawthorne's notion of Melville as a man who suffered for being unable to decide whether or not to believe in God.[4]

It seems finally that part of the difficulty with the study of Melville has been a reluctance to talk about humor, because humor suggests the contagion of sentimentality. After all that has been said about the American classical novel being in part a rebellion against the popular female sentimental novel,[5] what if it turned out that Melville's work only departs from popular fiction in creating the *male* sentimental novel?

This concern suggests the importance of recognizing the prose humor aesthetic in which Melville wrote. Richard Chase's important 1957 discussion of melodrama and romance [6] provides a beginning for an understanding of that aesthetic. Melodrama and romance suggest the proper context; it is in that realm of excess and extravagance that humor has its place. Humor historically has been associated with the lyrical and sympathetic, with the ordinary thrown into the extraordinary and back again. Humor is prosaic, deliberately so; and the subjective quirky monologue—at once erotic and asexual—is one of its key forms.

Humor has a highly subtle relationship to sentimentality. It plays off it. It moves through it. It catches up the reader in his most wishful thinking. Affectionately and systematically, humor denies the reader all his fatuous best hopes until he has nothing left but the humor itself to hang onto.

In the years since the Melville revival, Melville's humor has been written about, but much remains to be said. This study is about Melville's humor as the core of his achievement, about a tradition of prose in which humor provides the depth and vision. Melville's tragic awareness led him not to classical austerities, but to frontier legerdemain, lyricism, heresies, and flirtations. His career was short and intensely focused. His humor releases the tension of man's predicament in an ideal, democratic society.

II
Extracts and Etymologies

In the years of his fiction writing, 1844–56, Melville read voraciously and in a method recommended by Robert Burton and Samuel Johnson, as well as by Melville himself: read what you wish when you wish.[1] This chapter suggests one of the directions Melville took in his reading in this period, particularly in 1848–50, the years which led up to *Moby-Dick* and later masterpieces. It is generally acknowledged that in his reading from 1858 on Melville was teaching himself to write poetry. In his early years, it appears, he was teaching himself to write prose and specifically prose humor.

The works briefly evoked in this chapter provided Melville with forms, styles, and sometimes even sentences, paragraphs, and chapters. Most significantly, they gave him an aesthetic.

Critics often speak of frontier humor. Frontier humor, however, was not, as is usually suggested, just a subliterary folk phenomenon of nineteenth-century America, to be drawn on by great American authors. Frontier humor began as a mode of European literature early in the sixteenth century, when the frontier was originally opened by the discovery of the New World.

Beginning in the Renaissance and triggered by the dramatic

explorations of that era, frontier humor—or prose humor as I shall call it—was a response to man's new sense of his potential in a world with a new frontier. Medieval and early Renaissance forms of prose—the scholastic discourse, the sermon, and the chronicle—presented God and the church as the ultimate and fixed arsenals of certainty and authority. Prose humor plays off this old function of prose, and all the careful reasoning and earnest straightforwardness that were characteristic of it. In prodigious monologues and other new forms, prose humor celebrates man instead of God. It mocks the notion of a carefully protected authority. It toys with an image of man as the all-powerful explorer of the universe.

We should note that this image refers to man, not man and woman. The prose humorists take the liberty of leaving God behind them; similarly they say as little as they wish about women. While sexuality plays a key role in the way these humorists enjoy shocking their readers, and while eroticism is always in the air as one of many vehicles of man's insatiable desire, women as characters play minor roles in most of these works, and for good reason. The prose humorists from the Renaissance on are toying specifically with a new male self-image. What has excited them is themselves: man the explorer and traveller; and man the writer of almanacs, dictionaries, and encyclopedias.

In short, the great prosperity and new freedoms of the Renaissance allowed men to travel. They travelled together or alone—but they travelled. Sometimes their excursions were exiles resulting from their thinking and writing as they pleased. But whatever the purpose of their travels, the freedom of the traveller's mind is central to the prose humorist's bias on experience, his sense of himself as a giant, his endless pleasure in questioning himself, his teasing his reader and himself in the process of coming to wisdom and consolation.

Logically, then, the three words *extravagance, vagabond,* and *vagary*—all with the root *vaga,* "to wander or travel"—are central to the works at hand. Prose humor goes back and forth from extravagance to down-and-out vagabondage to the wry glory of the vagary. Particular humorists emphasize one or another of these commentaries on man the traveller, but all the humorists deal in equal part with braggadocio and defeat. The narrative is often shaped around a grand pointless quest, the style built up from encyclopedic long-windedness in a prose which doubles back on itself, celebrating verbal energies as it undoes itself with measured illogic, folly, and ultimate wisdom.

Specific works which provided this context for Melville are, from sixteenth and seventeenth-century France, Spain, and England, Rabelais's *Gargantua and Pantagruel* (1532–62), Cyrano de Bergerac's *Voyage to the Moon* (1657), Bayle's *Historical and Critical Dictionary* (1697), *Lazarillo de Tormes* (1554), Jonson's *Every Man Out of His Humor* (1599), and Burton's *Anatomy of Melancholy* (1621); from eighteenth and nineteenth-century England, Johnson's *Rasselas* (1759), Sterne's *Tristram Shandy* (1760–67), De Quincey's *Confessions of an English Opium Eater* (1821), and Lamb's "Imperfect Sympathies" (1821); and from nineteenth-century America, Washington Irving's "The Art of Bookmaking" (1820), *The Farmer's Almanack* (1842), and *Jonathan Jaw-Stretcher's Yankee Story All-My-Nack* (1852).

"Debt! why that's the more for your credit, sir," says Jonson's Buffone in *Every Man Out of His Humor* (in a passage borrowed from Rabelais).[2] Melville owed debts to—borrowed from—the works mentioned in central and peripheral ways, openly, playfully, teasingly. In fact, a wry borrowing played an important role in this aesthetic.

This chapter focuses on what the works mentioned offered Melville. Chapters 3, 4, and 5 discuss Melville's use of these works and their aesthetic in his development as a fiction writer.

In *The Lives, Heroic Deeds and Sayings of Gargantua and His Son Pantagruel* (1532–62) Rabelais projects an image of giddy desire. His book is a tall tale, an extravaganza, a prototype of frontier humor. Picture the young Gargantua, complete with codpiece:

> Being of this age, his father ordained to have clothes made to him in his owne livery, which was white and blew. To work then went the Tailors, and with great expedition were those clothes made, cut and sewed. . . .
> For his breeches were taken up eleven hundred and

five ells and a third of white broad cloth; they were cut in forme of pillars, chamfered, channel'd and pinked behinde. . . .

For his Codpeece was used sixteen ells and a quarter of the same cloth, and it was fashioned on the top like unto a Triumphant Arch, most gallantly fastened with two enamell'd Clasps, in each of which was set a great Emerauld as big as an Orange; for, as sayes Orpheus, *lib. de lapidibus,* and Plinius, *libr. ultimo,* it hath an erective vertue and comfortative of the natural member. . . .

And like to that Horn of Abundance, it was still gallant, succulent, droppie, sappie, pithie, lively, alwayes flourishing, always fructifying, full of juice, full of flower, full of fruit, and all manner of delight. I avow God, it would have done one good to have seen him, but I will tell you more of him in the book which I have made of the dignity of Codpieces. One thing I will tell you, that, as it was both long and large, so was it well furnished and victualled within, nothing like unto the hypocritical Codpieces of some fond Wooers and Wench courters, which are stuffed only with wind, to the great prejudice of the female sexe. . . .

For his Gown were employed nine thousand six hundred ells, wanting two thirds, of blew velvet, as before, all so diagonally purled, that by true perspective issued thence an unnamed colour, like that you see in the necks of Turtle-doves or Turkie-cocks, which wonderfully rejoyceth the eyes of the beholders. For his Bonnet or Cap were taken up three hundred two ells, and a quarter of white velvet. . . . For his plume, he wore a faire great blew feather, plucked from an Onocrotal of the Countrey of Hircania the Wilde. . . . [3]

In his chapter on the genealogy of Gargantua, we meet Alcofrybas, Rabelais's narrator, who inconspicuously asserts, "I cannot think but I am come of the race of some rich King or Prince in former times, for never yet saw you any man that had a greater desire to be a King, and to be rich, than I have."[4] The triumph central to this work, and one much simpler and far more direct than the old world's *veni vidi vici,* is *I desire, I am.* Gargantua, we recall, is the "Great Throat" born screaming for drink. As a child he dazzles his father with scatology; as a young man he builds the wonderful Abbey of Thélème. As an adult he fathers Pantagruel, the "All Thirsty," who in his birth blasts his mother to death and in his infancy, already outdoing Hercules, tears his iron-chained cradle out of its support. His invention of Pantagruelion, the herb unquenchable by fire, leaves the gods in a trembling fit. Prometheus only stole fire; Pantagruel has stolen the unquenchable. No wonder Pantagruel falls in love at first sight with the rogue Panurge, a giant in nothing but unquenchable desire which when thwarted turns him to brilliantly obscene, vengeful practical jokes.

Panurge attacks woman as the hardiest embodiment of nature's resistance to his desire. But revenge doesn't help him. He decides to marry if only he can, as he tries in the last three books, clear up the threat of cuckoldry. Of course he cannot. Nature's intransigence is nature's practical joke on the great practical joker, as is the imponderable but exuberant oracle "Trinc!"—the book's last word.

Rabelais writes about giants in a prose gargantuan with exuberance. As Panurge—trying to disprove Pantagruel's friendly premonition that a married Panurge will be cuckolded, beaten, and robbed—consults one authority after another, Rabelais indulges in a triumphant ventriloquism of all the pompous male mouthpieces of "wisdom": lawyer, poet, philosopher, physician, even wise fool and classic writer. But Rabelais's great rifling through experience is always punctuated by the same rap, like the monosyllabic "Trinc." Typically the narrator turns on his readers; it's their fault, he says, for wasting their time on such flimflam stories, not the author's for writing them.

Gargantua, Pantagruel, and Panurge embody a new freedom. As Gargantua sloughs off medieval scholasticism to embrace the new learning, as Pantagruel and Panurge voyage round a fantastic world, Rabelais himself celebrates the audacity of man pushing off and wrenching free of the old world and venturing out into the new. Typically, however, while he hacks back at the old world he hacks ahead at the new, which he knows will prove as preposterous as the old. Nonetheless, as Erich Auerbach suggests, in Rabelais "is developed an entirely different, entirely new and . . . extremely current theme—the theme of the discovery of the new world."[5] Rabelais's new world was a remaking of the globe so profound as to jumble rich and poor, aristocrat and folk. The excitement of Rabelais's prose lies as much in his deliberate use of the vernacular as in his turning inside out the popular form of the sermon.[6] Rabelais's choice of prose as his medium freed him from both the classical strictures on drama and poetry, and the burgeoning hierarchy of genres. Prose gave him all the liberties of the sermon, with its heritage of immediacy, its energetic entertaining oral quality, and its freewheeling shifting characterizations. In prose Rabelais could write as he would, with audacity changing the sermon's one requirement—preaching scripture—to teaching a new scripture, man's new excitement about his potential. Rabelais's humor voyages beyond to a new frontier where, if the image of man as a new world giant is a fantasy, it is one that "wonderfully rejoyceth the eyes of the beholder."

Melville read *Gargantua and Pantagruel* in January and February 1848.[7]

Written about a hundred years after Rabelais's work, Cyrano de Bergerac's *Voyage to the Moon* opens with some friends walking and talking on a moonlit night. "And for my part, gentlemen, said I, that I may put in for a share, and guess with the rest; not to amuse myself with those curious notions wherewith you tickle . . . Time; I believe that the Moon is a World like ours to which this of ours serves likewise for a Moon."[8] His friends responded with a great shout of mirth.

Within its first two pages, Cyrano's book carries the reader in a giddy progress from pedestrian cobblestones into space. The frame on which Cyrano builds his idea—at first a mere jest of one-upmanship—to an extravagance, is a burlesque of religious inspiration. To convince himself he provides a miracle of the open book, to convince his friends he quotes scientific scripture, and to conclude he allows himself God's shining benediction. Cyrano uses the paraphernalia of religion, however, not merely to burlesque it, but to suggest a parallel religion. Fully aware of the extravagance of his conceit, he worships the mind, the will, the imagination of man. Cyrano was a libertine who knew better than to publish his work during his lifetime. Cyrano's book is a by-product of the new explorers and new astronomers. It is certainly flimsy as a work of art, particularly compared to Rabelais's; and the new ideas, both philosophical and scientific, as they are presented, often do not even make sense. For Cyrano's purpose, however, they need not, just as the satire need not come home neatly and sharply to any particular targets. Swift would borrow from Cyrano to write his satire—just as Molière did to write his comedies. Cyrano's work as it stood, however, was neither satire nor comedy, but jeu d'esprit.

In a later section of the book, burlesquing Genesis, Cyrano tells a silly story of how, falling to the moon, he found and accidentally ate some apples. Pantagruel's ancestors had feasted on spectacular apples; Cyrano gets his story, as he gets much else, from Rabelais. As always, however, Cyrano's impish burlesque calls less attention to what it is dismissing than to what it is embracing, an image of man feasting on knowledge and getting giddy on his new sense of power. On his visit to the sun with its people of an all-powerful imagination, Cyrano expostulates, "But, cried I, is it not a Ravery to think that Monsieur Des Cartes, whom you have not seen since you left the World of the Earth, is now but Three Leagues off because you have imagined it to be so? I had just uttered the last syllable when we saw Des Cartes come."[9]

Descartes has come. The opening of the frontier that produced the humor of extravagance could also boil down and turn around the playful *I desire, I am* to the serious philosophical *I think, therefore I am.* Cyrano, like Rabelais and Melville, was no Columbus, no Kepler, no Descartes. But, like Rabelais, in a work of prose humor, he could make good game of man spiritedly eating his apple of knowledge and could send man off on extravagant voyages with dispatch and excitement.

Melville read Cyrano's book in the summer of 1849.

Pierre Bayle's *Historical and Critical Dictionary* of 1697 comprises all human history and gives us Bayle's personal running commentary on it. Bayle perpetually interprets and evaluates events, sorting through the opinions of all previous historians and commentators and providing his own modest reading of the facts. In his mammoth work, Bayle stays at home but by the all-encompassing vastness of his enterprise actually circumnavigates the world in a solo voyage that staggers the imagination—and was clearly meant to.

As Bayle scholar Richard Popkin writes, beginning with our century, an encyclopedia could "no longer amuse or cause philosophical and moral reflection; it had to inform and only inform." Yet reading Bayle now we "see how the world looked to an amazing man at the end of the seventeenth century, before everyone became 'enlightened.'"[10] Ultimately the light that Bayle reveals is that there is not very much light to reveal. Rewriting Maimonides' *Guide to the Perplexed,* [11] Bayle disentagled perplexities only to reknot them again. Bayle's five folio-volume dictionary tells us not just that we are full of vulgar errors, but that all reason is a vulgar error. It is in short a seventeenth-century shaggy dog story, dedicated to acatalepsy, the incomprehensibility of all things.

One of Bayle's articles is on King Abimelech. In passing, Bayle mentions how the king discovered that Isaac and Rebecca were not, after all, sister and brother; Abimelech accidentally saw them through their window "at a certain sport." Bayle glosses "a certain sport," debating at length and with an infinite show of scholarly patience precisely what it was that the octogenarian patriarch and his wife were doing when they were inadvertently spied upon. "And indeed," Bayle notes, "it is too rigorous to expect, that a Patriarch or a Bishop, if he is married should not recreate himself a little with his wife, without closing all his Window-Shutters. For we must have this good opinion of their Prudence, that if Nature inclines the greatest Men to a little indulgence, they will walk so cautiously upon this Slippery Road, as to take care that no Observation shall be made of them. . . ."[12]

In the Abimelech passage, Bayle brings his scrutiny to bear on one more exegetical question, typically sorting his way through the morass of critical ignorance. His commentary, however, does not just explicate or clarify. It teasingly elevates the subject and allows foolish commentators to have their say in such a way that in the commentary the loving couple is temporarily moved from their bedroom into the street itself. Finally it creates an image of the patriarch as a man closing, or not closing, his shutters, as a man upon "a slippery road." Indeed the essence of all Bayle's commentary seems to be precisely that: life is a slippery road. Bayle repeatedly refers to public sex because it undermines man's view of his own piety and decorum. There is an iconoclasm in public sex; so is there in public thinking aloud.

For all his quiet ridicule, however, Bayle never disparages man's love of his mind, man's love of thinking. His entire book seems actually to be his sport, a certain sport. In his seriousness he is the man he has described in his portrait of Arriaga, a subtle critical genius, the last of the great scholastics. In his humor he is more like the two characters he describes in his portrait of Hipparchia: Hipparchia herself—absurdly, preposterously, roguishly in love with the skeptic Crates—as well as the man who assaults her during an argument at dinner.

Bayle's sport is writing as he pleases, juxtaposing whatever incongruities he wishes, improvising, moving back and forth from the most scholarly erudition to the most colloquial, even nonverbal assaults, poking fun at the extremes of allegorical and literal-minded thinking. In defense of his obscenity, he typically piles up official-sounding arguments. He is a historian, he says, and it is his job to tell all. Then, not to tell such stories would be to omit what everyone knows and talks about anyway. And finally, with regard to his writing obscenities in the vernacular: it is unfair that monks should have the pleasure of reading such matters in Latin, and the rest of the world be shut out. If the monks insist on reading, for instance, a tract on the sounds women should or should not make, Bayle roguishly opens the book to all the world, and cannot resist adding his own advice, that women should not be grave and silent during conception unless they want their offspring to be dolts.

Millicent Bell would have us find in Bayle the same anguish that Hawthorne pointed to in Melville. She writes of Bayle, "A French Protestant, educated in Geneva, his is the essential Calvinist dilemma which Melville later re-encountered. The anguish is intense behind the words as he reviews the evil-doings of man from Eden on."[13] Richard Popkin seems to be addressing himself to these very remarks when he writes that "Bayle suffered, apparently, from no *Angst,* no fear and trembling. Unlike his nineteenth-century admirer, Herman Melville, Bayle was not desperately seeking God or trying to pierce the heart of Moby Dick."[14] If we may correct Popkin on Melville (as Popkin was perhaps correcting Bell on Bayle), neither was Melville "desperately" seeking God. Indeed, what Melville very likely admired in Bayle was not the anguish of a questioning Calvinism, but a certain orthodoxy transcended, a certain sport, a certain humor.

Melville did share a religious orientation with the French sixteenth and seventeenth-century writers discussed here, as well as with one other, Montaigne, but we should note exactly what that orientation was. In all four authors, the reader finds evidence of Christian as well as of Judaic concepts, of faith as well as heresy, of flirtations with Manicheanism as well as with Pyrrhonism. Critics struggling to define these writers' religious positions must eventually throw up their hands. These authors were not writing tracts; they only sought to explore their own minds, and to do so, they took every liberty they desired. Humor thrives on a certain blend of freedom and oppression, which sixteenth and seventeenth-century France provided in good measure. Melville was not the first to feel the exhilaration of writing a "wicked" book[15] of free thinking; nor the first to recognize the humor in that illusion of freedom. One finally cannot put a religious label on these men, because their labels are nothing less than the whole works themselves. Besides, these writers were not really talking about God; they were talking about man.

Melville's first contact with Bayle was in his schooldays in 1830. In April 1849, he wrote to his friend Evert Duyckinck, "I bought a set of Bayle's Dictionary the other day, & ... intend to lay the great old folios side by side & go to sleep on them thro' the summer."[16]

Lazarillo de Tormes's first master was a brutal blind con artist. His second gave him nothing to eat but onions, and nearly bludgeoned him to death for trying to steal a few pieces of bread from his master's hoard. Recovering from his wounds, the boy set out begging and thanked God he found a new master, a squire who was sure to treat him well, for the squire was not only well-dressed but thoroughly devout.

Written in 1554 in Spain, *Lazarillo* takes us from the humor of extravagance to the humor of the vagabond. Instead of the excitement of a wandering beyond, we have the oppression of being bound to wander. The picaresque novel in Spain came into being with the great prosperity and resulting growth and flurry of travelling both within and without the country during the early Renaissance. As *Lazarillo* suggests, however, the exhilaration of being on one's own and finding one's fortune is repeatedly, incessantly knocked down by the hardship and even brutality that reality brings to Lazarillo and other picaros. Lazarillo is a boy—a little Lazarus—who has been thrown out on the world to survive. The vagabond becomes a rogue in the hardest sense of the word. He learns early that as he will be the victim of practical jokes, he himself must practice them on others, even if in one of his early acts of this sort, the practical joke entails killing the blind man, his first master.

The chapter on the third master, in keeping with the rest of the book, sends the reader back and forth from expectation to recognition. God gives Lazarillo a wonderful master who turns out to be worse off than the boy is; Lazarillo gets ecstatic about his good fortune, becomes the happiest person in the world until it becomes clear that, after all, the cupboard was bare, and the new master, like the new world, is not much better than the old. The wonderful interplay—humorous and sharply pathetic—between master and boy, acted out punctiliously by both as they strive to outmatch each other with displays of showmanship, is an explicit dig at the showmanship of God who puts on a wonderful display but whose house is empty. Indeed it is not surprising that this book was placed on the Index. It is saturated with ironic gratitude to God. Here again, however, the "heresy" is not the point. In wrenching free of delusions, the author is only determined to see things as they are.

Nor is the point ridicule of one group above another. That the author has sympathy for both is especially clear in the encounter between the impoverished squire and the boy, but the author's sympathy in no way obstructs his image of the emptiness of living in this world. We should not be surprised that Lazarillo, in an ironic commentary on the heavenly reward given Lazarus in the New Testament, is rewarded ultimately with a civil service job—as town crier—and a wife for whom he pimps to the local archbishop. Lazarillo's ruthlessness and moral vacuity have been growing all through the novel. The book leaves idealism in shreds, but it does so with a sympathy for man denuded of even those shreds of idealism. Lazarillo's fastidious squire is not merely the target of a satiric attack, nor the emblem for a moral lesson, but one more fool trying to shield himself from a brutally empty world.

The humor of Lazarillo, the vagabond, projects the predicament of man being a vagabond on his own earth, constrained to wander, dreaming of food and enchantments, waking up to hunger and brutality, following in the pattern of God's hard moral neutrality.

Melville read *Lazarillo* in 1850. He also read other picaresque novels, for instance those of Smollett. Yet Smollett's source was *Lazarillo,* and ultimately it was the prototypical, concise, unadorned *Lazarillo* which was to have the most impact on Melville's fiction.

Every Man Out of His Humor is a weak play. It suffers from being a sequel rehashing the material of Jonson's grand success, *Every Man in His Humor.* It seems Jonson was so infatuated with his idea of a cast of humors characters (characters dominated by their particular humors) that in 1599 in the second play he let it stand alone, plot or fable becoming an unnecessary frivolity, the whole action consisting of the various characters speaking and acting out their foibles as described in the "Dramatis Personae." *Every Man Out of His Humor* is a parade of characters who mechanically scorn, razz, and gull each other by turns and who, in the end, all capitulate to sanity, relinquishing their humors in a predictable series of coming-to-their senses.

Indeed what Jonson adds here to his famous contribution of

the comedy of humors is his definition of humor not merely as an imbalance of personality, but as the affectation of such an imbalance. For this play Jonson took the unconventional tack, not only of publishing his script, but of prefacing it with a page of prose descriptions of the characters. The descriptions spell out the way the characters are not just passively foolish, but actively and thoroughly dedicated to their humors. They consecrate themselves to singularity, make a religion, a profession, an apoplexy of their foibles. Like Asper, the vagabond of a free rough spirit and the most important character of the play, they are as vigorous in criticizing others as they are in being fools themselves. Indeed the play as a parade does not just set up a cast of characters before an audience. It sets up a cast of characters before a chorus before an audience, when the characters' main occupation is watching and commenting upon the parade they make of themselves. They are all shifting critics and butts. In the end, by the way, even Asper—the character Jonson made to represent himself—gives up his critical humor and relaxes into amiable companionship with the audience.

In *Volpone,* also an apparent favorite of Melville's,[17] Jonson combines the ideas of *Every Man Out of His Humor* with a strong fable. Volpone not only has an overruling passion but a disguise which goes out of control with the help of that guiding genius, Mosca, whom Volpone would "embrace" and love as his own "Venus." And to Jonson even a Sir Politic Wouldbe is interesting; his disease is making himself, as Sogliardo says of Shift, a tall man. In Sir Wouldbe's diary, with its miniscule notes on beans and toothpicks and urination, we find the man preposterously busy, as many of Melville's narrators will be: "Sir, I do slip/ no action of my life, but thus I quote it."[18]

Although I am speaking here of Jonson's plays, not prose, particularly in the undramatic male-dominated *Every Man Out of His Humor,* we see a very proselike portrait of man in the Renaissance world of new aspirations and horizons. Jonson was a point of departure for amiable humor which fastened on the imbalance of the humor or foible and (turning Jonson's attitude inside out) glorified it. Like the author of *Lazarillo de Tormes,* Jonson basically ridiculed man for his desire to be *tall.* His image of the universe, however, was considerably more English—more hospitable and orderly—than that of the Spanish picaresque novel. As Jonson was an admirer of Rabelais,[19] Melville was of Jonson. Melville purchased a 1692 edition of *The Works of Ben Jonson* in November 1849.

In "Democritus Junior to the Reader," the preface of *The Anatomy of Melancholy* (1621), Robert Burton makes a "brief survey" to show us that "all the world is mad." After seventy pages of proving his point in as many areas as one in any state of mind could think of, he begins "briefly" to conclude, noting, for instance, that

to insist in all particulars were an Herculean task, to reckon up mad labours, mad books, endeavours, carriages, gross ignorance, ridiculous actions, absurd gestures; as Tully terms them, madness of villages [villas]; stupend structures, as those Egyptian pyramids, Labyrinths & Sphinxes, which a company of crowned asses, in the ostentation of riches, vainly built, when neither the Architect nor King that made them, or to what use and purpose, are yet known. . . . Shall I say Jupiter himself, Apollo, Mars, &c., doted; and monster-conquering Hercules, that subdued the world, & helped others, could not relieve himself in this, but mad he was at last. And where shall a man walk, converse with whom, in what Province, City, and not meet with [Jonson's] Signior Deliro, or Hercules Furens, Maenades, & Corybantes? Their speeches say no less. They were men sprung from mushrooms, or else they fetched their pedigree from those that were struck by Samson with the jawbone of an ass . . . as if they had all heard that enchanted horn of Astolpho, that English Duke in Ariosto, which never sounded but all his auditors were mad, and for fear ready to make away themselves; or landed in the mad haven in the Euxine sea of *Daphne Insana,* which had a secret quality to dementate; they are a company of giddy-heads, afternoon men, it is midsummer moon still, and the Dog-days last all the year long: they are all mad.[20]

The Anatomy of Melancholy is another of the Renaissance extravaganzas. Oxford-educated clergyman and scholar Robert Burton frequently mentions Hercules. Writing the Anatomy is first of all a Herculean task, the more so because it was the task of an era focusing on the disease of the era—spleen. Man's triumph, however, is once again a giddy, crazy business. Burton surveys all knowledge to prove that knowledge is futile. His subject, however, is specifically madness. Burton invents a persona—Democritus, Jr.—but he creates no dominant characters. Nor does he systematically portray biographical subjects. He begins directly with mad melancholy from which he, like Hercules, needs a distraction. Bayle's dispassionate sport here becomes a life-saving diversion. Burton's work finally is a humorous, paradoxical, encyclopedic consolatio. The paradox is that the illusion of triumph is both the cause and the cure of his madness.

In the quoted section, Burton adopts first one method then another to sum up his babbling survey. At first claiming ingenuously that all men are mad, he continues, as if to prove the rule by its exceptions, to make a wryly ironic list of nine exceptions, from Mr. Nobody to the Rosicrucians, in his descriptions juxtaposing the splendid and the banal, the erudite and the slang. Finally he quietly traps us in his wry illogic. He objects to calling Stoics sane, on the simple ground that those who have no perturbations must be bored. In other words you are mad if you do and mad if you do not have perturbations. Or perhaps anyone foolish enough to allow himself to be bored by this life must be mad?

Democritus, Jr. is many things but he is certainly never bored. The original Democritus, we recall, was the ancient world's radical scientist, the patriarch of those men Burton calls the "Copernical Giants" who have set the earth aspin and established between atomical motion and planetary motion the essential dizziness of man's state. The essence of his boldness, as Burton suggests, was in being free enough to apprehend his own unsteady situation, and—unlike Heraclitus, who wept for man—to laugh. Burton's persona, Democritus, Jr., who on the first page of his long preface is already by turns gentle, indulgent, and peremptory, who sings, "I am a free man born," makes the point of his book that all men, including himself, are fools, and that fools are all slaves. At the same time, however, for instance in his "Digression of Air," a spectacular magic carpet excursion to all the wonders of this world and universe, he gives us a preposterous, wish-fulfilling, self-undercutting fantasy of man lording it in the universe.

Where in Rabelais or Bayle we had an exhilaration offset by stinging ridicule, often heretical, sexual, or scatological, the Englishman Burton keeps his ridicule mellow, emphasizing with great sympathy the vagary—man's madness. Burton himself seems aware of the shift, for as Rabelais's characters love wine, Burton has his Democritus, Jr., good sober Englishman that he is, love water.[21] Indeed, Burton is the patriarch of English amiable humor.[22]

Melville's first allusion to Burton was in 1839 in "Fragments from a Writing-Desk."[23] In April 1847, Melville bought a volume of extracts from Burton's *Anatomy of Melancholy*. (It turned out that the secondhand copy he happened to purchase had belonged to his father twenty-five years before.) In February 1848, Melville purchased the complete *Anatomy*.

Johnson's Rasselas is not just a free man born. He is a prince, the embodiment of man's power to fulfill his wishes, young enough to have all of life before him, wealthy enough to satisfy his every wish. Furthermore he is a prince in a land of desire fulfilled, perhaps an old quintessential paradise or a perfected new world. It does not matter which; the fact is the place is surrounded by mountains, the prince is a prisoner there, and desire will not allow him to rest. "The mind, hurried by her own ardour to distant views,"[24] always sets man voyaging after impossibilities.

In a typical passage in chapter 4, Rasselas berates himself for being so sluggish in leaving the Happy Valley. Having squandered twenty months, he then passed "four months in resolving to lose no more time in idle resolves."[25] Awakened to this new loss, he spent time regretting his regret. Finally he set off. In this characteristic

Johnsonian moment, Rasselas's reticence is in a tug-of-war with his restlessness. But desire always makes an idiot of man. It sets him clamoring, with fine rhetorical flourishes, for both indolent snug security and the freedom of the road. Imlac's desire makes that of Rasselas seem piddling. Imlac's discourse begins by tracing his early observations, his ensuing resolution to be a poet, his growing hunger for experience, and his eventual voraciousness for travel, vision, and fame. His discourse builds slowly and imperceptibly until he outlines at overwhelming length the tasks and abilities required of a poet. He goes on and on, working himself up, laying one law upon another, one prescription upon another, until he sees himself as a god, an immortal presiding over futurity, and until Rasselas cuts off what Johnson calls this "enthusiastic fit"—"Enough! Thou hast convinced me, that no human being can ever be a poet. Proceed with thy narration."[26]

Neither Rasselas nor Imlac, however, attains his desire. In the Happy Valley, Rasselas meets a foolish man who wants to soar on mechanical wings. In his voyage round the world, Rasselas also meets the astronomer who has looked so long at the stars that he believes he controls them, and in a frenzy is concerned for the welfare of the world upon his decease.

Johnson does not attack man for his desire, however, for wanting even if he is born in paradise itself to voyage out of it, to consult one oracle after another, until the great new frontier that man has discovered yields to the inevitable recognition that there *is* no frontier. Johnson writes with equanimity. His favorite book was Burton's *Anatomy*.[27] Like Burton's, Johnson's humor is a quiet blend of ridicule and sympathy. But Johnson uses a considerably shorter form, the philosophical tale.

We have no date for Melville's reading of *Rasselas,* but the work was popular and highly respected in nineteenth-century America and Melville knew it early—most likely before he himself set out on his travels.[28]

In Diogenes Laërtius's *The Lives and Opinions of Eminent Philosophers,* each article runs a few pages, briefly summarizing the main biographical events and teachings of each of the great philosophers.

Rabelais toys with the genre of this ancient classic in his book, *The Lives, Heroic Deeds and Sayings of Gargantua and His Son Pantagruel*. So does Bayle in his dictionary, which provides so much commentary that it approaches being a monumental biographical portrait of the opinions of the eminent Bayle himself, more than of his subjects. Laurence Sterne's *Life and Opinions of Tristram Shandy, Gentleman* (1760-67), however, takes the biographical game as far as it can go; it is Tristram's six-hundred-page monologue of a biographical dictionary article on himself. No wonder Tristram tells the reader early in the book, "Don't hurry yourself."[29]

The egotism projects what Sterne wants us to feel: the absurdity of mind. In the first chapter, Tristram's zealously rhetorical paragraph wishing his parents had paid attention to his conception is cut short by a blunt ridiculous question, as was his conception. Here we have the pattern of the whole book which belittles rhapsodic syllogizing with interruption, forestallings, general ineffectiveness, and a lot of *"Lillabullero."* Indeed, Walter Shandy is an eighteenth-century embodiment of the Renaissance giant of mind utterly gone to seed. Walter is an amiable Gargantua of erudition and the new sciences, the most learned with regard to antiquity yet the most forward with regard to scientific innovation. He is as addicted to reading other encyclopedias, such as the exhaustive Slawkenbergian one, as he is to writing his own, the *Tristrapedia*. The latter is Gargantua's famous humanist letter to his son stretched to idiotic proportions. It has been so long in the writing that the longer he works on it the more his son has already grown up and the more useless it is. It is typical too that Shandy had wanted this son named after Trismegistus, that revered archetype of the Renaissance man—"the greatest king—the greatest lawgiver—the greatest philosopher—and the greatest priest."[30] All Walter's erudition and ambition go for naught, however. The boy is named Tristram, the sad one—the pathetic.

One of Tristram's digressions speaks directly to the central issue of learning and the mind:

> Thus,—thus my fellow labourers and associates in this great harvest of our learning, now ripening before our eyes; thus it is, by slow steps of casual increase, that

our knowledge, physical, metaphysical, physiological, polemical, nautical, mathematical, enigmatical, technical, biographical, romantical, chemical, and obstetrical, with fifty other branches of it, (most of 'em ending as these do, in *ical*) have, for these two last centuries and more, gradually been creeping upwards towards that Ἀχμὴ, of their perfections, from which, if we may form a conjecture from the advances of these last seven years, we cannot possibly be far off.

When that happens, it is to be hoped, it will put an end to all kind of writings whatsoever;—the want of all kind of writing will put an end to all kind of reading;—and that in time, *As war begets poverty, poverty peace,*—must in course put an end to all kind of knowledge,—and then—we shall have all to begin over again; or, in other words, be exactly where we started.

—Happy! thrice happy Times![31]

So much for the Renaissance dream of gigantic man. Like Rasselas, Tristram dreams of returning to the Happy Valley of our innocence. In Sterne, however, the real voyage to the outlands and back, the literal extravagance, is no longer physically possible. As the great untrismegistused Tristram is no longer capable of great exploits, so the book pushes on to the only extravagance possible for these characters—the vagary, an impotent wandering of the mind. Walter's hobbyhorse, fat as it is, takes him nowhere, as Yorick's lean Rocinante takes him to the grave. And the "Northwest Passage" which Walter discovers is not a great water but the auxiliary verb.

But poking fun at mind and body, Sterne puts another part of man upon the pedestal, the heart; and his doing so was what set all his humor—and all his popularity—in motion. Sterne was not the first to show the futility of knowledge or reason, but he may well have been the first to do so to demonstrate man's infinite lovability. If Tristram has lost, among other things, his great Slawkenbergian sexual credentials, he is above all a giant of heart. With him Sterne has begun and settled the famous division of head and heart.

Tristram, like the other characters of the book, is all impulse, self-gratification, and love to others—all sensibility, the more so because of Sterne's awareness of a great coldness blowing through the universe, blowing even through man's sensibility itself.

It is well known that two of Sterne's most important models were Rabelais and Burton. As an English clergyman, Sterne transformed Rabelais in much the same way as Burton had. Sterne mellowed Rabelais's humor. His work, like Burton's, is a ranting *consolatio*. In Sterne's book, however, Burton's only half-realized persona, Democritus, has become the full-blown amiable Tristram. Between the two, meanwhile, they have, despite all the talk of unmanning, fathered a prestigious enough line of pseudonymic humorists and monologuists—Geoffrey Crayon, Elia, Josh Billings, Artemus Ward, and many others—to say nothing of Redburn, White-Jacket, and, most of all, Ishmael.

Melville began reading *Tristram Shandy* in December 1849.

At one point in his *Confessions of an English Opium Eater* (1821), De Quincey peremptorily sets the stage with a "cottage, standing in a valley." He will shortly introduce a painter to complete the sketch, and a great number of books to place in the cottage; but first, the season is winter and it must be "winter in its sternest shape."[32] Indeed he puts up a petition for

> as much snow, hail, frost or storms of one kind or other as the skies can possibly afford us. Surely everybody is aware of the divine pleasures which attend a winter fireside . . . whilst the wind and rain are raging audibly without . . . I am not *"particular,"* as people say, whether it be snow or black frost or wind . . . but something of the sort I must have; and if I have not, I think myself in a manner ill-used; for why am I called on to pay so heavily for winter, in coals and candles and various privations . . . if I am not to have the article good of its kind? . . . Indeed so great an epicure am I in this matter that I cannot relish a winter night fully if it be much past St. Thomas' day and have degenerated into disgusting tendencies to vernal appearances; from the latter weeks of October to

Christmas Eve, therefore, is the period during which happiness is in season, which in my judgment, enters the room with the tea tray, for tea . . . will always be the favorite beverage of the intellectual; and, for my part, I would have joined Dr. Johnson in a *bellum internecinum* against Jonas Hanway or any other impious person who should presume to disparage it. But here, to save myself the trouble of too much verbal description, I will introduce a painter and give him directions. . . . Paint me, then, a room seventeen feet by twelve, and not more than seven and a half feet high. . . . [This is to be his drawing room-library] for it happens that books are the only articles of property in which I am richer than my neighbors. Of these I have about five thousand, collected gradually since my eighteenth year. Therefore, painter, put as many as you can into this room. Make it populous with books, and furthermore, paint me a good fire, and furniture. . . .[33]

No wonder De Quincey is having a rough time. Sixty years before, Sterne as Tristram had soothingly prophesied a great cataclysm of books—men would write and read no more—and here is De Quincey trying to cram his five thousand books into a modest cottage. Sterne's cataclysm could not be more necessary than it has become for De Quincey, because the great succulent apples of knowledge of the Renaissance, of Rabelais, Cyrano, and Burton, are in De Quincey's time beginning to rot and ferment. The full title of De Quincey's book of 1821 is *Confessions of an English Opium Eater, Being an Extract from the Life of a Scholar,* and early in it he explains, "I give this account at the risk of being pronounced a crazy enthusiast or visionary, but I regard that little. I must desire my reader to bear in mind that I was a hard student, and at severe studies for all the rest of my time; and certainly I had a right occasionally to relaxations as well as other people."[34]

The relaxation, of course, is opium, which taken in its liquid form fits De Quincey nicely into the tradition from which he is working, of the erudite and their beverages. For as Rabelais loved wine and Burton water, Sterne writes a brief treatise on the sexiness of water drinkers; and Johnson, of course, insists on his tea. De Quincey also loves tea, but in addition, had we followed his order to his painter a little further, we would have found he wanted "ruby-colored laudanum"—and served in a bottle "as much like a wine decanter as possible."[35] De Quincey must have them all, the water brewed with herbs, and the opium served up as wine; the futility of knowledge has become overwhelming. In the nineteenth century, it was no longer possible for one man to write an encyclopedia, which was what he wanted to do. Indeed, De Quincey's life consisted of a series of vast intellectual projects begun and not completed,[36] and his book is a grim song of eagerly embraced defeat.

In many ways De Quincey's humor is grimmer than any before, using patterns from his predecessors and taking them as far as they will go. It is first of all a picaresque, vagabond humor. The opening chapter of the *Confessions* tells a *Lazarillo*-like tale of a young boy fighting for survival in the streets. The practical jokes in De Quincey's tale, however, as in all overripe situations, are against himself, the greatest of them all being the final one, of his relaxing from mental excitation by taking opium. We see strong connections to Burton's humor in the ranting of the style, and the consuming imbalance of the impulse—melancholia in Burton, addiction in De Quincey—except that Burton pulls off his encyclopedic task, whereas De Quincey just gets by to tell us something of pleasure and pain. We know De Quincey is aware of Johnson. He puts his cottage in the happy valley; and like his mentor, studies that elusive thing, "happiness." De Quincey's persona, however, unlike Johnson's Rasselas or Imlac or astronomer, is the thoroughly vulnerable individual man, the bare ego bequeathing not the cosmos but his own private dream world to his readers and followers.

De Quincey gives his pain a gothic humor—he plays with his gothic. In one role after another in the quoted passage, he lords it, as a scientific analyst, an epicure, a scholar. Finally, just to save himself the trouble, he commands a painter to set his stage. The slave makes the joke of being the master; the writer makes the joke that his mountains and cottages are real. De Quincey jokes with the reader for believing that what we see in the universe we have created ourselves; and he jokes with himself for pretending to lord it in a snug cottage in an English happy valley. In December, 1849, Melville "at last" bought *The Opium Eater.* Reading it immediately, he found it "a most wondrous book."[37]

In Charles Lamb's essays, the apple of knowledge is still a thing of joy. In his town-versus-country musings, for instance, Lamb typically comes out for town.

O let no native Londoner imagine that health, and rest, and innocent occupation, interchange of converse sweet and recreative study, can make the countryside any thing better than altogether odious and detestable.[38] A garden was the primitive prison till man with promethean felicity and boldness luckily sinn'd himself out of it. Thence followed Babylon, Nineveh, Venice, London, haberdashers, goldsmiths, taverns, playhouses, satires, epigrams, puns—these all came in on the town part, and the thither side of innocence.[39]

While making a teasing judgment on Genesis, Lamb is really telling the reader his likes and dislikes, his whims. Indeed this is the essence of all Lamb's essays. To read them is to draw up a list of Elia's pleasures, including domesticity and Christianity, roast pig, memories of being a schoolboy, sociability, cities, ornery relatives, bachelorhood, grumbling housekeepers, revealing one's inner thoughts, Sir Thomas Browne, Robert Burton, books in general, and plumcake.

In fact, particularly in contrast to De Quincey, Lamb verges on the complacent and self-congratulatory. But we should not be misled. It is true that Elia prides himself on his indulgences. No one knows better than Lamb himself, however, that after all Elia is no free man but a slave—a "superannuated" thrall, a mere customs-house clerk. Lamb dearly loved his sister Mary, who had killed their mother. That Lamb never speaks of that matricide in his essays but converts her into a lovably dogmatic cousin Bridget does not mean that he ignored the latent chaos his sister embodied in real life. Spending an essay, "The Old Margate Hoy," on how he detests the sea, Elia plays a game of hating it because he knows its terrors all too well. Instead of merely giving in to them, he plays in one way or another that he is above them.

Lamb's key essay, "Imperfect Sympathies" (1821), presents this pattern in sharp relief. Discussing his prejudices of various racial and national types, Elia writes of Scotchmen (Caledonians):

> I have been trying all my life to like Scotchmen, and am obliged to desist from the experiment in despair. They cannot like me—and in truth, I never knew one of that nation who attempted to do it. . . . We know one another at first sight. There is an order of imperfect intellects (under which mine must be content to rank) which in its constitution is essentially anti-Caledonian.
>
> The owners of the sort of faculties I allude to, have minds rather suggestive than comprehensive. They have no pretences to much clearness or precision in their ideas. . . . Their intellectual wardrobe (to confess fairly) has few whole pieces in it. They are content with fragments and scattered pieces of Truth. She presents no full front to them—a feature or sideface at most.
>
> Hints and glimpses, germs and crude essays at a system, is the utmost they pretend to. They beat up a little game peradventure—and leave it to knottier heads . . . to run it down. . . . They will throw out a random word in or out of season, and be content to let it pass for what it is worth. They cannot speak always as if they were upon their oath—but must be understood, speaking or writing, with some abatement. . . .
>
> The brain of a True Caledonian (if I am not mistaken) is constituted upon quite a different plan. His Minerva is born in panoply. You are never admitted to see his ideas in their growth—if, indeed, they do grow, and are not rather put together upon principles of clockwork. You never catch his mind in an undress. He never hints or suggests anything, but unlades his stock of ideas in perfect order and completeness. He brings his total

wealth into company, and gravely unpacks it. His riches
are always about him. He never stoops to catch a glitter-
ing something in your presence to share it with you,
before he quite knows whether it be true touch or not. . . .
He does not find, but bring. . . .

He has no falterings of self-suspicion. Surmises,
guesses, misgivings, half-intuitions, semi-con-
sciousnesses, partial illuminations, dim instincts, embryo
conceptions, have no place in his brain, or vocabulary.
The twilight of dubiety never falls upon him. Is he
orthodox—he has no doubts. Is he an infidel—he has
none either. Between the affirmative and the negative
there is no borderland with him. You cannot hover with
him upon the confines of truth, or wander in the maze of
a probable argument. He always keeps the path. You
cannot make excursions with him—for he sets you
right.[40]

While in this passage Elia easily hates the Caledonians, in
other passages in the same essay he comes more problematically to
Jews and Negroes. Of Jews, he concludes, "Some admire the
Jewish female-physiognomy. I admire it—but with trembling. Jael
had those full dark inscrutable eyes." Of Negroes, Elia writes, "I
love what Fuller beautifully calls—these 'images of God cut in
ebony.' But I should not like to associate with them, to share my
meals and good-nights with them—because they are black." Of
Negroes also, "I have felt yearnings of tenderness towards some of
these faces—or rather masks."[41] Lamb's more typical ploy nonetheless is Elia's teasing the harmless Caledonians—for really all the
Scotchmen threaten is irritation and boredom. Lamb's picking on
an underdog here (and one which Johnson also loved to pick on) is
more of the story told above, of a man playing with his humors to
pretend that he is bigger than his fears.

But Lamb's discourse is wry. What Elia provides is an argument based on the simple proposition that he cannot like Scotchmen and they cannot like him. Upon the basis of this mutual
repellance, Elia systematically divides the world into Caledonians
and anti-Caledonians, making each of these labels a constant in an

equation that boils down to their always being offensive and his always being admirable. Elia cannot hover on the brink of truth in this matter; he asserts it with full deliberation. In fact, the more that Lamb presses his point, the more he becomes exactly what he is busy telling us that he doesn't like. It is not that the world truly doesn't have Caledonians and anti-Caledonians in it—earnest people and humorous people, for that is what his division boils down to—but that in writing his essay, Elia cannot help becoming as earnest and egotistical as those he detests. He too is part of some kind of machinery that he cannot shut off.

Meanwhile in his anti-Caledonians (the faction he definitely belongs to), Lamb gives us a helpful description of the prose humorists: "They beat up a little game peradventure. . . . They will throw out a random word in or out of season. . . . They cannot speak always as if they were upon their oath. . . . They seldom wait. . . . They delight to impart their defective discoveries as they arise."[42] Lamb's essay, by his own definition, is humorous. But it is also an expression of desperation. Those Caledonians will not wander with you in the twilight of dubiety.

Lamb is a twilight humorist, whose ploys beat up a game against the darkness. In his essays, we have the sense that the frontier is closed. Push as far west as you can, to the South Seas, and all you have is a hoax. No wonder the House (in Lamb's "South-Sea House," a Melville favorite), where that Hoax was negotiated is full of quirky humorous characters. The New World itself is the greatest hoax of all.

En route to England in October 1849, Melville came across a copy of Lamb's essays in the ship's library. He found Lamb "a rare humorist and excellent hearted man."[43] In London Melville acquired two volumes of Lamb.

It is an ironic reversal that to Washington Irving, Europe—not America—is the "land of promise." Knickerbocker's *History of New York* tells the story of the indolent pipe-smoking Dutch being defeated by the Yankees. To Irving, Yankees are conniving people who, constantly moving about and improving things, are rapacious destroyers of a man's ease. Knickerbocker finds America's free enterprise and glorious frontier awful impositions. When Knicker-bocker, now Geoffrey Crayon, Gent., in *The Sketch Book* (1820), finally gets to Europe, we should not be surprised to find a backwards frontier giddiness.

Irving finds in "our old home" a land where a man can be melancholy in the old style, and can write to dispel his own and others' melancholy. The *Sketch Book's* epigraph states the amiable bachelor humorist's position: "I have no wife nor children, good or bad, to provide for. A mere spectator of other men's fortunes and adventures, and how they play their parts, which methinks are diversely presented unto me, as from a common theatre or scene." The quote is from Burton, as is the epigraph of "The Art of Bookmaking," one of the *Sketch Book* essays: if " 'It is a greater offence to steal dead men's labor than their clothes,' what shall become of most writers?"

"The Art of Bookmaking" suggests Irving's part in the prose humor tradition. In it Crayon finds his way into the British Museum Reading Room. Leaning against a pile of ancient folio volumes, he succumbs to the soporific atmosphere and dozes off. He dreams of a ragged threadbare mob of authors stealing helter-skelter the clothes off the great literary figures whose portraits line the reading room walls, until in the height of this literary mas-querade, which he has described in lavish detail, "a cry suddenly resounded from every side of 'Thieves! thieves!' "[44]

The joke, of course, is that Irving here is not only the dreamer but the thief himself. He has taken Burton's epigram to write this very essay, as certainly as he stole from Rabelais, Cervantes, Fielding, and Swift to write his *Knickerbocker History*. Like his mentor, Burton, Irving knows how books are made—by thievery. Yet this knowledge, as with Burton, is the source as well as the target of his humor. If all writing is thievery and there is nothing new under the sun to be said, the question comes up again—why write? Irving's answer is the same as that of others before him: for sport, to relieve our melancholy and divert ourselves from the uncertainties of the slippery road.

Nonetheless, Irving does have originality. His essays are all humor and hobbyhorses; he rejects out of hand all that hard work of scholarship. To research Shakespeare, for instance, he visits an Eastcheap tavern. Rebelling against the vast Renaissance intellectual energy, as well as against its new world, Irving turns with a passion to indolence. In "The Art of Bookmaking," Irving typically drops Burton's erudition, steals a sentence, then fantasies it into a minute melodrama. Like De Quincey, Irving turns the melancholy futile world into a patchwork of instant dreams. Irving often gives us flimsy little games, yet ultimately in all of his work, the very indolence of the plan, all the napping, smoking, drinking, and trifling, is an important germ of originality.

Irving's attraction to Europe as a new frontier, as a place to escape to and return to, as the happy valley, draws a link between the amiable humorist of England and the frontier humorist of America. Irving wrote about Europe, but he gave America an image of indolence which would be its mental frontier in a world oppressed with the Puritan work ethic, oppressed with free dog-eat-dog enterprise.

Melville apparently knew Irving early and well; one finds bits and pieces of Irving through all of Melville's work.[45]

As unique in many ways as American folk humor was, it did not exist in a vacuum, but was the logical next step in the frontier humor which began in the Renaissance with the discovery of the New World. It is not only that American humor may be compared to earlier prose humor cited, but that American periodical humorists knew much of that earlier literature.[46]

American humor began to flourish in the nineteenth century, in the golden age of the periodical. Popular storytellers enjoyed seeing their tales in print. The stories themselves took on an excitement, self-consciousness, and rapid-fire worldliness quite unheard of in older cultures' folklore limited to oral transmission. This excitement is in itself part of what the humor consists of, that jaunty irreverent attitude of a people on the move who swap stories as they swap places, and who freely pick up new stories and learn to elaborate on the old ones by swapping and reading newspapers and almanacs.

It is generally agreed that the unifying characteristic of

American humor is its bent for exaggeration. Richard Dorson explains, "The initial urge to glorify had been there, but a compressed American history did not permit the slow, centuries-long weaving of sober heroic legend, nor the long retrospective glance that favors credence."[47] The pressure cooker, of course, was science. In the nineteenth century, prose humor was still riding out the beam of Renaissance optimism created by man's new scientific achievements. The nineteenth century in America was riding that optimism harder and faster than ever before, exploding into greatness man's image of his own capabilities. It was science and the literal fact of living in the New World that gave the periodical boom in America its burst of humor.

Almanacs were those popular New World folk encyclopedias designed to tell all about everything for the up-to-date American. There was a lot to tell. In the 1842 *Farmer's Almanack*, Robert Thomas's editorial "Fifty Years Ago!" was celebrating, with many exclamation points, the fiftieth anniversary of the almanac. This editorial gives us a glimpse into precisely what Americans were so excited about: "Fifty years ago, and cities, now full of thousands of souls, were the hunting-ground of the Indian, and covered only by the forest or the swamp . . . the city of New York contained but about 33,000 inhabitants; it has now 312,000. Boston, then about 18,000, now 93,000, Philadelphia then about 40,000, now 260,000. . . . " He lists America's presidents over the fifty years, then England's monarchs, then notes with the same exuberance, "France has had more changes, has been the scene of more violence and more exciting and terrible commotions, than almost any other part of the civilized world, and from which, thanks to a kind Providence, we have been measurably exempt." He notes the conversion of the South Sea Islanders, the peopling of the erstwhile barren wilderness of New Holland, and the Turks' recognition of the Jew as a human being and brother. Science "has added to the wealth and happiness of almost every class in our land," with the wonders of steam, "its boiling cauldrons traversing the land and water," improved breeds of cattle and swine, new varieties of seed, and improved implements from the apple-peeler to the steam threshing machine. Finally, "within the past fifty years commerce has made brethren and friends of the remote inhabitants of the earth, the cause of Peace has, as we trust, been progressing, that of Philanthropy and Temperance is rapidly advancing, and we trust as nations grow wiser, better acquainted, more civilized, that vice and ignorance will give place to virtue and knowledge."[48]

Here is that fine word *trust,* which comes in handy so often in nineteenth-century rhetoric and with which Melville will have such fun. But meanwhile, fifty years indeed! What could fifty years have meant to our European, Asian, or African ancestors? What in the old days could have possibly changed in a mere half century? It is as if Thomas is saying, "We are giants!"

Thomas's editorial is not humorous, but it just misses. He presents the humorist's material in the humorist's medium, the almanac. He had begun his almanac out of a fascination with astronomy, as almanacs, in fact, were originally astronomical diaries. But the annual also continually demonstrated an appreciation of both humorous saw and anecdote and it was typical that he mentioned enthusiastically Rabelais's burlesque of almanacs in the "famous" 1532 *Pantagrueline Prognostications.*[49] In the quoted editorial, however, moved by the prospect of his own death, he puts sentiment in the place of self-parody. As the editorial fades off into some lines on death, it suggests the thin but crucial line between sentimentality and humor.

The world *almanac* comes from the Arabic for the place where camels kneel: in that place, weather and terrain forecasts were swapped. Probably few Americans, however, knew the derivation. Many instead may well have read the word in good American English as one anonymous author translated it for his book title, *Jonathan Jaw-Stretcher's Yankee Story All-My-Nack* (1852). Here clearly is the work of a humorist, who is writing about all his uncanny abilities, or Yankees bragging about theirs, as in one 250-word selection, "The Very Latest Glimpse O' the Great Sea-Serpent, that for the last Fifty Years has Haunted Na-Hant!!, certified Affidavit o' Squire Varmifuge Vampose." In this piece, we learn that on a Monday morning "atween sunshine and clockstruck" a man "seed a figger o' a big snake . . . head a kind o' circumbendibously for Egg Rock." The knack here is in seeing the sea monster, and in describing him. The sport is in the juxtaposition of the concept of the conqueror of monsters with that of the big talker, of legal language with misspellings, of valor with bragging nonsense. As Varmifuge "deposeth as follers," the monster's diameter "in close kalk'lation, war as thick round as you can see," and the fellow "turned his tail intu his mouth, jumped deown his own throat, an' then *vanquished.*"[50]

This piece of foolery, a good introduction to the American tall tale, blends flagrant boasting with a strong sense of defeat. The fellow bragging has actually done no more than see the monster, and he can tell us very little about it. If the deposer is thus deposed, then at least the monster should have his glory as a gigantic ferocious creature who embodies what man in his greatest valor must confront. The great sea-serpent, however, turns out to be nothing but a humorist himself, drenched in sexual imagery, who flirts and spurts, seduces with his eyes, then picks his teeth on man's misfortune and spits out God's curse. The serpent, an embodiment of the humorous male ego, is just another rogue, who appears to turn tail, who has no pretensions about his honor, but who will appear again and again.

Discussions of American periodical humor frequently mention an 1854 *Crockett Almanac* passage, a gem of a tall tale about backwoodsman Davy Crockett.[51] In his *Autobiography,* Crockett recounted saving his life one freezing night by climbing up and sliding down a tree one hundred times; indeed tall-tale prowess often takes place amidst a lot of ice and snow. In this tale, however, Crockett saves not only his own hide and that of his bear, but the whole universe and all mankind. This tale goes as far as it can, not just mechanically up and down a very tall tree, but emotionally until the backwoodsman is lording it as the master, the universe first just its sluggish beast, but then—with a lyrical turn—a boon companion who salutes his friend with a wind of gratitude, as in turn the Promethean Davy salutes his friends, the people, with "a piece of sunrise" in his pocket.

When it is quoted, the almanac passage usually ends on that note. Yet it actually goes on a bit anticlimactically. And indeed, much of the periodical humor is not as fully realized as the two pieces mentioned here, or as T. B. Thorpe's story of 1845, another classic and one more sustained, "The Big Bear of Arkansas."[52] It would take a literary artist to amplify the vision of such pieces and develop them beyond the anecdote to a sustained and major work of prose humor. Nonetheless the vision is similar to what we have seen in the past in European prose humor: a vision of man's giddy triumph and futility, an ambivalent, continually self-balancing vision of man's potential, a fantasy that "wonderfully rejoyceth the eyes of the beholder."

III
Embarkations

After the above chapter, it would be anticlimactic to turn to Melville if he were a mere follower of any one of the prose humorists. He was more than that. As much of a borrower as Melville was, his humor has a striking originality which becomes clear as we set his novels against their context.

Melville had worried about his first five novels being "botches,"[1] and for good reason. George Stewart has written about the "Two *Moby-Dicks*."[2] Studying Melville's first five novels, one can count the number of *Typees, Omoos, Mardis, Redburns,* and *White-Jackets*. The reader of any one of these novels is thrown from one image of the work at hand to the next. It is as if Melville began with the intention to convey a certain experience in prose narrative, but every hundred pages or so came up with a different idea of what prose narrative at its best should be—travel narrative, romance, discourse, domestic comedy, the picaresque, and so on. Running those five novels together, one has a catalogue of forms. Eventually this botching worked as a technique for Melville. "I try everything" (*MD* 291) eventually became central to Melville's fiction. In his first five novels, however, this technique was only beginning to gel.

In the midst of them, what seems uppermost in Melville's image of prose is that it somehow be a vehicle for humor. In *White-Jacket* we meet Lemsford, a writer and fellow seaman. His genius includes a certain irritability, but as a writer, Lemsford has wit, imagination, feeling, and "humor in abundance" (*WJ* 41). In his first five novels we witness Melville's learning how to live up to this standard. These books certainly have other things in common. For instance, they are all first-person sailor narratives. But this element becomes a given. What Melville seemed to want was a way of working his basic materials so that they would come to life. He wanted his books to be memorable, bold, and—as he says in *White-Jacket* of the best books—"companionable" (*WJ* 169).

"Your letter was just what a letter should be," Charles Lamb once wrote to a friend in Paris, "crammed and very funny."[3] This remark suggests Melville's aesthetic. As in the letter, the place where the egotism and sociability of the writer meet and blend is humor. The only way for the writer to deal with the inherent self-congratulation in conveying his experience—as with the teller of yarns—is by recognizing and exploiting it in humor. That Melville shared this image of letter writing seems clear from his own letters which, in a natural habitual way, from his youth to his old age, were humorous—deliberately, appealingly, socially humorous on everything from the trivial to the profound, from the pleasant to the difficult. Melville, however, did not just wish to write letters or, as Lamb did, letters and essays. He sought a prose form with more vigor and stature. This ambition in turn made the integration of humor more difficult, for expressing humor in a letter is natural and in an essay or sketch only a little more demanding, but getting a crammed and humorous novel together is an entirely different task.

Melville's ventures at that task are the subject of this chapter. His second and fourth novels, *Omoo* (1847) and *Redburn* (1849), suggest something about the development of his humor. But of the five books before *Moby-Dick,* the first, third, and fifth are most interesting and I will speak of them first. In *Typee* (1846), *Mardi* (1849), and *White-Jacket* (1850), we see what is from the first so striking about Melville, what happens when he is at once humorous and artistically aggressive.

In *Typee,* he achieves the dramatic tension necessary for a great work of humor and falls easily into a style for expressing that humor. In *Mardi,* after some veering about, he creates a humors character (that is, a character dominated by imbalanced humors) who suits his temperament and artistic goals, and who has considerable originality. In *White-Jacket,* he places the humors character at the book's center from the beginning. In all three novels, Melville took strides toward a confident deliberate humor; in them, from the first, his humor is his vision.

It has frequently been suggested that *Typee* with all its humor was contrived simply to win popular appeal, and that not until later, serious books did Melville write as he wished.[4] Melville's comment that *Typee* was "certainly calculated for popular reading or for none at all"[5] seems to settle the issue. We should not, however, take an author's statement on his own work at face value. An author's motives are complex. Kostanza in *Mardi* did write to procure his yams, but a "full heart" was his motive "primus and forever" (*M* 592).

In *Typee,* it seems, Melville was doing very much what he wanted. What he achieved, under the exuberance of writing a first novel, set the style and method and vision of his later novels and stories. In *Typee,* Melville faced the question head on: would he be able to give his experience a narrative shape strong enough to support a texture rich with humor? In a sense he did so with more ease than he did again until *Moby-Dick. Typee* is in several ways a tentative book, but Melville's instincts were sound from the first.

Typee is neither mere entertainment nor a darkly profound history of a soul's journey, just as Typee itself is neither a purely pleasant place nor a land of extraordinary brutality. *Typee's* tone is bound at one end by Tommo's being a captive among cannibals, and bound at the other by his being a young man enjoying four months of feasting, chatting, sleeping, and dallying with naked ladies and gentlemen of the savage order.

With a bold stroke Melville apprehends in *Typee* the necessities of good humor—exuberance and defeat. From the first Melville avoided a humor which, merely "diverting" the reader from painful truths, ends by being depressing. He also avoided a provincial humor which clings to the here and now. *Typee* was written before Melville's reading spurt of 1848-50. Nonetheless in this, his first novel, Melville is already literary; *Typee* builds on old jokes, stories, and wisdoms.

In *Typee* Melville provides a menacing situation. A white man, Tommo, having jumped ship, is captive among cannibals. One does not know how extensively the Typees practice cannibalism; nonetheless, or even more so, the threat remains, of being butchered and eaten. This threat answers as much to an adventure tale's need for danger as to a reader's need to have a work of art deal with what he fears deeply. I avoid the word *evil* here, by the way, for that word with all its moral and religious baggage has done considerable damage to the reading of Melville. What we fear in the cannibals is not *evil,* but some irrational instinctive possessive cruelty; and we fear it in large part because it suggests a cruelty in ourselves. In an essay on the Dutch painters, Roland Barthes points out that art does not merely make a voyeur's spectacle, a shop window of experience, but creates an image of something, even if it is a merchant in his finery, which stares back unabashedly at the viewer.[6] *Typee's* story of captivity could not stare back at its readers any more potently than it does. By the book's end, it is the white man who, determined on escape, brutally stabs the one-eyed Mow-Mow with a boat hook. "Even at the moment," Tommo recalls, "I felt horror at the act I was about to commit" (*T* 252).

If one thinks of Raskolnikov's crime or Kurtz's "the horror! the horror!" one should not be surprised. Melville has started with the predicament of being pawn to a neutral and brutal will—and taken it one turn further. Instead of profoundly melodramatizing our fate, as Dostoyevsky does; instead of straightforwardly exposing it, as Conrad does, Melville retains the stark threat yet pokes fun at our continual efforts to neutralize or ignore it, to convince ourselves that we are well above it—or at least important and dignified for having to adjust to it. We may think of the two men in a Shel Silverstein cartoon, shaggy and painfully emaciated, bound hand and foot to chains bolted into the walls of a room with no door. "Now here's my plan," one says to the other. The language of *Typee,* Charles Feidelson tells us, does inhibit a symbolistic interpretation of that book.[7] Precisely, and we should keep this in mind for all of Melville's books.

And so we have the humorous mixture of joviality, self-pity, pride, and familiarity expressed in the outburst with which that novel—and Melville's career as a novelist—opens: "Six months at sea! Yes, reader, as I live, six months out of sight of land; cruising after the sperm-whale beneath the scorching sun of the Line, and tossed on the billows of the wide-rolling Pacific—the sky above, the sea around, and nothing else!" The loudly proclaiming excitability continues:

> Weeks and weeks ago our fresh provisions were all exhausted. There is not a sweet potatoe left; not a single yam. Those glorious bunches of bananas which once decorated our stern and quarter-deck have, alas, disappeared! and the delicious oranges which hung suspended from our tops and stays—they too, are gone! Yes, they are all departed, and there is nothing left us but salt-horse and sea-biscuit. [*T* 1]

From the first page, Melville takes the pressing sense of predicament and turns it into a joke on humankind. The heroic lament of the seafarer goes to seed. Dignified pride gives way to familiar hobnobbing with the reader, as reserve gives way to an irrepressible disposition to the exclamation point, and the *ubi sunt* motif to the absurdity of where are the sweet potatoes and bananas of yesteryear. It is not purely geographical, by the way, that bananas are so strewn around *Typee,* and yams around *Mardi.* One fruit for being phallic, the other for sounding like hams—they both have a way of undermining the dignity with which we attempt to console ourselves in our hardship.

They are also, however, simply tropical, exaggeratedly sweet and soft. They hint at an indolent sexuality that consistently colors the humor of *Typee.* We get a start on the indolence as the opening continues:

> Oh! ye state-room sailors, who make so much ado about a fourteen-days' passage across the Atlantic; who so pa-

thetically relate the privations and hardships of the sea, where, after a day of breakfasting, lunching, dining off five courses, chatting, playing whist, and drinking champagne-punch, it was your hard lot to be shut up in little cabinets of mahogany and maple, and sleep for ten hours, with nothing to disturb you but "those good-for-nothing tars, shouting and tramping over head,"—what would ye say to our six months out of sight of land?[*T* 1]

If we guess immediately that Melville is no Puritan here attacking the easy languor of the rich, but lusting after it himself in a dawdling, playful description, then the whole rest of the book in which Tommo gets to loll for four months in paradise is fair proof. The indolents are neither attacked nor merely parodied, but envied and even sympathized with. For here we have the characteristic twist. Just as the opening invocation ludicrously piles apostrophes one on top of the next—Oh readers, oh stateroom sailors, oh one-legged rooster, oh poor old ship—so it turns absurdly from one person's sensibility to the next. Finally we are left shut up in a luxurious little cabin, annoyed by people waking us, gorgeously oblivious to more far-reaching dilemmas.

A similar pattern of reversal exists through most of the book, except that the style changes. The style of veering excitability which Melville pitches into first is the same he will sustain for much of *White-Jacket* and for the whole of *Moby-Dick*. Here, however, after a few pages he subsides into a nuance humor which turns all human exertions into absurdities. This quiet style creates a realm in which language itself, most of all the desire to write, represents man's final absurd attempt at relieving his sense of being imprisoned in a sea of nothingness, whether on the forecastle or in a snug mahogany cubicle—or, as we shall see, within the hoops of the drawings upon our own faces.

Indeed the basic humorous shift of the book is from the vision of cannibals as embodiments of evil, to seeing them as human beings making shift with a lot of time on their hands. It does not take long before Melville himself is being regaled in the best manner of the stateroom sailor, or before we are made aware of the continual absurdity of man continually regaling himself. It does not take long to establish that Typee is a land singularly free of the petty vexations as well as of the serious hardships of civilized society. Even the idea of happiness, however, Melville turns inside out. As the Typees are not evil cannibals, neither are they noble savages basking in the joy of natural living. It is just that they have hit the breadfruit jackpot. Through a continual rotating of wry comparisons between the customs of primitive and civilized man—both of whom Melville pokes fun at—this book gets its humor.

Melville plays specifically with all the things we set up as pieties for ourselves to give us a sense of stability and order. His nuances are so quiet that we hardly notice how consistently he is knocking out from under us all the supports, all the patterns of thinking that give us a way of being in a perplexing world. The most immediate and direct of these is sexual. It is typical that Melville translates the word Typee not as cannibal or murderer but as "lover of human flesh." Indeed Melville in this book is one—and a flirt. Humor in this regard is not just an unmasking, but a literal undressing. Melville is a little heavy-handed, in fact, in the two incidents in which he throws up various ladies' skirts. He soon finds his characteristic balance, however, in giving us naked Fayaway as the mast for Tommo's canoe, or in speaking of the "bewitching ankle" (*T* 135) of a lady whose garment is certainly more than décolleté.

But sexual modesty is only one of many dandled toys. Melville at one point speaks of "a highly respectable cannibal education" (*T* 112), and *Perseverance* is the name of a whaleship sent by its owners on such a long journey that the sailors set out as babies and return—if ever—as old men, a ship last seen "somewhere in the vicinity of the ends of the earth" (*T* 22), somewhere near Buggery Island. Heroism is, in an aside, "the strong-rooted determination to have the biggest share of the pudding" (*T* 137), and gratitude a subject whose maxim may be easily turned inside out. "To be sure it was rather an inglorious thing to steal away privily from those at whose hands I had received wrongs and outrages" (*T* 23).

Sociability is a frequent target, and in ways suggestive for later books. Melville speaks of the Typees' "cordial hatred" for the French, of these gourmands' "taking it into their heads to make a convivial meal of a poor devil" or of the doctor's "confidential chat with some imaginary demon located in the calf of my leg" (*T* 16, 31, 80). In fact the wry phrase "confidential chat" is a favorite of Melvilles's from this book onward; it was only a matter of time before he wrote a whole book, *The Confidence-Man,* on such chats. If *Typee* opens with salty praise for the *Dolly's* hospitality, its cuts of meat "affording a never-ending variety in their different degrees of toughness" (*T* 21), Melville is more subtle and less cutting with his hosts ashore. Their warm lavish hospitality—or is it fattening for the slaughter?—is the central joke of the book. In a typical moment Mehevi "advanced at once in the most cordial manner, and, greeting me warmly, seemed to enjoy not a little the effect his barbaric costume had produced upon me" (*T* 78-79).

But any exertion, physical as well as social, is suspect. Melville indeed loves the natives' indolence. As his humor suggests, why should man embrace the penalty of the Fall with such passion? Thus he finds it "vastly convenient [that] whenever an enterprising islander chooses to emigrate a few hundred yards from the place where he was born, all he has to do in order to establish himself in some new locality, is to select one of the many unappropriated pipis, and without further ceremony pitch his bamboo tent upon it" (*T* 156).

"To many of them, indeed, life is little else than an often interrupted and luxurious nap" (*T* 152). Melville raises the question thus of what life is supposed to be—a rarely interrupted and oppressive work session? As if the Typees had caught a hint of that possibility, "it is a peculiarity among these people, that when engaged in any employment they always make a prodigious fuss about it . . . when they do work they seem determined that so meritorious an action shall not escape the observation of those around" (*T* 159). Yet it is these same people who at the Ti are busy "soothing the cares of Polynesian life in the sedative fumes of tobacco." (*T* 164).

In such a context, communication itself is an exertion. Tommo's body servant Kory-Kory "seemed to experience so heartfelt a desire to infuse into our minds proper views" (*T* 102) on various subjects that he and his "stunning gibberish" (*T* 103) are often appealing targets. On one occasion, pointing out to Tommo a variety of objects, he "endeavored to explain them in such an indescribable jargon of words, that it almost put me in bodily pain to listen to him" (*T* 160). He "had a great variety of short, smart-sounding sentences, with which he frequently enlivened his discourse; and he introduced them with an air which plainly intimated, that, in his opinion, they settled the matter in question, whatever it might be" (*T* 173). Mehevi also, disturbed by Tommo's meddling with taboo, "entered into a long, and I have no doubt a very learned and eloquent exposition of the history and nature of the 'taboo' as affecting this particular case; employing a variety of most extraordinary words, which, from their amazing length and sonorousness, I have every reason to believe were of a theological nature" (*T* 133). What a fine description, by the way, of an exposition Melville himself would write—*Moby-Dick*. The point here, however, is that Melville is making fun not only of Christianity or taboos, or even theology. The target is bigger—man's pretensions to logic and order.

Nonetheless, in toying with pieties, it is only a matter of time before we get to the piety of pieties, God himself—here, Moa Artua. "An unbounded liberty of conscience seemed to prevail. Those who pleased to do so were allowed to repose implicit faith in an ill-favored god with a large bottle nose and fat shapeless arms crossed upon his breast." In fact, Tommo continues,

> this funny little image was the "crack" god of the island; lording it over all the wooden lubbers who looked so grim and dreadful. . . . The priest comes along dandling his charge as if it were a lachrymose infant he was endeavoring to put into a good humor. Presently, entering the Ti, he seats himself on the mats. . . . As for the luckless idols, they received more hard knocks than supplications. I do not wonder that some of them looked so grim, and stood so bolt upright as if fearful of looking to the right or the left lest they should give any one offence. The fact is, they had to carry themselves "*pretty straight*," or suffer the consequences.[*T* 171, 175, 177-78]

Melville has not only turned the whole God-man veil of trembling inside out, but made all the world—from the smallest word to the highest god—a bundle of sensibilities, sensations, and humors. No wonder everything is constantly in a state of disrepair. The Typees, Tommo complains wryly,

> are sunk in religious sloth, and require a spiritual revival. A long prosperity of breadfruit and cocoa-nuts has rendered them remiss in the performance of their higher obligations. The wood-rot malady is spreading among the idols—the fruit upon their altars is becoming offensive—the temples themselves need re-thatching—the tattooed clergy are altogether too light-hearted and lazy—and their flocks are going astray. [T 179]

Indeed, with all these deflated pieties and meddlings with taboo, Melville in *Typee* is simply rewriting the *Young Men's Own Book*,[8] a conduct book which Tommo refers to midway through the novel. *Typee* is absurdly a conduct book for life among the savages, for life on this earth. We may go further, however. Melville in *Typee* is playfully, teasingly rewriting *the* young men's book, the ultimate conduct book, the Garden of Eden story, Genesis. In *Typee*, we are told, the penalty of the Fall sits as lightly on the inhabitants as the scriptural injunction to multiply. In fact in this Garden of Eden, untouched by Judeo-Christian myth, nakedness does not give way to embarrassment, God does not hover beyond the breadfruit trees, and Adammo does not hide in the palm tree's shadow. The natives instead dandle and put God in his place.

In spite, however, of all this happiness, from a nameless source comes something oppressive. Melville's relatively happy image of the Typee, like that of the stateroom sailor, is only a commentary on the state of man, and on the inevitability of man's imprisonment in this life, even in the paradise of paradises, that land of Typee where men do not even need to dream of heaven—and where perhaps they hold the white man captive because he is simply their only contact with the world outside their valley. Kory-Kory quietly becomes an emblem of man in this book. Tommo's turnkey—as hideous to behold as he was truly devoted and even loving—had on his proud warrior's face tattoos "which like those country roads . . . go straight forward in defiance of all obstacles." His countenance itself

> thus triply hooped, as it were, with tattooing, always reminded me of those unhappy wretches whom I have sometimes observed gazing out sentimentally from behind the grated bars of a prison window; whilst the entire body of my savage valet, covered all over with representations of birds and fishes, and a variety of the most unaccountable-looking creatures, suggested to me the idea of a pictorial museum of natural history, or, an illustrated copy of 'Goldsmith's Animated Nature.' [*T* 83]

Typee may have no tree of knowledge, and God there may be a rotted wooden idol, but the perverse force that is out there, making the paradox of human nature what it is, is unalterable. Kory-Kory inadvertently puts his head behind bars and lets his body become an encyclopedia, just as instinctively as the poor fly that Tommo swallows, possessed by a demythicized, debunked, simply instinctive determination, heads for Tommo's brain. The final impact of Melville's humor is to satirize neither savage nor Christian, but to teasingly rewrite Genesis with God and the devil taken out. We still have a hovering terror—man's barely controllable capacity for brutality; we still have the initial and underlying prodigiousness of nature's generosity—those glorious bananas the color of the glory of the sun; and we still have man's restlessness. But Melville gives us neither religious prescription nor moral recrimination with his debunked myth. We are left with nothing but the perversity itself: that raw universal principle.

Between the subliterary conduct book and the monumental Genesis is one other book we ought to mention, for Melville in *Typee* is certainly playing off Dr. Johnson's *Rasselas*. Melville's allusion to the "Happy Valley" and his sometimes Johnsonian style suggest that Melville's game of "Typee or Happar?" is a Johnsonian paradoxical play on the order of Rasselas's deliberation on seeking happiness outside the Happy Valley. Most significantly,

Tommo's desire to get out of the happy valley is built upon Rasselas's desire to escape his. This use of *Rasselas,* a work which was perceived as both literary and popular in nineteenth-century America, gave coherence and structure to *Typee's* exploration of the paradox of man's desire.

It is important also to note, however, the ways in which Melville went beyond *Rasselas,* playfully pushing even its paradox out of shape. *Typee* takes the exoticism of *Rasselas* as far as it can go, into the literal—and real—paradise of the Typee valley. It convolutes Johnson's paradox; it has the Happy Valley turn out to be the Typee instead of the expected Happar. It also provides, as a curative to the boredom of happiness, a penchant for the drama and spectacle of occasional cannibalism. Most of all, it adds a playful eroticism that spoofs the quiet control of Johnson's book. Johnson contented himself with kidnappings and corruption, and stiffly keeps his distance from sex. Melville, on the other hand, has for a narrator nothing less than a Peeping Tommo, and an adventure story that begins with a shipboard orgy, and then goes on to meddle with any taboo that presents itself.

In fact, particularly against the backdrop of *Rasselas,* we see that in its outer reaches, *Typee* is a love story. Tommo himself is as much a "lover of human flesh" as the people who have made him their beloved imprisoned guest. Ultimately, beyond the erotic play and reversal, Melville's book is a romance of the misbegotten for the misbecome. After all, the Typee is only a tribe which has insured its survival by perpetuating the most aggressive of reputations about itself; and Tommo is only a man who has bragged that he can do without home and mother, and then gone crawling back. That Kory-Kory and Fayaway weep for Tommo, and Tommo dreams of them, is ultimately no laughing matter. Nor is it humorous that the man who has felt threatened all along by the tribe of strangers is the one to strike the blow. In the extremity of man's alienation from man, however, Melville has given his humor grounding. Also, in projecting a love story between the alienated and the alien, he has expressed the lyrical component that gives his humor breadth. Tommo is a stranger, so are the Typees: strangers, prisoners, creatures in a paradox. It is both the fright and the love which create the tension required for humor, and which give the humor meaning.

I began this chapter speaking of botches, and *Typee* is one. Despite *Typee*'s achievement, in several respects it is a tentative work of art. The anxieties of the preface—is this to be a yarn, a travel narrative, or a classical literary work—are indicative of problems in the pages that follow. It was a little too much of a lucky hit that for his first novel, Melville actually found a Happar Valley upon which he could graft a *Rasselas*-like parable. Also, the anguish of Melville's infection in his leg suggests an individual pain that is not fully handled, just as the language of the escape scene at the end is too heavy after the nuance humor of the rest of the book. Finally, Melville can be clumsy in his desire to be amusing. As he himself tells us in reference to the purser's steward in *White-Jacket,* humor must come up quietly and straight-faced on the reader, or else, with waggery and high jinks, take the reader by storm. In various incidents like that of the popgun war, or of the two ladies early in the book, Melville is straining for comicality.

With regard to the latter, however, perhaps these incidents suggest Melville's clumsiness with male-female comedy. Although with Fayaway Melville transcends his usual self-consciousness about ladies, when he speaks of other women in the novel, he seems to be rebelling too hard or giving in too slavishly. On the whole, the book as a humorous romance, and a love story, even building on its teasing eroticism, is about Tommo, Toby, Mehevi, Kory-Kory, Marnoo—and the Ti, the place where the men regale themselves and where women are not allowed. Melville's humorous vision is a love story of men passing their time together in this life.

Mardi has none of *Typee's* ease. In many respects, *Mardi* is trying, is belabored. Babbalanja notes at one point in the book that "Genius is full of trash" (*M* 595). Clearly Melville was well aware of *Mardi*'s faults as he was writing it, for the book is full of such disclaimers and apologies. But we may look well into what is "trash" here. It turns out that in *Mardi,* Melville risks being so bad that he becomes good in new ways. Here his botching goes wild as he strives for one kind of effect after another. Yet eventually the botching takes hold and opens up into an extravagance which in turn opened up all of Melville's humor.

The main difficulty of *Mardi* is Melville's self-consciousness. He wrote it in 1847-48, when he was beginning to treat himself to a voracious reading of the classics. As his allusions suggest, he is thinking about Shakespeare, Dante, Spenser, Herodotus, Goethe, Coleridge, Chaucer, Browne, and so on—endlessly. Like his allusions, his ventriloquisms in their self-consciousness verge on the grotesque. A section like the visit to the holy oracle at Maramma, for instance, tries for a Bunyanesque intensity, Swiftian bite and Rabelaisian offhandedness, all at the same time. As a result, none of these styles is realized. It does not help that Melville tries to explain his harried infatuation with all these authors—"Like a frigate, I am full with a thousand souls. . . . Ay: many, many souls are in me" (*M* 367)—or that he defends "polysensuums" in a didactic "Nursery Tale." The tone is off. He is sentimental and anxious rather than wry and confident. Surrounded by all the greats, Melville seems to be worrying about competing, and straining to keep up. He finally does get something important from Rabelais, but the only author he really meets halfway is Burton. Melville "does" a beautiful Burton in ways and for reasons suggested later.

Meanwhile, on the narrative level, the book yaws. Melville is looking for what to do with prose narrative, for he has decided that this time he does not want to write a travel book. Particularly in the first third of *Mardi,* the reader is thrown from one course to another. Melville begins with the idea of a narrative with heroic, even Homeric, stature. As the book opens, the narrator is looking for a companion with heroic dignity, if only the dignity of calm silence. Then after he has his companion, and the two have jumped ship and set off, Melville veers suddenly to domestic comedy. On the derelict ship *Parki,* the two men meet Annatoo and her mate Samoa, and learn of henpecking, Polynesian style. This episode, which Melville refers to as a five-act drama, is the sexual comedy of *Typee*'s two opening incidents drawn out to tedium. Melville clearly threw it in for entertainment, but is uncomfortable with it. In *Typee* he had said that if one doesn't have something nice to say about a woman, one should say nothing at all. In *Mardi* he says a philosopher doesn't understand women.

Having gone from Homeric adventure to homey comedy, Melville now yaws back—to hubris. Annatoo is no sooner dispatched (with a fortuitous accidental blow on the head) than we have come back this way to meet her counterpart, beautiful white Yillah. Clearly Yillah was introduced to charm Melville's female audience (not least of all his new wife Elizabeth) and to repair the insult of such a negative picture of femininity in Annatoo. But most of all Yillah provided a fittingly melodramatic excuse for Taji's arrogance; he must rescue her from her savage captors. In this section, Taji picks up the guilt Melville left in *Typee.* Once again the main character brutally strikes a savage, and this time the savage dies. Melville picks up the guilt itself like a sledgehammer, however. While he was right to confront head-on this important theme from *Typee,* it seems he was not yet ready to handle it. We are suddenly given an exotic melodrama. Taji himself becomes the missionary Melville was exposing to ridicule in *Typee:* for it is Taji who attempts to correct the heathens, and he never recovers from this act for the rest of the book.

The conventional humor which goes along with this yawing is forced—coy and sugary—with many trying announcements of comicality. Indeed the straining reveals a wider problem, an irritability which depresses the book, as if Melville were forcing himself to be cheerful in a way he did not feel. The irritability is present from the first, in his preface; in the characterization of Taji who "throttling the thought" of his crime, "swore to be gay" (*M* 135); in the leer of the silenus-like figurehead of their canoe; and in the continual haunting by that half-Spenserian, half-German-romantic, Hautia.

The irritability builds to a kind of fury as Babbalanja explains that a poor slave cannot control the laughter of his body. On the night of the full moon, in fact, his gloomy talk makes Mohi's fastidiousness for the first time a wonderful relief. Mohi says, "He makes me crawl all over, as if I were an ant-hill" (*M* 613). But we should note that it is as wrong to call this irritability demonic as it is to call the Samoa-Annatoo comedy playful. No Prometheus, Taji is more like a young man pointing his finger (at Babbalanja) and bragging that he is more radical than thou.

The wonderful thing about *Mardi,* however, is that it survives its own failures. It is a case of ends and beginnings dovetailing. *Mardi* is ultimately a remarkable book. It is as if Melville has been straining so hard that when he relaxes, he is in a new place after all. With all its yawing, the book does hold a steady course to one principle, and that is sheer extravagance. In *Typee* Melville was teasingly rewriting Genesis. Here, in a book complete with Chronicles, Kings, Psalms, and Ecclesiastes, he seems to be rewriting the whole Bible. The outlandishness of such a project is the book's greatest achievement. It is not that at a given point, the book suddenly finds its balance. It is indeed better once the murder is behind us and Taji and his companion Jarl are launched on a great voyage in the company of historian Mohi, King Media, poet Yoomy, and philosopher Babbalanja. But the syntax to the end is exasperatingly involuted and Melville's aimlessness persists, as does his habit of telling the reader too much at every step of the way. Nonetheless, throughout, an extravagant humor is finding itself and building. It surfaces in several ways which eventually culminate in the portrait of Babbalanja. This character provides the Burtonesque Ecclesiastes of this bible. He also makes the greatest contribution toward Melville's awareness of how to build humor into the center of his novels.

The mood of this extravagant humor is suggested in the second chapter:

> To a landsman a calm is no joke. It not only revolutionizes his abdomen, but unsettles his mind; tempts him to recant his belief in the eternal fitness of things; in short, almost makes an infidel of him. At first he is taken by surprise, never having dreamt of a state of existence where existence itself seems suspended. He shakes himself in his coat, to see whether it be empty or no. He closes his eyes, to test the reality of the glassy expanse. He fetches a deep breath, by way of experiment and for the sake of witnessing the effect. If a reader of books, Priestley on Necessity occurs to him; and he believes in that old Sir Anthony Absolute to the very last chapter. [*M* 9]

The calm is a quiet version of the giddiness with which *Typee* opens. Threading through *Mardi* in phrases, sentences, nuances, and chapters, the calm suggests the essential humor of man at sea with his own mind.

In chapter 13, "The Chondropterygii and Other Uncouth Hordes Infesting the South Seas," Melville gives us an extended sample of *Mardi's* humor and happens on one of his central motifs. In the midst of classifying the wonders and inanities of the deep, he turns to the belligerents, the sharks. One phrase in particular gives us a sense of Melville's vision, of what sets his humor in motion: "God's creatures fighting, fin for fin, a thousand miles from land, and with the round horizon for an arena" (*M* 42). To put the situation in a landsman's terms, picture a vast desert crossed by one long endlessly empty highway, in the middle of which two cars coming from opposite directions have found each other and crashed. One would expect that, meeting in the middle of the nothingness, people would either tip their hats or rapturously hug one another. Often the latter happens and a good deal of Melville's humor is about the hug of fellowship. What Melville begins to relish here, however, is the flip side of the hug, the preposterousness of the fight. This was the basic joke of *Typee,* that Tommo and the cannibals loved each other—and that Kory-Kory, for instance, at once hideous to behold and the most devoted of valets, had a bear hug which, suffocating as it was, was an embrace.

In *Mardi,* in a haphazard way, Melville begins to explore this love-hate of God's creatures in a manner that is more original for being thoroughly outlandish. No wonder he quickly gets beyond a hackneyed humor of God's male and female creatures fighting. Once he leaves that behind him, as the chapter about sharks suggests he will do, once he leaves man and man and man and woman to go to fish and fish, and eventually man and fish, he seems to feel free to be truly extravagant. Men have something practical to gain from hugging women—sexual satisfaction and offspring— and the bear hug of fellowship between men certainly has its pragmatic side, as we see in *White-Jacket.* In the story of fish and fish, or man and fish, Melville suggests a love-hate pure and untainted by material satisfaction, a love-hate of thoroughgoing sensibility. Here Melville's touch can be light and exultant because the field is preposterous and, with the exception of American folk humor, which he builds from and opens up (even mentioning Davy Crockett), very much his own. In *Moby-Dick,* Melville will fully reap the benefits of a preposterous hug set at the center of the novel.

In this chapter, against a backdrop of the shark's menace, Melville characteristically plays with nuances. The blue shark is a "long, taper and mighty genteel looking fellow, with a slender waist, like a Bond-Street beau"; or the tiger shark is "a round portly gourmand; with distended mouth and collapsed conscience" (*M* 40). The sheer superfluity of sensibility is everywhere, until the chapter reads like a humors essay on hate. Melville keeps turning the issue of sensibility inside out, first earnestly arguing with Samuel Johnson for saying we should love a hater, then explaining dutifully that we should not hate at all, then returning scientifically to his ichthyology, then bursting out against the Algernine. But what, the question seems to be, should man *do* with his feelings? Repress them, stifle them, submerge them under science and morality: this is impossible. Letting them out, however, is just as absurd, for then we fall to waging war against the sharks. Human beings do want to be reasonable. But at the beginning of this chapter, we hear of Sir Thomas Browne who, while exploding "Vulgar Errors, heartily hugged all the mysteries in the Pentateuch" (*M* 39). Men do aspire to respectability and rationality, but dressing up as they do, like the sharks of Bond Street and the Pacific, will not do the trick, and Melville leaves us wondering if anything will.

Taji concludes, for he is narrator. "There is no telling all. The Pacific is as populous as China" (*M* 42). This sense of the inexhaustability of subjects Babbalanja will eventually take over from Taji, when the latter lapses into a taciturnity so brooding that his companion Jarl by comparison seems a very social fellow. First, however, we get the lord shark motif applied to the fish, then applied to Taji, himself by now a killer like the shark and by his own decision, a lord—a sun god, in fact. But his distinction only leads to wry recognitions: "Instead then of being struck with the audacity of endeavoring to palm myself off as a god—the way in which the thing first impressed me—I now perceived that I might be a god as much as I pleased, and yet not whisk a lion's tail after all; at least on that special account" (*M* 176). In other words, be he ever so much a god as he please, it somehow will make no dent in the universe. Nonetheless, if the moral here is that being a king or even a god does not help you, at the same time the game of the book is to play at being king, to play at *I desire, I am.* Taji has gone in fact in the first 177 pages from being in an open boat with a "king" for a companion to as far as he may go, to riding with a real King Media and to being himself a sun god. He decides to play the game to its hilt: "I resolved to follow my Mentor's wise counsel; neither arrogating aught, nor abating of just dues; but circulating freely, socially and frankly, among the gods, heroes, high-priests, kings and gentlemen that made up the principalities of Mardi" (*M* 177). This is an important aspect of the humor of the book, the sheer play of lording it.

In this sense Melville's main debt to Rabelais in this book is not for any particular scenes which have been identified as Rabelaisian in origin. When Melville borrowed particulars, as his contemporaries noted, he was often plodding. For instance, in *Mardi's* catalogue of the books, Melville is busy trying, not to be teasingly erotic, but to get Rabelais's obscenities under control. But at *Mardi's* appearance, Melville was called an American Rabelais.[9] What Melville does get of importance from Rabelais is the Gargantuan freedom to do as he pleases in the book, to let it run all over the globe, its main characters enjoying the aristocratic life of leisure. As Taji says, "Now, for all the rant of your democrats, a fine king on a throne is a very fine sight to behold" (*M* 182). Rabelais helped liberate this humor in Melville.

Before Babbalanja takes over the main thrust of the humor, however, Taji has one more outburst, and here Burton provides much of the inspiration. "Time and Temples" has that Democritan exultance at the "commotion" of things. The game in good part is in the promiscuous throwing together of temples and pleasure palaces, both wondrous to behold and taking ages to be built, Taji on two occasions in the midst of this catalogue affirming his "uttermost reverence" and assuring us he means "no derogation" (*M* 229, 230). What, however, is he revering? What is the point of his giddy rhapsody, which takes off on a mad voyage into space, adding new planets to the Milky Way? Is it that the infinite be "not less than more infinite now" (*M* 230)? It doesn't all quite make sense. We will need Babbalanja to straighten us out, and when he does, about fifty pages later, we can see he has already moved into center position. What we should know about time is that it mellows and softens. Babbalanja tells us this reclining, himself mellowing and softening with the leisure of his chat, as "frankly crossing his legs" (*M* 208) he had immediately taken King Media at his word in his social decree when the companions first set out on their voyage.

The most notable advance in Melville's humor is in the characterization of the Burtonesque Babbalanja. Taji is finally less interesting than Babbalanja, perhaps because Melville vacillates between making Taji a comic Prometheus and a romantic Prometheus. Ultimately Melville emphasizes the latter role and in it Taji leads to Ahab, but Taji is really a midpoint between the more subtle anguish of Tommo and the bold stroke of Ahab's arrogance. What ultimately made possible the development of Ahab was that Melville learned in this novel to separate out from the Tommo-Taji-Ahab character, the role of the affectionate skeptic—here Babbalanja, in *Moby-Dick* Ishmael—and to give that skeptic the reins of the book. But the characterization of Babbalanja is not just of interest with reference to Melville's growth. It stands on its own as an important element in *Mardi*.

That Babbalanja takes over Taji's initial role as humorous commentator is clear from the chapter in which the former "regales" the company with a geological "sandwich." What Babbalanja takes over from Taji and develops as far as it will go, is an open-endedly skeptical attitude toward himself, human nature, and the universe.

In addition to an attitude, however, Babbalanja has a spiritual journey. In fact he alone in the book has one, and it is presented very simply. It rests on his continual awareness and acceptance of his muddled state of mind. "Oh, my lord, I am in darkness" (*M*

389), he begins, but his discomfort steadily progresses. First he finds himself possessed by an impish devil, Azzageddi. Then he finds himself, as he says, rented out to an indwelling stranger, and finally finds his very head a madhouse. On the night of the full moon, his confusion builds to a climax. He eventually recants and settles down in the questionable bliss of Serenia.

Babbalanja's journey is saved from melodrama, however, by his other awareness—of the futilities—by his wry sensibility. What defines Babbalanja's journey is what colors the calm in the second chapter. To a landsman, a calm is no joke. To anyone human, Babbalanja's journey is no joke. It is the confrontation of man's mind with itself, man's desire with itself, in the calm of the nothingness of existence. What Melville does best, however, is to show us what is no joke with a quiet appreciation of its humor. So we have Babbalanja's sociability; his diverting of the company with his paradoxes; his regaling of the company with his talk; his conclusion after some raving and some Ramadan-like pondering that "an exclamation point is entire Mardi's autobiography" (*M* 581); his Azzageddi's "fugle-fogle-orum"; and his fine sense that you may turn people down in many ways, but should never, as Bardiana says, refuse their yams.

As Media reminds us, whereas Yoomy's province is poetry, Babbalanja's is prose. Basically Babbalanja is a prosy Democritus, Jr.—the man to whom life can be endlessly anatomized. Indeed, if we note the way *Mardi* stops short of being fully Rabelaisian, a prudish self-seriousness often getting in Melville's way, we see that in being Democritan, Melville feels at home. Babbalanja's humor lies in his indefatigable attempt to take Burton to his own conclusions.

As with Melville himself, for Babbalanja, prose is the vehicle for man's direct experience of shaking himself in his coat to see if he is still there. The joke of the book rests on Babbalanja's statement of what, after all, is our only certainty: "All I am sure of, is a sort of prickly sensation all over me, which they call life; and, occasionally, a headache or a queer conceit admonishes me, that there is something astir in my attic" (*M* 456). This is the "Descartian vortex" Melville speaks of elsewhere, rendered with a humorous sensibility—not *I think therefore I am* nor even just *I desire, I am,* but finally *I feel and that's all I know.* Even conceits in this prosy Democritan realm have sensibilities and touchy feelings—Babbalanja's conceits *admonish* him. We need add one additional point here, that Babbalanja introduces a nice humorous perspective on the brutality of man's will as the central menace. With Babbalanja and Media, as with lavishly imprisoned kings like Donjololo, Melville suggests that the main menace hovering over man is not brutality but boredom.

Perhaps another way of approaching Babbalanja, as well as *Mardi*'s other characters, is by introducing the concept of the humors character. That term, however, can be too easily tossed off with little regard to the way humors characters function in a novel; the way they demand, like children, to be the center of attention; the way they absorb, like the very sponge that White-Jacket becomes in his quilted padded coat, everything in sight. Humors characters demand that in the prose in which they appear—very differently, by the way, than in the drama in which they appear—that sensibility be "primus and forever." It is as if the prosaicness of prose predisposes both humors character and reader to the world of sensibility.

Babbalanja is a humors character, but we should note how Melville humors him. Indeed, each prose humorist handles his humors characters differently. Dickens, for instance, sets his down in the degenerating machinery of society and lets them struggle to be more than machines themselves. Melville sets his against the panoply of the American adventure. In the old world one man was king; in the new every man thinks he is king—or at least entitled to be one. It is the democratic egalitarian fantasy that makes Melville's humors characters rise as if heroically to their own idiosyncrasies; and that gives the vision of the humors character a new scope. Melville draws considerably from Burton's Democritus, Jr. The style of the anatomist has opened up to a large extent the egalitarian joke of the humor. In Babbalanja, Melville goes further, however, in presenting a man who works through in all his personal vulnerability what it means to be a humors character. Finally what Melville has learned with Babbalanja will in large part account for the success of *White-Jacket* and *Moby-Dick*. Working out the humors character until he has him for his own, Melville makes humor central to his novel in a rich and profound way.

Taji began *Mardi* "pining for someone who could page me a quotation from Burton on Blue Devils" (*M* 5). The coherence of *Mardi* is that it is such a "page" done in Melville's own hand. Melville builds on the freedoms of discourse, especially as they are impinged upon by blue devils, or (as we have shortened the name) the blues, by irritability, dyspepsia, love passions, solitariness, delusions—in short, all the ups and downs of a "sanguine melancholy," the particular type of melancholy which was Burton's,[10] and Babbalanja's.

Both Taji and Babbalanja are humors characters. They share the mood swings of the sanguine melancholic, but by the end of the book, Melville has sent the two their separate ways. The disentangling of approaches to experience into king, poet, chronicler, and philosopher (Media, Yoomy, Mohi, and Babbalanja) represents a similar impulse to disentangle into separate characters separate sensibilities. But of utmost importance is the way Melville separates out the babbling angel from Taji's initial role as commentator, comic Prometheus, and romantic Prometheus.

Mardi does pay the price of Melville's inexperience and experimentation. It is typical that the fate of the two main characters is at once histrionic and flimsy—Taji turns his prow into the racing tide, Babbalanja suddenly resolves all his doubts and goes to live happily ever after in Serenia.

Mardi is a book that alternates between humor and irritability. We should note that the title itself creates a world, a planet, named after Mars, god of war. Indeed this is a warring book about God's creatures fighting; and Melville often fails to be aloof from that fighting. But if *Mardi* releases an unbridled aggressiveness in Melville, it also allows him, in the long run, to find a deeper, more expansive humor.

In *White-Jacket,* Melville takes another step toward working through his novels' being "botches." The jacket which the narrator makes for himself is a metaphor for the book as a patchwork of borrowings. These borrowings are not just sentences, paragraphs, and incidents, but—as before—types of prose narrative. If the novel on one level is a humorous battle between Melville's jacket and himself, in destroying the jacket as he does at the end of the book, Melville exorcises its hold over him. The outcome, oddly enough, is that for the future he is free to borrow as he wishes without fear of losing his identity. In this novel, the narrator rescues not the inaccessible beautiful lady, but himself. In many respects *White-Jacket* is a tentative book, but it also rings with self-recognition.

In this novel, Melville gives the Babbalanja character the central role of narrator, and makes the entire book subservient to him. White-Jacket, like Babbalanja, is a man who lives with all his questions about him, but whose instinctive response to them is to search out the comfort of human fellowship. True, White-Jacket is given neither a spiritual journey nor spiritual problems to solve, but the jacket itself deftly embodies Babbalanja's entire predicament, of feeling himself alone in his own mind. And if White-Jacket is less confident and more vulnerable than Babbalanja, he is at the same time more accessible and better realized as a character. White-Jacket need not indulge endlessly in theological speculations. His dilemma is shifted to a ludicrous battle between a man and his jacket. In the calm of *Mardi,* the landsman shook himself in his coat to see if he was alive; now Melville takes up the coat itself. *White-Jacket* presents the human dilemma as it is expressed concretely in the way a man feels in his clothing, in his own skin.

Melville is not a novelist of ideas. As this shift demonstrates, he is interested less in ideas than in what it feels like to have ideas, to have something particular going on in your head—your attic. Ideas in Melville come from and lead to questions. They are not stable entities but animated embodiments of what interests him, the experience of having a mind. Never a philosopher, just as he is never a historian, Melville tosses out to us many a philosophical idea, as well as many a fine historical document. He gives us life on a cannibal island just before white civilization moved in, on a frigate just before flogging was abolished, on a whaleship at the moment when the whaling industry was at its peak. He likes to catch philosophy and history at a critical juncture, when they are pushing man to revolutionary new sensations of what life is. Then his main character sweats it out with those fine new sensations.

So White-Jacket, like Babbalanja, is unable to repress his talk, his encyclopedic rambling. He insists on trying everything, that is, on trying to describe everything. Referring to the book's opening, a critic has warned us to pay attention because when Melville is facetious something is usually going on underneath.[11] The playfulness, however, is no diversionary tactic. Melville is simply introducing a persona who will "in all conscience" tell us everything at every point of the way—even, to begin with, that the white jacket of the title is not so very white after all. The opening suggests the book's humor: in a story of rejection and acceptance, loneliness and sociability, a man is assiduously trying to figure out and explain what sort of sensation life is. Here, ichthyology reverts to anthropology. White-Jacket deferentially catalogues all the people on the American warship *Neversink,* their tempers, ranks, personalities—humors. He even longs for a directory at one point.

If *White-Jacket* had only the narrator's conscientious attempt as a documenter, and his fight with his jacket to depend upon for drama, it would be a flimsy book. It has more. Melville's triumph is that he finds a concrete image of God's creatures fighting. It was suggested above that Mardi may be translated as a warring world, a planet named after the god of war. In *White-Jacket* we have, as the logical next step, "the world in a man-of-war," or life in our man-of-war world. Indeed, Melville could not have found for himself a more apt subject than a frigate. It gets immediately to the heart of the absurdity Melville talks around in *Mardi,* but cannot quite enact except through a lot of conversation and some histrionic gestures. It takes Melville a while in *White-Jacket* to get to the topics associated with war—the flogging, the articles of war, and the superb motto: "Burn, Sink and Destroy." Similarly, *Typee* is obsessed with the wonders of a breadfruit paradise to the frequent neglect of the cannibalistic menace. But in both books it is the menace which provides the dramatic tension.

The humor in *White-Jacket,* as in *Typee,* is neither lighthearted nor darkly oppressive. *White-Jacket* mainly differs from the earlier book in that the humorous excitability of *Typee*'s opening pages is here sustained for thirty chapters. Especially in the first third of the book, White-Jacket thinks in terms of grandiose desires and ideals. For instance, he takes a humorously bragging pride in his role as the looser of the mainroyal sail, as well as in his achievement in being accepted into Jack Chase's mess, the Forty-Two Pounder Club, the place for life and commotion, the place to be gentlemanly and jolly. He does not merely hug his friends, however: "yes: I fairly hugged myself, and reveled in my jacket" (*WJ* 37), he says, having just described the jacket in terms that build from a Caledonian earnestness to a lavish extravagance.

The narrator already guesses that his jacket (among other things) may have failings. Nonetheless, his intoxication with good companionship and high ideals rubs off on every meditation. We hear of the grand democratic cookery, of White-Jacket's ambition to make the best of all possible "duffs," and of days "spent among oranges and ladies" (*WJ* 32). In chapter 12 Melville himself speaks of the "free, broad, off-hand" style (*WJ* 47) which has made a melodrama of everything from the construction of a garment to the swabbing of the deck. In fact the Fourth of July theatricals are only a climax of what has been in progress all along and it is not surprising that they build to this height: "At length, when that heart-thrilling scene came on, where Percy Royal-Mast rescues fifteen oppressed sailors from the watch-house, in the teeth of a posse of constables, the audience leaped to their feet, overturned the capstan bars, and to a man hurled their hats on the stage in a delirium of delight" (*WJ* 94).

The game is making believe freedom is possible, and getting drunk on one's desires. Even, however, when the Percy Royal-Masts of the world have far to go in freeing the oppressed, the complaint is rendered in lavish terms: "There is no calling for a mutton chop and a point of claret for yourself; no selecting of chambers for the night; no hanging of pantaloons over the back of a chair; no ringing your bell on a rainy morning, to take your coffee in bed" (*WJ* 35). Or the complaint is sung out in rhapsodies, for instance, as in White-Jacket's thoughts on the seamen's meal hours:

Twelve o'clock! It is the natural centre, key-stone, and

very heart of the day. At that hour, the sun has arrived at the top of his hill; and as he seems to hang poised there a while, before coming down on the other side, it is but reasonable to suppose that he is then stopping to dine; setting an eminent example to all mankind. The rest of the day is called *afternoon;* the very sound of which fine old Saxon word conveys a feeling of the lee bulwarks and a nap; a summer sea—soft breezes creeping over it; dreamy dolphins gliding in the distance. [*WJ* 28-29]

Throughout the book, we come back to this joking. Melville identifies the law of gravitation as the only victor of modern mechanical warfare. Nonetheless, afterwards, he takes off again: "I have no doubt that, had I and my gun been at the battle of the Nile, we would mutually have immortalized ourselves; the ramming-pole would have been hung up in Westminster Abbey; and I, ennobled by the king, besides receiving the illustrious honor of an autographed letter from his majesty through the perfumed right hand of his private secretary" (*WJ* 66-67). The joke is not just that we cannot be kings, or even ennobled by kings, but, as in *Mardi,* so what if we were? Even our visions of the past, with their elaborate hierarchies, like those of Arabia that Melville is always teasing us with, are illusory. If we think war was better then, and life was finer for being more heroic, we should listen to White-Jacket, for example, regarding "that Thracian who, with his compliments, [sending] an arrow into the King of Macedon, superscribed 'For Philip's right eye,' set a fine example to all warriors" (*WJ* 66).

Especially, however, because the past is not more glorious than the present, we can dream of being free in ways that never were possible and never will be possible in a world ruled by a law of gravitation. In such a world, Melville may well boast, in the midst of his complaining, "I would not exchange my coarse canvas hammock for the grand state-bed, like a stately coach-and-four, in which they tuck in a king when he passes a night at Blenheim Castle" (*WJ* 79).

The purest embodiment in *White-Jacket* of the high jinks of idealism is the man who plays Percy Royal-Mast in the theatricals—Jack Chase. Frequently called a romantic hero, he is also exultant and rhapsodic, a cosmopolitan yarn-spinner. Jack Chase deserts ship to fight for the Peruvian rebellion, then is miraculously accepted back. He saves White-Jacket from a flogging and tries to save him from his fall. But it is not just what he has done that makes him such a hero in this book, it is the showmanship of how he has done it; not just the stories he tells, but the flair with which he tells them.

"Were mine the style of stout old Chapman's Homer, even then I would scarce venture to give noble Jack's own version" is the key sentence in White-Jacket's description of Jack recalling the battle of Navarino. In an offhand way, Jack is said to surpass not Achilles but Homer. But as Jack's story unfolds, we discover it has nothing to do with either Chapman's or Homer's style. Instead, it suggests the rhapsodic prose of Melville's opening in *Typee*: "We bayed to be at them," said Jack; "and when we did open fire, we were like dolphin among the flying fish. 'Every man take his bird' was the cry, when we trained our guns. And those guns all smoked like rows of Dutch pipe-bowls, my hearties!" (*WJ* 318).

This sort of showmanship is the heart of the book. It is sustained by Jack Chase as well as by the commotion of the ship "rolling like the world" (*WJ* 115); by the grand state reception of the commodore; by the purser's steward's auction of the famous white jacket; by an absurd man-of-war race in which the *Neversink* loses all sight of its rivals; and finally by the fall from the yardarm completed by an ascent from the realm of the water of the coiled fish, to the air, to the deck, and within ten minutes aloft again to the rigging. A sailor who read *White-Jacket* shortly after it was written complained that, after such a fall, White-Jacket certainly could not have returned to the rigging within ten minutes.[12] That is precisely Melville's game, to make a profound, breathtaking circus act out of a physical fall and ascent.

Sustaining this exultation, as in *Typee*, is a vision of evil as vacuous brutality. But here the vision is presented more forcefully and deliberately, less exotically. Instead of remote savages we face a tyrannical American sea captain who, however, like the Typees, is not evil in any grandiose way, but merely swaggering, foolish— and as if in an attempt to fill his own vacuum—sadistic. Claret's cruelty is inadvertent, as if some gravitational law were operating through him. At Cape Horn, he tumbles out of his cabin looking "like a ghost in his nightdress" (*WJ* 106) and stumbles on precisely the wrong order. (It would have been catastrophic but, luckily, Mad Jack is sharp enough to countermand the order and save the ship.) Or, having been attacked by flying objects, Claret decides to let his men play checkers after all. Captain Claret is only a man who looks pretty inconsequential, after all, at a cocktail party. The commodore is even less in evidence, a scarecrow embodiment of the articles of war, who sticks to his cabin for nearly the entire voyage. Even Bland, well known for his serpentine evil, should be noted for his name. One of the adjectives Melville affectionately uses for his jacket is "very tasty." Bland is surely evil, yet Melville's point about him is that he is bland, "even more luckless than depraved," a man whose corruption was casual, unmomentous, even rote. He "did wicked deeds as the cattle browse the herbage" (*WJ* 188).

It is only incidental, however, that the main targets in *White-Jacket* are the people in power. Melville mocks the officers of the ship not because he sat down to write a propagandistic attack on the undemocratic American navy (although this was certainly part of his purpose), but because men of high rank have access to the biggest whips, and wear their pretensions most ostentatiously. White-Jacket's critical eye on his superiors is essentially a comment on the absurdity of mankind.

> The officers generally fight as dandies dance, namely, in silk stockings; inasmuch as, in case of being wounded in the leg, the silk-hose can be more easily drawn off by the Surgeon. . . . An economical captain, while taking care to case his legs in silk, might yet see fit to save his best suit, and fight in his old clothes. For, besides that an old garment might much better be cut to pieces than a new one, it must be a mighty disagreeable thing to die in a stiff, tight-breasted coat, not yet worked easy under the arm-pits. At such times, a man should feel free, unencumbered, and perfectly at his ease in points of straps and suspenders. No ill-will concerning his tailor, should intrude upon his thoughts of eternity. [*WJ* 68-69]

This nuance, by the way, is more subtle than the famous Dr. Cadwallader Cuticle incident. Bound twice, once by slavish devotion to fashion and once again by mortality, man quirkily diverts himself by emphasizing the most literal stricture, the pull on the underarm.

The sympathy, though, that makes this attack on the officers subtle, comes from the speaker's being not just the boy who sees through the emperor's old clothes, but himself a fellow in a worthless garment. The men in short are not much better than the officers. Chapter 10, "From Pockets to Pickpockets," traces precisely this reality. In it Melville moves from the pockets he has lovingly built into his castle of a jacket to the reason for their ineffectuality, *"the people's"* pickpocketing. White-Jacket wryly describes all the ingenious ways the sailors have of stealing from one another: "It is a good joke, for instance, and one often perpetrated on board ship, to stand talking to a man in a dark night watch and all the while be cutting the buttons from his coat" (*WJ* 38). White-Jacket concludes, however, with his usual philosophicalness, "To enumerate all the minor pilferings on board a man-of-war would be endless. With some highly commendable exceptions, they rob from one another, and rob back again, till, in the matter of small things, a community of goods seems almost established" (*WJ* 39).

In other words, after I have stolen your gold piece, you will steal mine, and for all our efforts we shall each have gained nothing except an outlet for our perversity. Like the officers, *"the people"* themselves are outlandish. While Melville certainly clarifies that the inhumanity of the articles of war has had a large role in demoralizing *"the people"* into pickpocketings and worse, and while it is certain that Melville is on one level arguing for considerable reform of those articles, on another level Melville is simply confronting the reader with a certain intransigence of reality, the component of "God's creatures fighting."

In this book, then, Melville balances dandies with pickpockets, barbers with barbars, Captain Claret's toping with tyranny. If we laugh at the Polynesian Wooloo's mistaking snow for flour, hailstones for glass beads, and raisins for bugs, we are reminded that we are all Wooloos, and the world constantly turning. Sometimes Melville wryly takes this reflection to more serious proportions, as when White-Jacket dreams of a sphere "where to break a man on the wheel is held the most exquisite of delights you can confer upon him . . . where to tumble one into a pit after death, and then throw cold clods upon his upturned face, is a species of contumely, only inflicted upon the most notorious criminals" (*WJ* 186). Baldy, harried in his duties aloft, finds falling to the deck (where "he was picked up for dead. . . his bones. . . like those of a man broken on the wheel" [*WJ* 196]) far from the most exquisite of delights. And yet again if Baldy painfully falls to the deck, White-Jacket miraculously falls not to the deck but to the ocean, which receives him and sends him back up.

We should return for a moment, however, to Baldy's fall, which has been given little critical attention and which has been attributed to some actual happening: the log of Melville's ship indicates that a man, after a fall, was put into a body cast to heal.[13] However, Melville may well have gotten the idea of the fall from the Mercier and Gallop book, *Life in a Man-of-War, or Scenes in "Old Ironsides" during Her Cruise in the Pacific, By a Fore-top-man,* to which critics generally only attribute *White-Jacket*'s amusing material.[14]

Crude as it may be, this source is actually a piece of prison literature. It is true that "the Fore-top-man" says almost nothing about flogging, and generally does not criticize the officers, that he prides himself on his patriotism and piety, and does not know what to do with his sense of the sailor's hardship. However, early in this book—which is dedicated to his fellow sailors as if to fellow sufferers—the Fore-top-man tells a story of a sailor who jumps overboard because he cannot stand the prospect of the voyage ahead. Once in the water, this fellow decides drowning is not so pleasant and lets himself be saved. We are told by way of a moral that "Second Thoughts are Best." If this is just what we would expect, the authors quickly follow it up with Bill Garnet's yarn of a man so harried by a cruel officer in his work aloft that he falls from the yardarm and, unlike the suicidal sailor, refuses to be rescued by the men in the boat. He shakes his fist at them as he drowns, and that night sends his ghost up to hurl the mate to his death. The story may well be the source for Baldy's fall, as well as the source of another incident. After Bungs has fallen to the ocean and died because his life raft was so shoddy, White-Jacket is mistaken for the ghost of Bungs in the yardarm, in the first of the two times that his jacket is almost the death of him.

Both expanding the Fore-top-man's mirth to a theatricality and absorbing the hardships which the Fore-top-man did not know how to handle, Melville invigorates Mercier and Gallop's glibly philosophical humor of defeat. Ultimately Melville devotes a character, Happy Jack, to embodying the false servile humor which that of the Fore-top-man must have represented to him. Indeed, Melville makes it clear how different Happy Jack is from the book's other humorists, the purser's steward and Lemsford. To make up for Happy Jack, Melville also gives us, with his characteristic balancing in this book, on one side, Mad Jack, vigorous but a drinker; and on the other, courageous spirited Jack Chase. In the middle finally is another "jack," the narrator, White-Jacket, who in all his sensibility embodies precisely the humor that Melville would most want an author to have in his work.

But a well-balanced book is not necessarily a consistently bold and effective one. Newton Arvin's comment still holds, that although *White-Jacket* is rich, substantial, and taut in many respects, it is flawed by "the solid and sometimes lumpish blocks of straight exposition and description" and by an overassertive moral passion.[15]

In *White-Jacket* Melville has temporarily lost the knack he had found so easily in *Typee* of sustaining his humor. *White-Jacket* sags heavily in the middle while the ship sits in Rio's harbor. Indeed, the problem with the Dr. Cuticle episode is that it is contrived to relieve the boredom of the middle section of the book, and made as grotesque as it is not because Melville is fascinated with the man himself, but because Melville is searching for an extreme to gain the reader's attention in some startling way. The floggings, especially the flogging of the fleet, are described painfully well, but lack the dramatic focus that comes from sharp characterization. Claret, a drunken rerun of Taji, thinking himself master of the moon and sun, is a character in absentia like the commodore himself. When Melville pitches upon Cuticle, he does so with too much weight for this suddenly introduced (and just as suddenly dropped) character to bear.

White-Jacket is weak in one other respect, in the narrator's timidity. The most telling remark that White-Jacket makes about himself is that he has politely decided never to mention whaling around Jack Chase because the latter hated to hear of such a demeaning trade. As much as *White-Jacket* emboldens both the exultation and the brutality of the Fore-top-man's tale, it is thinly developed. Melville has the idea of expressing his humor, but it is as if he has not realized that he has the idea. Not until *Moby-Dick* does the reader feel that the author is both committed to his humor and sufficiently in control to make that humor viable.

Just as Melville's humor played off the manic-depressive swing of sensibility as the "sort of sensation" life is, so his novels themselves swung noticeably in response to the public's criticism of him and to his own feelings of what he had or had not achieved in them. His responsiveness to his audience accounts for the great showmanship of most of his novels. In *Omoo* and *Redburn,* however, Melville seems distracted by his concern for his public. In these two books, he is not at his strongest. His second book, *Omoo* (1847), is his response to the success of his first, *Typee;* and his fourth book, *Redburn* (1849), to the pitfalls of his third, *Mardi.* In looking briefly at *Omoo* and *Redburn*—as well as at his articles on "Old Zack" (1847)— we see how Melville's desire to please his public affected his humor. Also we find developments which enlarged his humor for later works.

Omoo has the shortcomings of a sequel. In this book it seems Melville tried to hold onto *Typee*'s success and at the same time to correct all of *Typee*'s weaknesses. Specifically, *Typee* taught Melville that the public likes humor, publishers demand authenticity, and critics dislike attacks on missionaries. As a result, in *Omoo* Melville is too determined to be funny. He is less daring than in *Typee.* He clings to a day-by-day authenticity rather than seeking a larger fictional design so effective in *Typee,* and as a result *Omoo* lacks the drama necessary to sustain the humor. What is more, to show he really meant it in *Typee,* in *Omoo* Melville plunges head first into the attack on the missionaries, and the polemic grates.

In the first two-thirds of this South Seas travel narrative, *Omoo* alternates between jauntiness and axe grinding. The fault at both extremes is the same. The narrator, Paul, ridicules the captain of the ship which picks him up at sea, and he ridicules the natives and European missionaries he meets ashore in Tahiti. But he rarely parodies himself. Instead, he is a Danaesque figure, who straightforwardly identifies himself with gentleman stock, tries reasonably to talk the men out of the mutiny, and only writes up the round robin because he needs some way of appeasing an anarchic crew. A pragmatic man with no quirks, Paul is not even humorously priggish, as Redburn is intended to be. It is as if Melville sought to solve the problem of authenticity by providing a normal sort of man for a narrator.

Perhaps the vagabond, Dr. Long Ghost, takes the burden of being the humors character from the narrator; but I think not. Melville chooses to narrate in the first person; his narrator cannot simply be wished out of the way. Melville's novels are as far from Henry James's kind of craft as one could go. As in *Tristram Shandy* or the essays of Elia, the narrator in a Melville novel—off to the side telling the story—is actually at the magnetic center of the book. Paul's feeling stifled by Dr. Long Ghost's continually stealing the show suggests a central problem. Paul (perhaps like Melville here) is getting swept under a bit; and because Paul is too weak a character for us to laugh at, the humor of the whole book, wonderful as it is at moments, turns thin. The anticivilization polemic may even fall flat because mild Tahiti, like Paul, is too easily stepped on. Indeed *Typee* is the stronger book because the Typee culture was that much more fiercely protective of itself—at a considerable price, of course, but nonetheless protective. Such a question with regard to either Paul or the Tahitians would be irrelevant if the protection of selfhood—and the threat of disintegration of selfhood—did not fascinate Melville so much elsewhere and bring forth such originality and vision. In *Omoo* Melville has little of this fascination.

But in addition, as a character in his own right, Dr. Long

Ghost is less interesting than critical opinion makes him seem. It is true that his failure to woo a young lady or gain audience with the queen makes him sympathetic as a character. Also, it is to his credit as a rogue that he is as happy to leave the plantation job as he was to make sure Paul got the heaviest share of the work there. Yet ultimately he is too complacent to make it as a rogue. He is watered-down Smollett without the initial sense of hardship that makes Smollett's picaresque bracing, and Smollett's rovers rogues. Melville's allusion to Smollett with reference to Long Ghost, we should note, is to associate the scamp not so much with the roguery of jumping ship as with a predilection for the ladies. But Long Ghost's dallyings are dull, as is Paul's infatuation with the English-woman, Mrs. Bell. Humorous passion in Melville does best with the hugging of self that we get so much of, first in *White-Jacket* and later in *Moby-Dick:* you hug yourself, your jacket, your cannibal bedmate, and all the mysteries of the Pentateuch. In *Omoo,* the narrator's inability to experience this absurd fundamental emotion throws off the other relationships in the book.

Nevertheless, and beginning with chapter 51, or for the last third of the book, Melville does find a rich vein of humor, though it is more like *Dharma Bums* than like Smollett. This part of the book is the happy part, the song of indolence. In the first fifty chapters, Melville's narrator, Paul, is the prudent Yankee. Afterwards Zeke, the yam-planting Yankee, takes the burden of being hardworking and prudent from the narrator, so that Paul is free to be a rover. The book from that point on is more relaxed. The rovers rove; we recall all the walking around, Paul's inglorious adventure of being shadily offered a pair of pants, the visit with Po-Po, the marvelous unstinting hospitality, the delusion of becoming consul to the Tahitian queen, the living off the breadfruit of the land, and—most of all—the encounter with the native personality where it is still free of the anxieties and mental contortions introduced by for-eigners.

This is what Melville has happened on here, the native temperament which is antithetical to earnest sentiment, and con-ducive, above all, to amusement. The indolent savage speaks to the unsanctimonious, improvisational approach to life. Melville spells out why he has to go to the last frontier, the Pacific Islands, for this easy love of motley. It is as if the earnestness of America has rubbed off on its aborigines. What Melville prefers is not noble savages but savages like the inland Tahitians, who "only tolerated your company when making merry at your expense," and "laughed in your face when you looked sentimental" (O 268). It is this very love of anti-Caledonian motley which makes Melville come down so hard on the officious missionaries, because the natives in contrast are so zany. Once Melville writes about them positively instead of portraying civilization negatively, the book begins to work.

The counterpart of *Omoo*'s humor of motley spontaneous outdoor living is the humor of the snug cottage, which Melville begins to develop in *Redburn*. Embodied most of all here in Redburn's priggishness, snug cottage humor forms a key element in Melville's fiction at its best. Here, however, Melville is only beginning to understand this sort of humor.

To detail the way it works in *Redburn,* we need to begin with another element in the book, the intelligence and power of its descriptions of nineteenth-century wretchedness, when Redburn, arriving in Europe, views the squalor of Liverpool and the steerage. Melville achieves a voice of clarity and authority in these scenes which make them memorable above much else in the book. The intelligence of his description lies in his recognition that even the seemingly clear response to the squalor, that it is terrible, is full of paradoxes. Of course, laws must be passed, income distributed, economies restructured; but as Melville's tone often suggests, ameliorate one inscrutable hardship and it will but lead to some new one. The sensation of being alive is not just a matter of seeing hardship and plunging into reform, but of being burdened with the intractability of things; see, for example, Melville on slavery in *Mardi*'s Vivenza. Man quite simply does not live in a breadfruit paradise where sustenance grows on trees, and where he need do virtually nothing to be fed, except indulge in the pleasure of cooking and eat.

What then is Redburn's connection to all this hardship? In this story of a poor boy's first voyage in the merchant service, we are led to think that the boy, Redburn, has had a particularly hard time. Yet for all that, on one level, he hovers on the brink of suffering, on another level he really does all right for himself. He certainly is poor and he gets ribbed quite a bit by the sailors for his inexperience at sea. We are never given the sense, however, that Redburn is seriously threatened by his experience. Hard work does not hurt him, he loves climbing the rigging, the ship does not go near Cape Horn, and his stay in Liverpool is essentially a vacation with free room and board; the fact is that Redburn more than others has his options even if he is poor. A sign ultimately of how Melville wants us to read Redburn's story is the history of Redburn's friend, Harry Bolton, who—despite his money—is much more up against the brutality of things than Redburn. When Redburn at the close of the voyage is hurrying happily home to his mother, we recall he glibly suggests a copying job to Bolton; and Bolton eventually dies crushed between a ship and a whale.

Redburn's problem as a novel, as William Gilman shows in detail,[16] stems from inconsistency in the portrayal of its main character. As in *Omoo,* Melville tackles the problem of authenticity too vigorously. Though poor, Redburn is clearly a gentleman's son, and we are told exactly why this son has gone to sea. Clarifying these practical details leaves other problems, however. Primarily, how can such a naive fellow, who is nearly idiotic regarding sea usages, become for a time not only intelligent but levelheaded and mature? Melville's lucid descriptions of poverty destroy the characterization which he takes such pains to establish in the early part of the book.

In the final analysis, Melville alternates between satire of Redburn's complacency and respect for his sagacity, between a sympathetic interest in his adventures as a tenderfoot and a simple dislike of the young man. Redburn often bears the brunt of Melville's anger at his audience for wanting so much to be mollified. It is not that Redburn begins a priggish youth and matures, or that he is essentially priggish with flashes of perceptivity. Rather it seems that Melville cannot decide whether to make Redburn in essence smugly naive or intelligently enlightened—a mirror of his audience at its worst or a mirror of himself at his best.

But Melville's problem is not sheer indecision. He is beginning to be fascinated by Redburn's smugness. Had he realized it, Melville might have been more subtle about it, more sympathetic—as he will be in his later works, most notably with Captain Delano in "Benito Cereno," and the lawyer in "Bartleby." Here, however, we get Redburn's unrelenting talk of mother and sisters and our sweet little cottage and street, all that reverence for papa, and that fine touch of the defunct guidebook drawn out twenty pages too long because Redburn is too naive to accept the reality that things change. It is not just that Redburn is a member of the temperance and nonsmoking societies, and that he preaches to others, but that Melville provides a sugary tone of voice for him, as if the boy were telling the story in his mother's arms. "The reason why I did this, was because" (R 23), Redburn typically begins with a puckering wordiness—he is explaining why he threw his last penny away. Or he notes that Tom Legare kept the Juvenile Total Abstinence Association funds "in a little purse that his cousin knit for him" (R 42). These mannerisms lead up to larger false-ringing pieties about how the Holy Bible was the only timeless guide, about how he should not look into things that only God could understand, and—most flagrant—about how he has remained a bachelor because of his infatuation with three pretty girls he saw in a cottage on the road to London. This last is so silly it forces us to ask what Melville means by this character.

In later works, Melville has learned to use cozy cottage humor to better advantage. The mistake of overdoing Redburn's smug desire to live out his life in a cute little cottage, preferably with his mother, will surface even more painfully in *Pierre*. In "Bartleby" and "Benito Cereno," however, subtle and evocative studies of complacency will provide the brilliant core. There Melville will know well how to separate the strands of response into separate characters, making Redburn and Bolton into the lawyer and Bartleby in one story, and into Delano and Babo in another.

In addition to satirizing the smugness, however, Melville learns eventually how to enjoy his cozy cottage. In *Redburn* he is thinking too much in terms of a cottage on land. His distinctive contribution to the humor of cottage pretensions is to move that cottage out to sea. In *White-Jacket,* then, for all its failings, Melville profits from his oath to keep the book at sea, even in Rio. On shipboard, the Forty-two Pounder Club and the foretop provide the cottage where man may hug himself, his illusions, and his friends. When Melville is in control of cozy cottage humor, it does not pall because it is his own Cape-Horn-weathered foretop cottage, not an English countryside cottage. In *Redburn,* however, very much as later in *Pierre,* Melville is still playing with English cottages and English girls eating muffins. Also, in the future with the exception of *Pierre,* Melville will not force the reader to decide whether the prevailing attitude is satire or sympathy. Instead he will blend the two with consummate tact.

This chapter will conclude with a brief look at Melville's ten "Authentic Anecdotes of 'Old Zack.'" (Zack was Zachary Taylor who, in the summer of 1847 when these articles appeared, was a Mexican War general—and to some people, a great hero.) The articles, originally published in the Duyckinck circle humorous periodical, *Yankee Doodle,* have not yet been reprinted in full. They have been rarely mentioned and then only with a certain reluctance.[17] The assumption seems to be that they represent an embarrassing and unique experience in Melville's career, because Melville wrote them to keep himself in good favor in the Duyckinck circle, and hence associated them with a great humiliation. We have, however, no evidence of Melville feeling anything of the kind. Even if we had, were we to listen to Melville's every scruple with regard to potboiling, we would have to scrap four of the five novels written before *Moby-Dick.* What is illuminating about these articles is that, on the contrary, they were written under conditions and with intentions very similar to those prompting Melville's first five novels. Written expressly to be funny, they embody in small the artistic task that Melville faced in writing his fiction, and they suggest how Melville characteristically handled his humor.

The real weakness of the anecdotes is their heavy-handedness. They use low-grade conventional jokes to an embarrassing degree. For example, Melville emphasizes Zack's oversized posterior, and gives us unimaginative practical jokes like the tack placed upon

Zack's saddle, even though this sort of circus humor does not fare well in print. In addition, in case we have missed the joke of the supposedly rough-and-ready general being a fastidious effeminate (he does his own washing and mending), Melville calls him at one point "modest as any miss";[18] this is lame. Finally, Melville plays with language in a standard American way: "In all cases we give the old man's very words. If they show a want of early attendance at the Grammar School, it must be borne in mind that old Zack never took a college diploma . . . and rather glories in the simplicity and unostentation of his speech. 'Describe me, Sir,' said he to our correspondent—'describe me Sir as I am—no polysyllables—no stuff—it's time they should know me in my true light.'"[19]

Once again the man of gumption and monosyllables makes fun of his large-worded countryman, but in this case his doing so reveals him as a nincompoop, not a hero. The reversal, however, is hardly ingenious. We are still left with the same overworked material—the rivalry between sophisticate and backwoodsman.

In these articles Melville seems to have worried about publicly and directly attacking a particular individual. Melville had not yet been much attacked in reviews. It was only two years later, after *Mardi* came out and he began to understand too well the pain that critical attacks could bring, that he vowed he would never attack any man's work.[20] This vow, however, does not represent a change, only a realization of what Melville felt all along and what accounts for the distinct character of his humor from *Typee* to *The Confidence-Man*. That is: merely converting hostility into cleverness is a tedious game, as literal-minded as it is narrow. What interested Melville was the absurdity of human nature and the absurdity of the universe to which human nature is a response. His way of dealing with what interested him was to find the right balance between ridicule and sympathy, and to see the individual as part, even if an ornery or misanthropic part, of the human condition.

In the Zack articles, however, Melville could not allow himself such a broad perspective. He was supposed to attack one man, Taylor. The easiest way for him to have released the strain on his humor would have been to remove the individual target, and with it the assumption that after all most men are better than those few god-awful ones. Indeed in his novels he has done precisely this, taken the heavy-handed sting out of his attack by broadening it to the entire human race, and being careful not even to put in writing to Richard Dana the names of the prototypes of the *Neversink* officers. Thus one can see how the awkwardness of Melville's attack on Zack's clothing[21] prefigures the subtle play and lucidity of the section quoted above in the discussion of *White-Jacket*. That passage, beginning "Officers generally fight as dandies dance," attacks all officers and shows the absurdity of mankind in muddling thoughts of eternity with ill will toward its tailors.

But even in these articles, however, and this is what is illuminating, Melville finds a way to avoid a narrow attack on a single man. It was neither original nor difficult for Melville to parody P. T. Barnum's enterprise and advertisements. But in allowing most of the ten articles to build quietly from an attack on Zachary Taylor to a parody of P. T. Barnum, Melville has achieved a characteristic freshness. Barnum is not just one more fool, but as Ishmael would say, "the sign and symbol" of what utter fools we all are. Melville's repeated introduction of Barnum here is his way of deflecting the attack from Zack to ourselves, to show us that if we think we can call this backwoodsman an idiot, we should look again—to ourselves, to the average person who so enjoys a Barnum spectacle or a Barnum museum cataloguing the great excitements of the age.

Beginning with the intention to be funny, Melville starts by being so in the most uncomfortably hackneyed ways. Ultimately, however, he finds a way not just to please his public but to please himself by sympathetically and subtly poking fun at his own audience, at himself, and at all of human nature in its desire to lose itself in spectacular fanfares and the idlest of curiosities. One of Melville's concluding touches here is a letter from Barnum asking the general to allow himself to be displayed in one of Barnum's cages. In this negotiation, nicely conveyed and sustained, we see again Melville's preoccupation with the delusion of power, and with the inevitable predicament of our all being mere prisoners in cages. More significantly, returning to Roland Barthes's notes on what distinguishes great art, we see how in using Barnum, Melville makes the spectacle stare back at the spectator, who is fool enough to pay his money to see what we all are, prisoners in cages.

As we see in Melville's "Anecdotes of Old Zack," his early steps involved some clumsy toying with conventional humor. But even when it seemed that Melville was most giving in to the public, he was working at finding his own humorous voice.

IV
Whales and Confidence

With *Moby-Dick,* Melville comes into his own. True, he fumbles in the opening hundred pages with a nervous comicality, and toward the end he is heavy-handed with portents of disaster. Nonetheless, here is Melville's first novel in which, from the beginning, the reader has the clear sense that Melville has not only found his subject, but knows that he has. Here from the first, as he plays with the humor of extravagance, Melville has found his free-ranging voice.

Whaling as a subject is effortlessly right. It combines the modesty of describing the industry one does well with the bragging of a young nation showing off its achievement. The whaling crew, while conveniently limiting the focus to the male sex, projects a profile of the emerging democratic adventure with all America's ambitions to be egalitarian—and rich. As a hunt, whaling provides the stuff not only for robust physical action but for immediate and sustained dramatic conflict: man against whale. Only in *Typee,* with white man and cannibal, had Melville found such a workable dramatic tension. *Moby-Dick* avoids the veering of *Mardi* and the diffuseness of *White-Jacket* without being merely, however, the happy hit of *Typee.* From the first page Melville sees the potential of his subject, the exultation and the dread, a humor grounded in a sense of death. And he knows from the start how to give this humor its leeway; he gives us a narrator who is as assertive as he is stable, and as stable as he is affectionate. Unlike Babbalanja, Ishmael need not quote his way tediously through Seneca, try skepticism, then learn faith. Ishmael begins with a "decoction of Seneca and the Stoics" (*MD* 15) under his belt, and the knowledge as well that even that wears off in time. Unlike self-effacing White-Jacket, as entrammeled in the folds of his own coat as he is in admiration for Jack Chase, Ishmael does not hesitate to mention whaling. Whaling is Ishmael's subject from beginning to end, and he finds a friend who not only wants to talk whaling but to go whaling with him.

Ishmael sets out with a simple impulse. He has noticed and wishes to say that something exciting is going on. He opens his monologue with a list of words with which to name and worship the whale in thirteen languages. His collection of extracts from all over the globe and history conveys his transcendent wonder regarding whales and other prodigies. His first chapter of "Loomings" expresses his sense of forms rising before us with an appearance of great and portentous, indeed exaggerated, size. Later chapters suggest that Ishmael could not have seen a more sublime painting than that in the Spouter Inn, made a better friend than Queequeg, or heard a better sermon than Father Mapple's. Ishmael's impulse is to say not that this is the best of all possible worlds, but that this is nothing less than the most magnificent of all possible universes. His point is not simplistic optimism—it is rhapsody. Everything bows before this impulse, everything comes to seem subservient.

What Melville has arranged, however, is that Ishmael is always losing ground to his excitability. Ishmael would like to have modestly and deferentially said that the whale is a grand and mighty creature. His superlatives, however, take on a life of their own, his invocations trip over themselves. In the midst of straightforward etymologies spring up pompous orthographical maxims; in the midst of joyful songs to the whale, there are pedantic irrelevancies like "The whale is a mammiferous animal without hind feet" (*MD* 7). Ishmael ever waxes warm, even in an address to a sub-sub-librarian:

So fare thee well, poor devil of a Sub-Sub, whose commentator I am. Thou belongest to that hopeless sallow tribe which no wine of the world will ever warm; and for whom even Pale Sherry would be too rosy-strong; but with whom one sometimes loves to sit, and feel poor-devilish too; and grow convivial upon tears; and say to them bluntly, with full eyes and empty glasses, and in not altogether unpleasant sadness—Give it up, Sub-Subs! . . . Would that I could clear out Hampton Court and the Tuileries for ye! [*MD* 2]

All things in this universe become grand, all things wonderful. The more Ishmael says, the more he must say to stay on top of his remarks; but the more he says, the more he ends up submerged. Indeed, not until the very last page when he is almost actually submerged—by water—will Ishmael have said his fill.

In the meantime we cannot be surprised that what Ishmael's peremptory commands in "Loomings" would have us look at from Corlears Hook to Coenties Slip is nothing less than a world of men bewitched, overcome by the ineffable, lost to ocean reveries. For, even while he describes what he sees, here and throughout, he is continually trying to get a footing amidst the current of his statements, until finally: "Once more. Say you are in the country; in some high land of lakes. Take almost any path you please. . . . There is magic in it. Let the most absentminded of men be plunged in his deepest reveries—stand that man on his legs, set his feet agoing, and he will infallibly lead you to water, if water there be in all that region" (*MD* 13). Stand Ishmael on his legs, and he will infallibly lead you to the magnificent uncertainties of this watery world. He is like those brave and daring Nantucketers, who first caught crabs in the sand, then grown bolder, waded out for mackerel, then "at last, launching a navy of great ships on the sea, explored this watery world; put an incessant belt of circumnavigations round it; peeped in at Behring's Straits; and in all seasons and all oceans declared everlasting war with the mightiest animated mass that has survived the flood; most monstrous and most mountainous! That Himmalehan . . . " (*MD* 62).

In the first twenty chapters, however, before the *Pequod* sets sail, Melville had the problem of how to direct this enthusiasm gone haywire. He tries comicality; he spikes the monologue with comic bits. These are not bad, but they do not stand up as well as the rest of the book. We have the landlord gulling Ishmael, Mrs. Hussey quarreling with Queequeg, Ishmael breaking down his roommate's door, Bildad and Peleg doing a nineteenth-century Laurel and Hardy routine, Aunt Charity bustling aboard her pickles and flannels. Accompanying this standard sort of buffoonery are explanations that tell a little too much. "A good laugh is a mighty good thing, and rather too scarce a good thing; the more's the pity," Ishmael says, for example. "So, if any man in his own proper person, afford stuff for a good joke to anybody, let him not be backward, but let him cheerfully allow himself to spend and be spent in that way" (*MD* 35). Statements like these confirm for us our reading of Ishmael's attitude, but they spell out the game too clearly, just as the bits between the obviously comic characters grate by their very insistence upon being funny.

Melville's achievement in *Moby-Dick* has to do less with the game of little interchanges than the game of long talk. The book is full of sermons, full of "the best contradictory authorities" (*MD* 306) giving us their spiels. We have Ishmael's to Queequeg on fasting and fanaticism, Ishmael's to Bildad and Peleg on the First Congregational Church, Father Mapple's to the whalemen, Stubb's to Pip, Stubb's to Fleece, Fleece's to the sharks, and—above all and beneath all—Ishmael's from start to finish on one whaling voyage with one Queequeg, one Ahab, one Moby Dick. The humor at the beginning fumbles, it would seem, because the book is not yet firmly at sea. It is not just that the water itself puts everything in a continually, reliably precarious state of rocking and motion, but that the water is also the territory that Melville has for his own. There was much land humor, and there were many sea stories, but a watery prose humor of old salts and oceangoing isolatoes Melville had to himself. Once at sea also, Ishmael may take a more comfortable working position, less at the center of the action than at the side, as narrator, observer, anatomist, stand-up philosopher. His whole action from then on can become the talk, as it should be. He will occasionally take part in the action or talk about himself, but mostly what we have from "The Advocate" on is Ishmael as the schoolmaster with the full "boggy, soggy, squitchy picture" (*MD* 20) before him, the picture of ultimate fascination, importance, and drama.

In "The Advocate" Melville gets into the heart of his subject and sets up the novel as a prodigious long piece of talk about one of man's activities. Thereafter Ishmael never needs to hesitate to find something to describe or explain. He hardly need turn his head, from Starbuck to Stubb to Flask to Ahab, to the whale, to a system of whales, to the whale's fin to his blubber to his organ to his tail, from the sighting of the whale to the killing of him to the boiling of him to the carving of his teeth, from one gam to the next to the next. So much to talk about! In *Moby-Dick,* Ishmael gets excited about many things; he invokes many gods and kings, and gives us many visions of heaven. "This is Charing Cross; hear ye! good people all,—the Greenland whale is deposed,—the great sperm whale now reigneth" (*MD* 118). Or he invokes that "democratic dignity which, on all hands, radiates without end from God; Himself! The great God absolute! The centre and circumference of all democracy! His omnipresence, our divine equality!" (*MD* 104). Or he dreams up a vision of a heaven of angels each with his hand in a jar of spermacetti. But truly Ishmael's image of glory is being able to talk, and from "The Advocate" on, he may go on as long as he pleases. No wonder the whale is, according to one of Ishmael's final etymological flourishes, "the Macrocephalus of the Long Words" (*MD* 120). *Moby-Dick* is not only a tall tale, but a long story, by another macrocephalus (big head of the long words), by Ishmael himself. And finally, if one notices the quiet inanity of Ishmael's description of Starbuck as a "long earnest man" (*MD* 102), one begins to see that Ishmael knows we are all long, earnest men (unless we are short, stubby ones). We all seek to defend our-selves—or match wits with the universe—by going on as long as we can.

Chapter 82, "The Honor and Glory of Whaling," is central to the book. Here Ishmael typically takes impossible leaps of logic as if he were merely crossing the street. He conjures up for our pleasure the gallant Perseus, who in a fine and lovely act rescues and marries a maid. He conjures up St. George and with a quietly dazzling verbal legerdemain makes over the "tutelary guardian of England" and his dragon into whaleman and whale. Of Hercules we are told, "At any rate the whale caught him, if he did not the whale. I claim him for one of our clan." And finally Vishnoo is brought gently and firmly into the fold. "If I claim the demi-god then, why not the prophet," Ishmael asks, moving quickly and naturally on to the gods themselves. "Perseus, St. George, Hercules, Jonah and Vishnoo! there's a member-roll for you!" (*MD* 306).

Ishmael takes such liberties in the procedures of his talk that the reader's response in part is like Queequeg's, as that benevolent cannibal sits counting by fifties the pages of the incomprehensible book in his lap, "a long-drawn gurgling whistle of astonishment" (*MD* 51). Ishmael, however, has explained of man what is true of himself: "Nothing dispirits and nothing seems worth while disputing. He bolts down all events, all creeds, and beliefs and persuasions, all things visible and invisible, never mind how knobby" (*MD* 195). If Ishmael entangles the reader in the crisscrossing harpoon lines of his suggestibility, he has no choice. Considering the difficulty of getting a grip on that elusive thing called reality, considering that the whale cannot be simply stared in the face because he has none, Ishmael will try anything and with consummate energy and infinite good graces. He will let himself get carried away with a redundancy of alliteration, exclamation, and allusion. He will tell one part of his book as a set of Shakespearean soliloquies, one as a cetological catalogue, one as a visit to a tropical temple surrounded by fierce but indolent natives, and the book as a whole as an anatomy of the world on a ship of fools. He will let Stubb inculcate "the religion of rowing" amongst his men, Flask whip up his to an atheistical orgasmic fury, and he himself get caught up in the current of fifty different sects: Christian, cannibal, Moslem, Hindu, ancient Hebrew, pragmatic American, and more. Ishmael is the predecessor of Beckett's Lucky, but when Ishmael commands himself "Think!" he has let himself in knowingly, willingly, and even happily for the foolishness he will make of himself.

At the end of *Moby-Dick,* the chapters fall off to what we may call tragic relief. Finally all talk gives way to the death song at its core—as "The Hyena" chapter liberates the clean ghost with a quiet conscience sitting snugly in the family vault, the clean ghost who is Ishmael at his best. Finally everyone dies except Ishmael who swims off with the sharks, padlocks on their mouths—and, in effect, on his. The book that begins by following funerals and ends with the death of a nation is from beginning to end a song about what it is like to have survived your own death.

Indeed death is just a shorthand for the vulnerability that is at the core of man's sense of himself in this universe. Ishmael not only sympathizes with our plight, but slowly and lovingly revolves it before our eyes, sees it everywhere, projects it onto anything in sight. A felonious looking whale "has a lovely tail and sentimental Indian eyes of a hazel hue. But his mealy mouth spoils all" (*MD* 127). A white man before Daggoo is a white flag come to beg truce of a fortress, as the "Cabin Table" leaves fearful Starbuck cutting his meat "tenderly" (*MD* 131). In the definition and description prefatory to the first of the nine gams strung through the novel, "the captain, having no place to sit in, is pulled off to his visit all standing like a pine tree. And often you will notice that being conscious of the eyes of the whole visible world resting on him from the sides of the two ships, this standing captain is all alive to the importance of sustaining his dignity by maintaining his legs." Indeed dignity is always the catch; if we did not insist upon it we would never be quite this vulnerable.

> Nor is this any very easy matter; for in his rear is the immense projecting steering oar hitting him now and then in the small of his back, the after oar reciprocating by rapping his knees in front. He is thus completely wedged before and behind, and can only expand himself sideways by settling down on his stretched legs. . . . Then, again, it would never do in plain sight of the world's riveted eyes, it would never do, I say, for this straddling captain to be seen steadying himself the slightest particle by catching hold of anything with his hands; indeed as token of his entire, buoyant self-command, he generally carries his hands in his trouser's pockets. [*MD* 207]

It is typical of Ishmael, by the way, that in this description he is not only busily tacking one thought to the next, but that in doing so he lets slip in new juxtapositions. It is not only how wedged in is this figure of impressive authority, but how courteous the after oar is in *reciprocating* the raps of the steering oar.

What Ishmael calls the "universal thump" in this book in fact goes round and round, alternating only with the kick. Poor devils on shore "that happen to know an irascible great man" only "make distant unobtrusive salutations to him in the street, lest if they pursued the acquaintance further, they might receive a summary thump for their presumption" (*MD* 176-77). In "Merry Christmas," Ishmael, presuming only to worry to himself about Ahab, is kicked in the rear by Peleg. Stubb, thinking he is dreaming of being kicked by Ahab, is actually dreaming of Ahab being kicked by Moby Dick; for in his dream Stubb kicks his leg off trying to get back at a mute immovable pyramid (while a seaweedy Mr. Humpback urges prudence upon him and then swims off). Ultimately it is of course Ahab, having become the "old sea-captain" himself, who is kicked and thumped by the great universe itself in the body of Moby Dick (who in turn like many another whale has been continuously thumped by mankind). The fact that Ahab, unlike "wise" Stubb, continues to kick back and loses not only his leg, but his life, his ship, and all his crew but Ishmael, no more means that Ahab is a fool than that he is actually the wise one. Ahab's response simply attests to the absoluteness with which Melville understands and estimates that thump. The thump is finally the starkest revelation of our predicament as human beings. No wonder we humor ourselves. Humor is our grand consolation.

Ishmael's monologue, however, is not merely an abstract extravaganza of a *consolatio*. The "Love Partition" which was Melville's first purchase of *The Anatomy of Melancholy*[1] presented love as one of melancholy's causes and cures. Ishmael goes further. At the center of the whole book is what may be referred to as the hug. It is not just that Ishmael is affectionate and friendly, that he is inclined to rub shoulders and be sociable, that the first of his adventures is befriending the patchwork-tattooed pedlar of heads. The whole book is built upon the magnetism between the inmates of the universe. *Moby-Dick* is permeated with the imagery and paraphernalia of love, marriage, sex, generation, and lactation; *Moby-Dick* is filled with gigantic phalli such as queens worship in their secret groves, with sperm, wedding candles, wedding cakes, wedding beds, cream, sugar, and strawberries. It is not just that Moby Dick is celebrated on one level as a great bull, nor that "The Cassock" ceremoniously undresses the whale's private parts upon the deck. It is not just that Queequeg throws his arm over Ishmael in the bed in which the landlord and Sal were "spliced," nor that the reader is invited with Ishmael to watch the amours of the deep. Most like *Typee* is this respect, *Moby-Dick* is saturated with a teasing sexuality which comes across as wonder at erotic bounty. Finally what we realize is most pathetic about Dough-Boy is that his father was a breadless baker, and his mother a sterile creature of a hospital nurse. Ishmael's song of triumph is an exultation in sexuality, climaxed rapturously and onanistically with his squeezing his own hands in the oleaginous tubs of "sperm."

Indeed Melville here has found his game. You hug yourself, you hug your cannibal bedmate, you lick your paws, you even hug your agony (Ahab for the latter two). In those great hugs, squeezing hands, you dream of all of nature's bounty, all the creams and milks of sperm and gold, without ever touching your precarious individual selfhood or engaging in the fruitful—hence pedestrian—business of sex. It is not merely fortuitous that no women were on board the *Pequod*. Rather, it was the very fact that whaleships were all male which made them perfect touchstones for Melville's humor. There he could dwell upon the asexual hug and the asexual dream of plenty, and the very asexuality of the hug would establish and maintain the important elements of self-parody and absurdity.

Of course the biggest hug in the book is that of Ahab and Moby Dick. We have heard at length about the way young bull whales still "swelling with noble aspirations" (*MD* 303), cruised around together. Ahab, like the hunted whale himself, is no young thing but one of the older isolatoes. Melville makes fun of these for their flaunting neglect of Montaigne's good advice in "Du Repentir."[2] The old worn-out bulls brag of their virtue and repentance, when really all that has happened is that they have run out of hormonal drive. Moby Dick, however, is beyond that. Old and wise, he brags to no one, talks with no one, has no confidentiality or intercourse. All he wants, it would seem, is his peace, not to be hunted. It is as if the course of existence had been boisterous and rugged enough. The requirements should be behind him and something gained, some respect due him from the universe for having endured, and for having refused the dependencies and self-delusions with which many pacify themselves in old age.

Moby Dick, of course, is not given this modicum of respect. It is fitting that the one who would know best how much Moby Dick wants it is Ahab, an old man who has also endured, refused himself every sort of illusory sentiment, and also demanded a certain bowing to his will from the nature of things. Ahab is another lone old bull in this story. Melville at one point calls him a "heart-stricken moose," at another "the lone Missouri Grisly," at a third a "mute, maned sea-lion" (MD 143, 134, 131). Yet it is not merely ironic that the two who demand the most respect from the universe should end up in a fatal interlocking bear hug, a death embrace, Ahab's Parsee even lashed to Moby Dick's bosom as an emblem of that hug. This is the other marriage, the other splicing, of the book. It is the other side of the coin of Queequeg and Ishmael's genial bear hug and splicing at the opening of the novel.

If, in this bear hug, Ahab is more to blame than Moby Dick, since Ahab is the hunter and Moby Dick the hunted, that is not the issue. Nor is it that the "stricken" Moby Dick, for all we know, may live on. The point is that both are presented as creatures, grand and mighty creatures, but creatures nonetheless. Their equality is suggested not only by their mutual exasperation and ferocity, not only in all Ishmael's playful anthropomorphic descriptions of whales—and cetomorphic descriptions of men ("I have swam through libraries," [MD 118], etc.), but even further by Ishmael's fundamental love and respect for the whale. His is a love which transcends anthropomorphism to another realm, where man loves fish because man and fish are fellows in a simultaneously and ceaselessly magnificent and awful universe. Ahab and Moby Dick, after all, are God's creatures fighting, just as they are man and fish in mid-ocean, in the nothingness together, God's creatures loving.

But finally also the hug leaves us recognizing, as the chapter on "The Tail" makes clear, that while Ishmael begins as a spoony-eyed romantic, in love with the transcendently wonderful universe, at the same time he begins as a flirt, a dirty old young man looking for any chance he can get to parade before us his sexual bravado. Indeed in "The Tail," Ishmael makes repeated and noisy reference to the connections between the elephant and the whale, for their respective trunk and tail. Surely while celebrating the glory of the whale and of the universe, while letting himself and his humors celebrate and engage in the most heartfelt and passionate of embraces, Ishmael is also, to use the nineteenth-century phrase that Melville knew well,[3] taking his reader "to see the elephant"—to see the whale. That is, Ishmael is skylarking with his reader and skylarking with himself. *Moby-Dick,* after all, celebrates the great hoax we perpetrate upon ourselves. Our busy, earnest, conscientious heads celebrate ourselves, while our tails assert themselves. And finally, for an additional twist, as we learn of the whale in Ishmael's "Heads and Tails," if we cut ourselves into head and tail, as we repeatedly do, we shall find that there is nothing left.

Part of the sustained achievement of *Moby-Dick* is that Melville has not only found exactly the subject to talk about, but a way of talking about it. One of his distractions in earlier novels was finding a form when available ones such as the travel narrative and the sentimental novel were wrong—unresilient and constricting. Richard Chase has suggested forms and motifs which Melville found in American folklore;[4] these indeed were instrumental in liberating Melville's humor by providing him a way to talk about his very American subject. I suggest, however, that American folklore is only one part, the final part, of what Melville was absorbing and building upon. This was the whole tradition of prose humorists who, from the Renaissance on, played with the excitement of the opening of the frontier, of land and knowledge, of the new man of infinite potentials. Indeed, Melville is not only relieved to find available to him all the forms of the past, but even seems to enjoy the showmanship of incorporating and building upon all the male frontier monologues he knew and admired: the Renaissance tall tale of Rabelais; the melancholy anatomy of Burton; the humorous novel of sensibility/cock-and-bull story of Sterne; the humorous essay of sensibility of Lamb, De Quincey, and Irving; and finally the periodical tall tale or twister of popular American culture.

In his extravaganza, Rabelais gave Melville a way of spelling out the feeling of prodigiousness and bounty that is at the heart of frontier humor. Rabelais created Gargantua and Pantagruel, giants of body, mind, and heart who are described in an affectionate extravagant vernacular and sprung from native folk legend. Like Pantagruel, the whale in Melville's book is a vast creature, described and admired in a spirited colloquial tongue, one who as an infant consumes in a day thousands of gallons of milk, and as an adult, travelling whither he pleases and turning up everywhere, takes the whole world for his province. Moby Dick, in addition, as one particular whale, is sprung very consciously from native legend and, like Pantagruel, is male, important, and importantly dressed in white. Gargantua's enterprising love of learning and independent thinking meanwhile has encouraged Ishmael's bragging, central to *Moby-Dick,* of the grand sweep and scope of his research and knowledge. And so contagious is the love of learning in Rabelais's book that even Panurge, obscene practical joker that he is, first wins Pantagruel's heart in the beginning of their long friendship by saying that he is hungry in thirteen languages. Is this perhaps why Ishmael in his overture to his reader translates *whale* into thirteen languages?

For all the friendship and affection, however, neither in Rabelais nor in Melville is the bounty strictly benign. At heart also it is an aggressiveness, not just threatening women, but men and sheep, too, and in this regard Panurge's practical jokes were sources for Melville's inclusion of Stubb's in *Moby-Dick.* Alcofrybas also, let us recall, is always on hand as the subservient fellow so small he could live for six months in Gargantua's throat without that giant even noticing. Indeed this important episode in Rabelais is related to the image of man being swallowed by the whale that figures so large in the mythology behind *Moby-Dick.* Giants, in short, are wonderful but they may swallow you, just as all the marvelous dreams of man's democratic and egalitarian potential may swallow you and leave you a "pale loaf-of-bread" faced steward (*MD* 130), tremblingly serving at the "Cabin Table" the voracious, superb, baronial "giants" (*MD* 133), the harpooners.

The great throat swallows, the great mouth talks. Rabelais's book, like Melville's afterwards, is a teasing ventriloquistic performance. Panurge through three volumes only wishes to know whether he should marry or not, as Pip later in an incident central to *Moby-Dick* only wants to know if he is supposed to jump from the whaleboat or not. All they both get is talk—long, endlessly pompous, contradictory sermons. Moving from physician to poet to philosopher to lawyer to scholar in one book, and from First Congregationalist to Shakespearean soliloquizer to Poor Richard to a tale teller in Peru in the other is a sign that none of the oracles' advice can shield us from uncertainties, particularly because all the ventriloquism is served up with a sexual and religious teasing. Indeed Rabelais helped liberate Melville's humor in this regard. Pantagruel's buoyant sexuality, St. Victor's vast pornographic library, Panurge's making a shambles of feminine niceties and sexual pieties: these are all a great source for Melville in *Moby-Dick*. In *Mardi,* Melville had backed off into a prudish irritability. Here, however, he does not hesitate. In addition to the wide open jokes of a book about "sperm" and a tale of a tail, we get a quiet succession of teasing innuendos and one-liners about unicorns, prizes to queens, and elephants in the marketplace softly caressing ladies' "zones."

That Melville had Rabelais in mind for a many-sided teasingly heretical independence is clear from a crucial chapter that he borrowed from Rabelais, the whiteness chapter—about Pantagruel wearing, and Moby Dick being, white.[5] The business of these chapters is a theatrical redefinition of the word *white,* Rabelais and Melville each ceremoniously rejecting meanings from the past, insisting upon his own interpretation of things, and officiously cataloguing all the evidence supporting his view. If Melville emphasizes dread to Rabelais's joy, we should keep in mind that Rabelais in that chapter tells us that the "lion, who with his only cry and roaring affrights all beasts, dreads and feareth only a white cock,"[6] and ends by speaking of white as the color of a joy so extreme you could die from it. Similarly Melville in his milk-white steed gives us a creature of royal magnificence which, like that of the Milky Way itself, affrights us, but only by being the greatest of spectacles of this universe. It is certainly true that Rabelais never emphasizes the dread which haunts Melville's novel, that atheism to Rabelais never seems the truly terrifying spectre it does to Melville, that Melville in turn takes Rabelais's catalogue of the previous meanings of white up past Rabelais, through Coleridge (and Poe) to his own. We do have a contrast in tone and fable between the two books. But in some basic concept of the bounty of the universe and of the sociability of friendships like those of Pantagruel and Panurge, Gargantua and Pantagruel, in the excitement of gigantic man as a New World creature of possibilities, and the bounty of nature's gallons of milk, white and endless—Melville found a great source in Rabelais.

Robert Burton gave *Moby-Dick* not just the form of the anatomy,[7] but his subject and a purpose, to cure his own melancholy by writing. "When I first took this task in hand," Democritus, Jr. writes, "this I aimed at: to ease my mind by writing, for I had a heavy heart and an ugly head, a kind of imposthume in my head, which I was very desirous to be unladen of, and could imagine no fitter evacuation than. Besides I might not well refrain, for one must needs scratch where it itches."[8] Ishmael goes to sea for the same reason: "It is a way I have of driving off the spleen, and regulating the circulation. Whenever I find myself growing grim about the mouth: whenever it is a damp, drizzly November in my soul . . . especially whenever my hypos get such an upper hand of me. . . . This is my substitute for pistol and ball. With a philosophical flourish Cato throws himself upon his sword; I quietly take to the ship" (*MD* 12). One for his anatomy, the other for his journey, the purpose is the same, to drive off the spleen, the ugliness in the head, the haziness around the eyes, the heaviness of the heart. Indeed in *Moby-Dick,* as in *The Anatomy of Melancholy,* the imposthume of the head is a central obsession; it is not incidental that Ishmael, while he turns to other things, enjoys leaving the sperm whale's prodigious head hanging on the *Pequod*'s side for, as in

Burton, the story begins with a prodigious head (the persona's) caught, suspended, and turned into a helpless monstrosity waiting upon its master. "Too many heads" (*MD* 25), says the landlord of the Spouter Inn, and Melville loves to let us see the steam rising both from whales' heads and philosophers'. "While composing a little treatise on Eternity, I had the curiosity to place a mirror before me . . . " (*MD* 313), Ishmael writes.

Democritus, Jr., we should note, by legacy has good reason for his melancholy. The original Democritus, Burton reminds us, was nothing less than the patriarch of those "Copernical giants";[9] he was the radical scientist who conceived of the universe as all in perpetual atomical motion. The original Ishmael also was no mere anonymous orphan and outcast, but the father of a whole new tribe, a whole new heretical religion, Islam. Melville, in choosing such a name, is following Burton's suit here as the later spate of humorists, by the way, will not. By legacy, then, in both Burton and Melville, it is as if at the start of their books, both men are beyond pat and hackneyed orthodoxies ranging from the Senecan to the Christian. No wonder their heads are steaming and prodigious. No wonder also in both works the speakers at once brag of being a free man born, a schoolmaster, a lording anatomist—and a fool, a slave, a prisoner. "Who aint a slave?" (*MD* 15), Ishmael teases at one point, while Democritus, Jr., "the free man born," tells us that "we are slaves and servants, the best of us all," that he is a giddy fool giving us his "confused lump," his "phantastical fit," and asks "What's our life but a prison?"[10] One needs to know a lot and to be a perseveringly independent thinker in order to have achieved the full title of vulnerability to the chaos of the mind and this universe.

The cure for the imposthume in the head is much the same in both works. Ishmael, like Democritus, Jr., consoles himself with absorption in some monumental all-defying project; it hardly matters that one uses a voyage at sea and the other a voyage of the mind. Ishmael's voyage after all is only grist for his mill, and Democritus, Jr. in his anatomy also, among an eventual myriad of proposed remedies, recommends voyages. Democritus, Jr. takes his readers in fact on a whirlwind tour in "A Digression of Air" to "many strange places, Isthmuses, Europeuses, Chersones, creeks, havens, promontories, straits, lakes, baths, rocks, mountains, places and fields, where Cities have been ruined or swallowed, battles fought, creatures, Sea-monsters, remora, minerals, vegetals."[11] The important thing about the cure is that neither the wonders of travel nor the spectacles of the extravaganza anatomy are mere curatives to the disease, but its cause to begin with. In a popular American song, a doctor prescribes lime and coconut for the patient who is sick from drinking lime and coconut. The madness itself is a product of the original excitability. What Melville borrows from Burton is the underlying preposterousness of the cure. Burton cites Felix Plater, who went on a seven-year voyage to rid himself of the chattering Aristophanic frogs in his belly, but what are Burton's *Anatomy* and Melville's *Moby-Dick* but more frogs chanting splendid impossible "wicked" nonsense, "Breccex, Coax, coax, oop, oop," a fine promiscuity of erudition and jabber, of fancy scientific words and slang. What indeed is the whole anatomy but "never a barrel better herring?"[12]

Comparing Burton's central proof that all men are mad with Melville's that whaling is noble gives us a concrete image of how all this works out through the two books. Just as Burton makes up an absurd list of exceptions to prove the rule, such as Monsieur Nobody and the Stoics who must be mad for not being so, Ishmael as the "advocate" conjures up a great melodramatic courtroom scene in which, to vindicate the nobility of whaling, a hodgepodge of absurd logic, grandiose allusion, and general fast-talking is thrown at the reader while the speaker works himself into a frenzy of assertion. Burton's frenzy is quieter and more archaic in its tone, but he is doing the same thing.

> *No dignity in whaling?* The dignity of our calling the very heavens attest. Cetus is a constellation in the South! No more! Drive down your hat in presence of the Czar, and take it off to Queequeg! No more! I know a man that, in his lifetime, has taken three hundred and fifty whales. I account that man more honorable than that great captain of antiquity who boasted of taking as many walled towns. [*MD* 101]

The odd thing is that while the rowdy exaggeration would seem to undermine the argument, the more it parodies itself, the more it nonetheless convinces us. Say no more, indeed! All men are mad! Whaling is noble! Can we possibly disagree? Can we possibly not submit to the acataleptic fervor? The Burtonesque geological sandwiches of *Mardi* have expanded. The whole of *Moby-Dick,* with its perpetual fossil whales, cetologies, and masthead exhaustive researches, endlessly anatomizes the whale, the whaleship, and this watery world.

Laurence Sterne's *Tristram Shandy*[13] is a rewriting and reshaping of Burton's *Anatomy* which gave Melville another handle for *Moby-Dick.* That Tristram writes in the same vein as Democritus, Jr. is clear. "If 'tis wrote against anything,—'tis wrote," Tristram says of his book, "against the spleen."[14] Sterne, however, has made several shifts. Dropping Burton's discreetness, he has revived Rabelais's open sexual and religious teasing in time to encourage Melville to do the same. In addition, Sterne has turned Burton's dignified melancholic philosopher into the domesticated pathetic men of the Shandy household, who are as infatuated with learning as Democritus, Jr. ever was but, in addition, ceremoniously castrated and mechanized, deprived of their noses and names. Indeed, since Melville was responding as much to Sterne as to Burton, it is crucial that we do not speak of Melville's fixation on unmanning without reference to its central place in all the Sterne-based humorous male monologues of the nineteenth century.

Most importantly, however, Sterne has tightened Burton's unwieldy extravaganza *consolatio* to the form at its core, the novel of sensibility/cock-and-bull story, a form surely, by the way, the English ancestor of the American twister. It is most of all the form of Sterne's novel that Melville has worked from; for Sterne's book, unlike Burton's, devotes itself to a series of plotted splenetic events. From the very opening when Walter is interrupted by his wife to every other event of irritation that follows, *Tristram Shandy*'s plot itself is hardly more than a series of disconnections and exasperations.

It is in this conceptual sense that Melville's book is a novel of sensibility. The author is not only willing to dispel his own hypos—

morbid blues—but to expiate them, not with a plot built upon a series of frustrations, but with a plot centered on one major exasperation. Indeed the word *exasperation* occurs regularly in the book, like a chime, beginning with the picture of the exasperated whale impaling itself upon the dismantled masts of a ship, like Cato upon his sword. Luther Mansfield has noted a perverse skepticism in Melville's interpreting Cato's great act of courage as mere cure for the spleen.[15] This, however, is the humorist's perspective, establishing from the start a vision of man as a creature beset by hypos and exasperations, and needing continually to get himself from one to the next. So we see other whales, later in the novel, their hunters in the midst of "the serene, exasperating sunlight"; we hear of Ahab's "intellectual and spiritual exasperations," and of Radney at a crucial moment being in a "corporeally exasperated state" (*MD* 159, 160, 212). One may object that all this suggests tragic recognition rather than the exasperation of sensibility. We would not speak, however, of Oedipus or Antigone or Lear as being *exasperated.* The word connotes something unheroic and essentially melodramatic; it describes a creature literally *roughened up*—and by the extremes, not of hubris, but of hypos. We cannot be surprised when Melville turns this sensibility inside out, showing us sulking right whales with their embarrassingly limp lower jaws hanging down, or punning about grim old bull whales who will fight you "like grim fiends exasperated by a penal gout" (*MD* 330).

This is not to say that Sterne and Melville do not have their differences, and use the cock-and-bull story/novel of sensibility in different ways. Melville's humor is grounded in a way that Sterne's is never intended to be; Melville is utterly determined to take the hypo, spleen, and exasperation to their sharpest, so that we most need the humor that is the staple of the book, so that it is in no way gratuitous. Nonetheless, there is a certain similarity that is important, not just incidental. The final thing we must say about Ahab is astonishing to come upon. We have seen him described as one sullen animal after another—all comparisons that are grim jokes on man's idealization of his misery. Even further, however, what we must come to terms with is the hum: "While the mate was getting the hammer, Ahab, without speaking, was slowly rubbing the gold piece against the skirts of his jacket, as if to heighten its lustre, and without using any words was meanwhile lowly humming to himself, producing a sound so strangely muffled and inarticulate that it seemed the mechanical humming of the wheels of his vitality in him" (*MD* 142).

This is balder than the confidence man later humming to himself an "opera snatch" (*TCM* 61) as he goes down the hall to gull the old miser. This is closer to Henri Bergson's mechanical man at the root of all humor.[16] This is related to Walter Shandy's winding up the clock and his marital relations the same one night a month at the opening of Sterne's book. Ishmael too will become the mechanical man of warp and woof, the mere shuttle in "The Mat-Maker," as does the carpenter at the end of the book in a short, brilliant sketch. Finally Moby Dick also in the last moment before Ahab's death: "Suddenly the waters around them slowly swelled in broad circles; then quickly upheaved, as if sideways sliding from a submerged berg of ice, swiftly rising to the surface. A low rumbling sound was heard; a subterraneous hum; and then all held their breaths; as bedraggled with trailing ropes, and harpoons, and lances, a vast form shot lengthwise, but obliquely from the sea" (*MD* 464). Melville's mechanical exasperated creature—man or beast, cock and bull—is a creature of sensibility and grim humor. Melville takes the joke of the hypo absolutely and deliberately to its limit, but the pattern in which he does so is the novel of sensibility/cock-and-bull story.

It was in Thomas De Quincey's book that Melville found this sensibility gone to seed. Indeed, De Quincey often uses the word *sensibility* to describe the extreme hypos which pushed him to his own extreme remedy, opium addiction. The braggadocio of extremism, the determination to encounter the worst, provided a model, a novel of grim humor, which we cannot be surprised that Melville found "wondrous" in 1849. Specifically, De Quincey's book, *Being an Extract from the Life of a Scholar* (as it was subtitled), gave Melville a monologue of a man proudly miserable in the midst of his myriad of books, a monologue of a modern worried child of Burton and Johnson. De Quincey, much like Ishmael after him in the Spouter Inn, begins with a deliberate and clumsy attempt to produce an amusing situation, his trunk willfully spiriting itself downstairs as he tries to steal away quietly from the house where he is staying. Buffoonery, however, gives way quickly to the mainstream of his confessional and the steadier wryness of passages like the one in which De Quincey peremptorily asks an artist to paint a cottage in order to spell out a theory of happiness ineluctably tied to a demand for a good strong terrible winter. That Melville enjoys this approach is suggested by his taking up the same theme in very similar language:

> But here is an artist. He desires to paint you the dreamiest, shadiest, quietest, most enchanting bit of romantic landscape in all the valley of the Saco. What is the chief element he employs? . . . Go visit the Prairies in June, when for scores of miles you wade knee-deep among Tiger-lillies . . . what is the one charm wanting? . . . there is not a drop of water there! Were Niagara but a cataract of sand, would you travel your thousand miles to see it? [*MD* 13]

In De Quincey the article, the goods, is winter; in Melville, it is water. In Melville also, however, his theory of happiness resounds to cold outdoors as Ishmael and Queequeg sit up in bed together "very nice and snug, the more so since it was so chilly out of doors. . . . The more so, I say, because truly to enjoy bodily warmth, some small part of you must be cold. . . . For the height of this sort of deliciousness is to have nothing but the blanket between you and your snugness and the cold of the outer air. Then there you lie like the one warm spark in the heart of an arctic crystal" (*MD* 55). Melville takes up De Quincey's playful perversity here by conscientiously reasoning upon a subject that boils down to a question of taste. Indeed, it seems Melville not only had De Quincey in mind, but deliberately enlarged upon the bit. Melville must have water nearby his cottage in the happy valley, he will tolerate no fire on his most wintry of eves, and, above all, he wants his nose cold.

It is in Melville's chapter 35 that De Quincey's opium is introduced. Ishmael tells us riding in the masthead produced a trance very much like that produced by opium. The trance in turn produces a giddy, wry monologue with historical, philosophical, and emotional commentary upon mastheads; with a mock earnestness cataloguing all possible entrants in that category; teasing pious narrators like Scoresby; and above all celebrating the snugness of this cold, vulnerable, lonely perch which might easily throw a man to his watery death hundreds of feet below. The masthead, indeed, with its opiumlike trance, is Melville's De Quinceyan cottage of happiness par excellence, perfectly fit out to supply the theory of happiness. Here we not only deny ourselves fire, counterpane, and tea (although Ishmael chides the arctic Scoresby for omitting to mention his flask), but windows, walls, and roof.

Indeed, finally here is the difference between De Quincey's and Melville's wry humor of vast vulnerability, of being out in the cold—that De Quincey actually takes a drug to induce his giddy wryness, whereas Ishmael induces his own without help from any of the beverages which humorists have so depended upon to soothe their melancholy souls. In *Moby-Dick,* Melville leaps from the standard humorists' ploy of drinking a beverage to mentally fixating on one. The liquid in *Moby-Dick* is water, but instead of physically drinking it, Ishmael mentally takes it in and becomes obsessed with it, as if he has taken the whole "watery world" and got drunk on it. In contrast to De Quincey, because his trance is only opium-like, and not actually opium-induced, Melville has all the freedom of its intense vision and all the depths of its vulnerability which are the realm of the humorist, but none of the disadvantages. "That De Quincey is a very conscious (at . . . moments one would say conscientious) humorist is obvious," writes Jean-Jacques Mayoux. "What seems to me much less certain is that he knows the way his humor is going, or that he guides it."[17] Melville does guide his book's humor; neither Melville as author nor Ishmael as narrator-humorist is forced into the bondage produced by a chemical actually in the blood. Thus the fine wryness that is so spotty in De Quincey—as in the footnote in which he earnestly discusses whether a druggist may "evanesce," or tosses off a thought about it being a disagreeable thing to die—is intrinsic to Melville's work and steady in it. Similarly, where disturbing childhood events such as a trance over the death of a sister may sprawl out cloyingly over pages of "Suspira Profundis," Ishmael's trance over the loss of his dinner, a very similar type of evocation of a child's utter sense of isolation in an adult world, passes within a page or two, evoking the traumatic material from which humor is built, but never pressing it, providing a source for the humor without ever getting out of control.

Much more in control than De Quincey, although turning the game from deliberately confronting to deliberately evading the extremes of human vulnerability, is Charles Lamb. Elia is an important source for Ishmael. Elia is male, a bachelor, melancholy, domesticated, all oddities and quirks, and pleasures and displeasures, yet overridingly sociable and amiable, with affection especially for other ornery types like his grumbling housekeeper. Elia besides is a customshouse thrall, "poor Elia," who is continuously drawing our attention to the pathetic distance between man's illusion of mental control and the actuality of dependency and slavery, between theory and practice: "My theory is to enjoy life, but the practice is aginst it."[18] Elia, all sensibility, consoles himself with the joys of roast pig and plum pudding. Sympathetically he pokes fun at our Caledonian earnestness. Indulgently he lets himself out for wandering in the "twilight of dubiety" where he will "cry halves" for the bits of truth that he may find, allowing himself only "hints and glimpses," "crude essays at a system," "wanderings" in the maze of possibilities, for "truth presents no full face," a "feature or side face at most."[19]

Ishmael, like Elia, is male, a bachelor, in his own way on board ship domesticated, puttering about among the try-pots and all his likes and dislikes, making friends with other isolatoes—those ornery and intimidating, but ultimately most affectionate, types. Ishmael, too, tells us his foibles and his loves: for whaling, chowder, forbidden seas, cannibals, following funerals, the whale as a dish, confidential chats, dipping his biscuit, holding mock debates, unraveling parodic dissertations and anatomies upon the whale who never shows his face, and turning over his endless thinking as neither infidel nor believer. Ishmael, the whaleship thrall, takes up Lamb's crude "essay" in both its meanings. Duyckinck was one critic to notice the essayistic quality of many of *Moby-Dick*'s chapters,[20] and indeed in this perspective we may recognize them as fine examples of humorous essays—monologue bits in the method of Lamb, Hazlitt, De Quincey, and Irving. In addition, however, Ishmael in all his staggering ambition is in a constant hubbub of crude attempts—essays—at a system. "I am in earnest and I will try" (*MD* 118), he says of his cetological system, that vast array of surly mouths and seductive young bulls. "I try all things; I achieve what I can" (*MD* 291), he says while hopelessly phrenologizing the whale whose head turns out to have no face, just as its spout turns out to be only a mist. Ishmael always busies himself with his desire "to approve myself omnisciently exhaustive" (*MD* 378), as if one could, through mere well-meaning conscientiousness, actually sort out all the chaos of the universe, and as if he had caught onto exactly the "system" of how that was to be done.

Like Elia, Ishmael is always dishing up some earnestness to respond to the absurdity. "That mortal man should feed upon the creature that feeds his lamp, and, like Stubb, eat him by his own light, as you may say; this seems so outlandish a thing that one must needs go a little into the history and philosophy of it" (*MD* 254). One must? Even if Melville were speaking of actual history, we could not assume that the history of a thing can remove its absurdity. Melville is not even speaking of actual history, however, but making up ludicrous prescriptions of blubber as nutritious for infants, and letting calves' heads, helpless upon the carving board, look up quoting Shakespeare into the face of their executioner. In Melville as with Lamb, ideas are mere absurd pretensions and consolations against the darkness, until heads themselves become things to pity. "Meantime, there was a terrible tumult. Looking over the side, they saw the before lifeless head throbbing and heaving just below the surface of the sea, as if that moment seized with some momentous idea; whereas it was only the poor Indian unconsciously revealing by those struggles the perilous depth to which he had sunk" (*MD* 288). The poor Indian, the poor head, the poor essayist. The joke is that we are creatures possessed by the idea that our heads can save us, and as a result possessed by our heads, which in turn are possessed by momentous uncontrollable ideas.

The problem, however, is that man must worship something. In "The Whale as a Dish," Ishmael takes a different line from Elia in his "Dissertation on Roast Pig." One insists upon giving us a full history and philosophy, the other a dissertation on origins. Both, however, are playing on a finger-licking-good self-indulgence, both establishing the absurdity of a lyricism—and an erudition— devoted to succulence. But what is this infatuation? Let us recall that Ishmael, early in *Moby-Dick,* in an aside on the glory of being paid, says, "I never fancied broiling fowls;—though once broiled, judiciously buttered, and judgmatically salted and peppered, there is no one who will speak more respectfully not to say reverentially, of a broiled fowl than I will. It is out of the idolatrous dotings of the old Egyptians upon broiled ibis and roasted river horse, that you see the mummies of those creatures in their huge bake-houses, the pyramids" (*MD* 14). "Idolatrous dotings" is the key. Lamb's whole dissertation on roast pig builds playfully and quietly up to the image of the pig on the platter as meek and beautiful as Christ on the cross. De Quincey told us he worshipped his druggist. We not only are what we eat; we worship what we eat. But only because in the "twilight of dubiety" what else shall man worship?

We must not omit to notice an important difference between Elia and Ishmael, which gave Melville an opening to improve upon his model. Elia says of Negroes that he is drawn to them but he "would not spend his good nights with them." Ishmael, very much as if in reply to Elia upon this exact point, immerses himself in the comic predicament of being forced to spend his good night with the terrible apotheosis of the Negro, a tattooed, shrunken-head-toting cannibal. It is crucial that Ishmael resolves this confrontation in a kind of marriage, so that his night becomes a good night indeed, but it is characteristic too of Ishmael that he takes his humorist self as far into his depths as possible. The humorously joyous denouement of Ishmael's encounter with the black cannibal prefigures, of course, the joy of Ishmael's surviving the encounter with the white whale. That the ship and all its crew descend into the maelstrom (to use Poe's phrase) or over the verge of the Descartian vortex (to use Melville's) is awesome in its horror, but then no humorist worth his salt can avoid calling upon the horrors of the deep, the vacuities beyond man's seeming mental grasp. Elia seems very much at the core of Melville's conception of Ishmael, even if Melville has consciously taken Elia a good deal further.

Washington Irving was another humorist essayist who seems to have been in Melville's mind during the writing of *Moby-Dick.* We may notice details that Melville lifts from Irving, such as Plato's "honey head,"[21] and Manhattan as the isle of "Manhattoes."[22] We may notice that as Irving has written about the Neversink Indians (thus giving Melville the shipname for *White-Jacket*), so Irving had written at length about the Pequod Indians. More to the point, however, Irving's pathetic schoolmaster Ichabod Crane, as well as the Burtonesque bachelor Geoffrey Crayon, provided humorous prototypes for Ishmael; and the tyrannical peg-legged Peter Stuyvesant provided one for Ahab. We must say immediately, of course, that Irving's tyrant turns out to be most kindhearted after all, and Irving's pathetic types are often thin in their appeal, resting too much upon their settings, or rallying a bit too easily after all. Ichabod, for instance, after the headless horseman fright, goes to the city and becomes, within sentences, a successful businessman. Nonetheless, Irving seems to have been in Melville's mind as a novice of an artist. It is as if Melville becomes Irving and survives him, becomes him and transcends him. In "Bartleby," we may see the relationship between the two authors more clearly. For the moment, let us simply note that it must have been important to Melville to find an American working the Democritan extravaganza vein of humor in its romantic essay form.

Considering the Americanness of *Moby-Dick,* it was certainly important that Melville found, in addition to Irving, a thriving American periodical humor which he could tap. Indeed, no one questions the essential Americanness of *Moby-Dick.* That the brave, generous, and dependable Queequeg is called a "George Washington cannibalistically developed" (*MD* 52) sets the mood. All the whalemen, be they from whatever lands or tribes, are George Washington's progeny, translations of the idea of America—just as the showmanship of "The Masthead" chapter, like all Melville's writing, takes us home to America with a final absurd masthead of

George Washington on a pedestal. The question is exactly what did Melville take from developing American humor to flesh out the Americanness of his book, and to develop his own humor to its quickest, brightest level.

Richard Chase makes some important suggestions along these lines.[23] He points out that Melville borrows American folk figures—Ishmael, for example, being a composite of the Yankee, the frontiersman, the comic Promethean demigod of a trickster, the jack-of-all-trades like Sam Slick, and finally the elusive soliloquizing yarn-spinner. Stubb is a typically American screamer, using the standard techniques of the American trickster, razzing Negroes and gulling Europeans; and finally out of the comic realm, Ahab is the ultimate screamer, a folkloric embodiment of Manifest Destiny, an American Prometheus. For both his central fable and its spin-offs, Melville also uses, Chase tells us, the American predilection for comic metamorphosis, an instantaneous transformation back and forth that makes the whale into an albino and then into a god; the story's heroes into titans, beasts, and machines; men into animals and back again, as Ahab is made into a grizzly and Ishmael into a May grasshopper. It is only the beginning to recall that Crockett, for one, was half-horse, half-alligator, and half-man, or that he went so far as to call himself an entire zoological institute. Chase shows that in *Moby-Dick,* Melville was working from a grab bag of standard American tall tales built upon exaggeration, sudden or eventual violation of the laws of nature, or the whimsy that shows the utter impracticality of human endeavor.

Within this typically American flight of fantasy, Chase finds a very American emphasis on and undercurrent of fact and practicality, so strong that it sometimes camouflages the fantasy, just as Ahab being above all a successful whaling captain is in good part what wins the loyal adherence of his crew. This underlying bias toward fact is as responsible for the workings of the central fable as it is for the book's whole style. This style has its roots in P. T. Barnum showmanship, American magniloquent oratory, and the theatre of the 1830s and 1840s in which a blank mask, omnipresent from the Yankee pedlar, allows the tale-teller to move freely back and forth from sales pitch to scientific razzmatazz to dramatic action.

Two problems arise with the suggestions Chase made in 1949. To begin with, it was Chase's ultimate point about all this material that Melville exploits Americana to provide a fabric for his historical-tragic allegory, the comic material giving a "low enjoying power"[24] to the higher stuff as Melville transmutes "the language of the screamer" into an apostrophe "to space and freedom."[25] The P. T. Barnum hoax, Chase says, Melville turns inside out. Barnum was exploiting the desire of the audience to be comforted by the destruction of any fierce emotion. Melville, on the contrary, uses his hoax to insist on that emotion. When Melville neither transmutes nor turns inside out the Americana, Chase feels its tastelessness needs apology. For example, regarding Stubb's callous gulling of Fleece, Chase explains that, unpleasant as this sort of play may be, we must accept it as cultural fact.

The main problem with Chase's analysis, however, is that most of what Chase refers to as distinctly American is simply essentially humorous. The American folk tradition, we should realize, is only one part of the background of the comic trickster Prometheus. The European literature which Melville read was full of comic Prometheuses and demigods, like Pantagruel inventing his omnipotent Pantagruelion, Panurge inventing his *libertin* tricks, or de Bergerac inventing his moon machine and calling himself a Prometheus as a result. The literature was full as well of pure rogues and tricksters, from Lazarillo to Volpone to Mosca. For sources of Ishmael as a soliloquizing monologuist, we have already said much here of his literary paternity—Alcofrybas, Democritus, Jr., Tristram Shandy, Elia, and Geoffrey Crayon. The comic metamorphosis, too, is only partially American. We have not only the tall tale of Renaissance humor to cite, but the humorist's whole game of *what I desire I am*. Humor depends upon continuous expansions and contractions, continually thrown back to back. Democritus, Jr. is a free man and a slave, Panurge a giant of desire and cowardice—and later Alice in Wonderland will be a giant, then after a sip of "Drink Me," a mite. The only particularly American characteristic of Melville's metamorphoses may be the predominance of animals in the transformations. Otherwise, the shuffling back and forth is simply the humorist's insistence on writing as he pleases, showing he is boss, submitting to no logic or dogma, continually indulging his fantasies.

Finally to recognize that the showmanship of a literary-scientific extravaganza is not merely American, we need only mention *Gargantua and Pantagruel, The Anatomy of Melancholy,* and *The Historical and Critical Dictionary.* In each of those works of peremptory showmanship, the author is, above all, determined to outdo anything prior in scope and method, as well as to suggest continually the farce of this sort of determination. This is what makes it so important to see beyond the Barnum roots of Melville's humor; while with Chase we may condemn the ultimately shabby artistry of a P. T. Barnum, we may respect and admire the shaggy dog encyclopedias of such great writers as Rabelais, Burton, and Bayle. Their hoaxes need not be turned inside out; their humor needs no "transmuting." The actually literary literary-scientific extravaganza is built upon a fundamental bleakness and the "fierce emotion" it can inspire. It is built upon the uncertainty that Panurge faces, the slippery road on which the patriarchs walk, the bleak lot of a Lazarillo, the whiteness of acatalepsy, the all pervasiveness of mad melancholy, and the trance, finally, of opium. It is always there, that atheistical whiteness. In short, as Chase seems to have begun to suggest in his few pages in 1955 on *Moby-Dick,*[26] humor need not be, and in fact is not, a stepping-off point for this book. It is its center.

Still, once we have recognized that American humor only added one more element to the humor that is central to *Moby-Dick,* let us see what that element is. First of all, America provided the allusive materials for many of Melville's exaggerations and reversals. As a white American, Ishmael need not spell out that he is a free man born, but may jump ahead to the turnaround of "who aint a slave?" So, too, while the squire and Lazarillo or Volpone and Mosca, as master and servant types appropriate to their era, gull each other by turns, it is only fitting that in America, the two parties turning tables on each other—the Cabin Table, for one—should be white and black, or American and European, or Lakeman and Vineyarder. It is fitting also that Melville's metamorphoses jump back and forth not only from erudition to slang, or from rhapsody to the thump, or from piety to phallicism, but from man to animal; America was a land in which the animals were only then in the process of being subdued, conquered, and exterminated. In addition to the incidentals, however, American humor did indeed provide a grab bag of yarns and twisters to help Ishmael, a sort of King Midas, transform details into braggadocio. More importantly, the yarn helped Melville shape the central fable as a fish story of one man hunting down one particularly monstrous fish. Melville uses the yarn to transform and tighten the spacious voyage of Rabelais, the anatomy of Burton, the encyclopedia of Bayle, the rambling novel of Sterne; and he uses it to open up the small essay of sensibility, the melancholic sketch of De Quincey, Lamb, and Irving.

But beyond the paraphernalia for the quick allusiveness which humor always demands, and beyond the form both peripheral and central of the yarn or twister, Melville gets something which is distinctively American, a game of immediacy. The American hallmark of *Moby-Dick*'s humor is a certain journalistic predilection that moves us from Rabelais's fantasy of the giant Pantagruel drinking thousands of pails of milk a day to the actuality of a whale sucking that much from its dam; from Rabelais's fantasy of Pantagruel's arch of triumph to the actual six-foot-long pride of the whale. Chase had hinted at this essentially American aspect when he spoke of the particularly American reliance on fact and practicality. Practicality is too broad because all humor depends upon the play between the lofty and the banal, the theory and the practice, the soaring desire and the menial actuality. The fact part is right, however, and crucial. In the Renaissance frontier humor springing from the explorations of that era, the New World is very much in people's minds and very strong in creating the braggadocio and self-parody of that literature, but the authors themselves are not actually *in* the New World. With the earlier non-American humorists, the idea of the frontier is what sets them going, but with those in America, it is as if the joke has been suddenly accelerated and escalated into actuality. In American humor, we are not just given the remote idea or the willful fantasy, but the literal physical frontier, the experience of the land, the Indians, the animals, and the sea.

It is the periodical journalistic aspect which Melville borrowed most from American humor, a certain literal-mindedness, a stubbornness of the persona's insistence on having been there. *And I only am escaped to tell you* is part of the song: I alone was there and saw it with my own eyes. That the almanac, periodical book of timely and pragmatic knowledge as well as of humor and entertainment, was the standard American household book is not surprising, nor is it that the humor there is that of factual experience and deposition braggadocio. In the excerpts given above in chapter 2, Robert Thomas was in raptures that *he was there,* and that those "Fifty years!" which America had just lived through were surely the greatest in all history. This spirit rendered humorously gives us the "Deposition of Varmifuge," the literalness of the joker insisting he has seen the sea serpent with his own eyes, and giving us his ostentatiously legal statement; the misspelling used in the piece even forms a sort of verbal literalness, the insistence on sticking as close to reality—via phonetics—as one can possibly get. And finally in the famous Crockett excerpt, we get not just the practicality of how an American typically takes the impossible in hand for his survival, and not just the sense of his being present at the Creation, but of his having initiated it. To see that Melville was responding to this spirit, we may look at central chapters like "The Affidavit," which reveal the book as the bragging deposition that it is. Ishmael calls himself at one point "a veritable witness" (*MD* 373); at another he speaks of procuring for every snow crystal "a sworn affidavit" (*MD* 231). I cannot help thinking that, finally, part of the fun of the title *Moby-Dick* was that the word *dick* in the slang of Melville's day—not yet into the explicitness of our own time— not only signaled fellow (as in Tom, Dick, and Harry), and the dictionary, but declaration or affidavit.[27] *Moby-Dick* is Ishmael's wordy bragging, in effect, "I was there, ladies and gentlemen, this man was there and saw all this with his own eyes."

Although as a doctor, Rabelais teases us with a lot of close-up physicality, he has a certain distance from the low life he describes. Burton, one feels, has isolated himself in his study. Even Sterne and the Romantic essayists have a certain remove. In Melville's humor, however, if only to be able to brag that you were there in the most complete fashion, you are forever "putting your hand into the tar-pot" (*MD* 14); *Moby-Dick* is a total immersion in universal social, economical, political, and physical realities. The central conflict gives us all the innards of fish cleaning and fish stories, while it plays off a history of the peaking of one of America's first extraordinarily successful commercial enterprises. Melville's Ishmael, too, is not only directly at the masthead watching over all the watery world, not only at the helm once with the entire survival of the ship at his hand, not only in the whaleboat privy to the inner circles of the whales copulating and giving suck, but in chapter after chapter on board ship wresting the oil from the captured whale, at the end of the monkey rope, and with his hands, his whole body immersed in the smell and realities of the whale. Indeed the humor of "A Squeeze of the Hand" is that the exultant image of the felicitous brotherhood of mankind is pinned to the most physical and inane of immersions.

Melville is never afraid of getting his hands wet or dirty. His very American humor not only anatomizes the world and presents a melancholic idiosyncratic persona, but gets "these visible hands" (*MD* 118) into the actual physicalities of the whale—and squeezes. Yet, and this is important too, for it makes the whole difference, American as Melville was in his deposition, in his bragging journalistic immersion, at the same time, by his leaning on and listening to earlier and highly literary voices, he avoids the reductionism, provinciality, and claustrophobia of American periodical and almanac humor, whose joke of literalness and insistence on petty regionalist rivalry can quickly begin to pall.

Finally, then, *Moby-Dick*'s giddy sense of triumph evolves out of Melville's building upon a tradition of the giddy sense of triumph. It rests upon his awareness that he is building upon other humorous literature that has gone before, quickening the European fantasy with an American eye for physical and economic realities, sustaining the American quick turn of periodical humor by giving it a longer form and a substantial vision, broadening the American game of provincial literalness with a truly literary and catholic teasing and sense of play. Besides, however, doing all of this, we may ask if Melville adds anything to the long line of developing humor, or whether his whole achievement lies simply in impersonating and stretching. To be sure, the building itself is characteristically Melville's. That he takes everything he looks at into the superlative of the modern, and metamorphoses all that he has read into the present, is itself the game of his humor. In addition, however, it is the intensity of the hug which brings all of Melville's book into focus and distinctively shapes his originality. Against a frame of absolute universality, Melville opens up what he calls the "spheres" of "fright" and "love" (*MD* 169) to two sustaining hugs, Ishmael and Queequeg at one end, Ahab and Moby Dick at the other. To transform the humorous male monologues of the past into his present, and impose upon them the preposterous hug: here is the achievement of Melville's humor in *Moby-Dick*.

Like *Moby-Dick,* "Bartleby" has its grimness. The scrivener's predicament exists through no fault of his own, but rather through some perverse law that requires that some men be at the top and others at the bottom, and that those at the bottom submit themselves to the will of those at the top. Like Harry Bolton, Bartleby is definitely at the bottom. We may recall that in Melville's fourth novel, Redburn had blithely suggested that his friend Harry earn his living as a copyist; Bolton later dies a grim death.

If, however, we accept the seeming assumption of the story, that there is a top and a bottom, the first catch is that there is no top. For all his being employer, attorney, and former master of chancery, the narrator is as lost as Bartleby, as little in control yet with the added problem of the illusion of power. The lawyer is as much a piece of flotsam in the great Atlantic as the man he feels so sorry for. That he busies himself in all earnestness, conscientiously telling us a tale that is diverting, strange, moving, and comical, is only a sign of how much he would like to think himself in control. Yet the more he talks, the more he reveals himself as a man of nothingness, with no faith, no emotional ties, nothing but the barest essentials for a false sense of survival. Meanwhile, the second catch is Bartleby's imperturbable self-sufficiency. Bartleby has a wry eloquence, dedication, and refinement. The refrain "I would prefer not to" has all the pride of Yankee terseness, and he sticks to it unto death. If we hear a long-drawn whistle of astonishment here, it is for the steadfastness of Bartleby's self-sabotage.

In fact, the narrator envies Bartleby. The more the narrator talks or clowns or works at befriending the reader, the more elusive Bartleby becomes in his wry understatement and independence. Bartleby's star of nothingness is on the ascension, just out of the narrator's reach. If only the narrator could achieve such class; "The beauty of my procedure seemed to consist in its perfect quietness" (B 40), the narrator brags to himself one night, thinking he has ousted the offender and succeeded in adopting Bartleby's cool. "There was no vulgar bullying, no bravado of any sort, no choleric hectoring, and striding to and fro across the apartment, jerking out vehement commands. . . . Nothing of the kind." His interior volubility, however, makes hash of his goal of superb simplicity. It is just not true that the more one explains oneself the more subtle one becomes.

Nor is it true, as the narrator attempts to console himself the morning after when he guesses he has failed after all and that Bartleby will still be there when he arrives, that the two cannot communicate because one works by "assumption," and the other by "preference." Actually we could find no greater man of preference than the narrator himself. True—and here the word *prefer* takes on its inevitable momentum—the narrator would *prefer* to believe himself a man of assumptions rather than of preferences, but actually as we listen to his tale we see it is little more than a list of preferences: I could tell you about many a scrivener, but I prefer to tell you about this one; I would prefer for Bartleby to remove himself from my premises, but I would prefer not to take the final step of having him removed by force; I would prefer not to have Bartleby angry with me. The lawyer's consolation boils down to nothing. The narrator is neither as good as, nor somehow miraculously better than, his self-proclaimed prisoner. Both have nothing but their preferences, some vestige of the old great desire, *what I desire I am.*

In fact the story ceremoniously goes nowhere. The passage referred to ends with the attorney walking downtown after breakfast "arguing the probabilities *pro* and *con.* One moment I thought it would prove a miserable failure, and Bartleby would be found all alive at my office as usual; the next moment it seemed certain that I should find his chair empty" (B 40-41). If the essence of the lawyer's response is his envy of Bartleby, the humor partly grows out of the pathos of watching this elaborate veering back and forth in the mind of this "rather" elderly, most ordinary of men walking home from his office and back again. In one of Lamb's essays we are told that the once destitute show girl Barbara has now become rich and need not engage in any more "landing-place moral dilemmas"; one day when she was a poor child, she had to debate with herself on the stairs whether to go back up to tell her employer that he had given her too large a coin by mistake.[28] This moment in "Bartleby" bears something of that stamp. The lawyer's dilemma as he walks home, goes to bed, and wakes up, is grossly beside the point; and yet, in the very spirit of his self-deluded self-illumination, touching.

The narrator's involvement with Bartleby grows finally to climactic proportions. "'Stationary you shall be, then,' I cried, now losing all patience, and, for the first time in all my exasperating connection with him, fairly flying into a passion. 'If you do not go away from these premises before night, I shall feel bound—indeed, I *am* bound—to—to. . . .'" The reader expects that, even coward that he is, the lawyer is bound to and finally can and will call the police, but he continues:

> to quit the premises myself!" I rather absurdly concluded, knowing not with what possible threat to try to frighten his immobility into compliance.
>
> Despairing of all further efforts, I was precipitately leaving him, when a final thought occurred to me—one which had not been wholly unindulged before.
>
> "Bartleby," said I, in the kindest tone I could assume under such exciting circumstances, "will you go home with me now—not to my office, but my dwelling—and remain there till we can conclude upon some convenient arrangement for you at our leisure? Come, let us start now, right away." [B 49]

Finally, after all the exasperation, in the manner of true comedy, the only solution to the fight is marriage. Instead of Benedick and Beatrice, instead of man and woman, however, in the manner of the prose humor finale we have man and man, lawyer and scrivener. Come home with me! If the lawyer has learned anything about his partner in this adventure, it is that the "till we can conclude upon some convenient arrangement" might as well be—and turns out to be—till death do us part. Melville has even hinted at giddy desire here, leading up to the directness of "come, let us start now," like poet and shepherdess turned Beckett's Didi and Gogo. Indeed, if Bartleby does not go home with the lawyer, it is because he has been home with him all along, in the office between the blank walls, at one end the white blank wall "deficient in what landscape painters call 'life,'" and at the other end, the "lofty" soot-blackened wall which "required no spy-glass to bring out its lurking beauties, but, [which] for the benefit of all near-sighted spectators, was pushed up to within ten feet of my window panes" (B 17).

Between the blank walls, it is the preposterous hug again. Bartleby terse, the lawyer talky—here is our couple. If in the midst of their hug, the attorney looks to the reader for assurance, he need not worry. For all his understandable envy of Bartleby, the narrator does fine also. His is a slower death, to be sure. Also his wit is less brilliant. But he too is worthy of our sympathy; and he too has his self-sabotage.

Three short prose pieces seem at the root of Melville's "Bartleby." Indeed, it is building upon the solid foundations of Irving's "Rip Van Winkle," Hawthorne's "Wakefield," and Lamb's "South-Sea House" which gives Melville's short story the roundness of artistic mastery. The artist need not so much invent as perform; "Bartleby" is a brilliant performance.

The Washington Irving joke of American indolence was suggestive for "Bartleby." Nowhere does Irving enjoy it more than in his character Rip. Rip wants nothing more than to do nothing, to sit all day, or go out and hunt squirrels, but above all, not to do whatever it is that his wife, the "boss" in the story, demands that he do. Whether or not she is just an embodiment of necessity, which Rip is determined at all costs to evade, in any case it is to Dame Van Winkle and her loud-mouthed berating that Rip characteristically replies with the tersest of responses: "He shrugged his shoulders, shook his head, cast up his eyes, but said nothing."[29] This sort of interchange culminates in Rip's practical joking triumph over his wife; he oversleeps by twenty years and returns to his town, bewildered, but eventually to gain the position, his lifelong goal, of unmolested town patriarch. In short, he returns to his male cronies of the bench, one of whom, Nicholas Vedder, in his morning-to-night shifts in position to avoid the sun and keep in the shade of a large tree, informs the neighbors as accurately as a sundial of the hours of the day, very much as Turkey in Melville's story tells the hours with the changes in his flushed facial color. And sit from morning till night, Diedrich Knickerbocker tells us that Rip could well do also. For all his aversion to profitable labor, like Bartleby after him, he had no lack of "assiduity or perseverance."[30] Rip's story is told also by an earnest, talky man. Knickerbocker's scholarly historical notes form the framing device for the supposed Catskill folktale. Of course Knickerbocker in no way involves himself in the story he is telling, except to assure us pedantically of its authority. Yet, like Melville's lawyer, he ends by being another of this tale's humors characters.

Hawthorne's "Wakefield" tells the same story as Irving's "Rip." The target again, at least the ostensible target, is the wife, except that this time our man is, as his name suggests, *awake* during his twenty-year absence. Also his act is deliberate; Wakefield knows he is gulling his wife. Confining his parting remarks and explanations to a wry, teasing smile, Wakefield leaves his London wife on a supposed few days' journey, only to take up a London residence of his own on the next street to hers, and not return for twenty years. The day he comes home and passes in through his door, we have a "glimpse of his visage, and recognize the crafty smile which was the precursor of the little joke that he has ever since been playing off at his wife's expense." Of course it is not just a joke on her; as with Rip before him and Bartleby afterwards, the joke is in large part upon himself. Wakefield, we should recall, in changing his hair, his clothes, and his residence, actually "banishes" himself. He "exposes himself to a fearful risk of losing his place forever."[31]

Hawthorne's version is, of course, much more subtle and wry than Irving's. We have no termagants and no good-for-nothings. Instead of slapstick and buffooning fantasy, we have wry circumlocutions and a literary air of teasing understatement. Hawthorne also uses a frame, only without creating a ridiculous narrator. He tells us he is writing an "article" intended as "food for thought," in which he is conjuring up the details of a story that he has heard about a man who left his wife for twenty years. This narrator, while sometimes playful and teasing, is essentially straightforwardly articulate; he does not intend to mock himself or to be mocked—he is not a humors character. Rather, he is just an embodiment of the author, a man who is giving his version of how he imagines the story, and incidentally inviting the reader to do his own: "If the reader choose, let him do his own meditation."[32] Melville, I suggest, was one who would do so, although he as usual takes his model as far as he can go. Bartleby with a wry persistence makes his "fearful risk" into a certainty.

While we have evidence that Melville found Lamb's "South-Sea House" memorable,[33] one might question if it is relevant here. Lamb's piece is decidedly more an essay than a story, and indeed provides no central fable of an antihero of passive resistance playing a practical joke upon a female embodiment of necessity. The essay is a series of portraits of the pathetic creatures working in that pathetic house. True, Lamb writes of Evans, a Cambro-Briton with a choleric complexion, that he has a "tristful visage clearing up a little over his roast neck of veal at Anderton's at two . . . but not attaining the meridian of its animation till evening brought on the hour of tea and visiting."[34] Melville's playful description of Turkey borrows actual wording here.[35] Irving, however, had given Melville a pathetic set of self-indulging bachelor cronies, complete with one in whose face we could read the "vedder"; Melville could as easily have worked from that.

But Melville may well have had Elia's "introductory sketch" open on his desk, because Lamb was tapping something which

Irving had touched on slightly and which Hawthorne had evaded, the issue of economic vulnerability, a level of perception central to Melville's humor. Irving had strewn his tale with Rip's untended vegetable gardens, unpainted roof, and poorly dressed children, but that was all; Hawthorne had protected both man and wife with an impermeable London prosperity. Lamb, alone of the three, quietly set economics at the center of his piece, and his piece at the center of finance, as Melville would set his. Lamb does not have to say much about the South Sea Bubble itself, as an emblem of economic speculation, desire, illusion, or fantasy; or of the bubble bursting, a bubble tied in every way to Europe's dreams of a New World paradise. He just chooses the South Sea House and lets his sketch whimsically float out beyond the economic realities it is based upon. He chooses that "House," however, for a specific reason. He is affectionately remembering not only the greed but what lies tucked within it, beneath the layers of dust, the long-buried mysteries of "that tremendous HOAX whose extent the petty peculators of our day look back upon with the same expression of incredulous admiration, and hopeless ambition of rivalry, as would become the puny face of modern conspiracy contemplating the Titan size of Vaux's superhuman plot."[36] Beneath the commiseration for the pathetic is sheer admiration for the hoax. In fact, Lamb is celebrating the practical joke on the grand scale, the communal hoax.

Of course, a practical joke is nothing without a victim, and specifically what Lamb enjoys is that when the hoax is done on the grand scale, the schlemiels will line up on the grand scale, in all their paltry meagerness. Lamb's sense for this meagerness on the grand scale, in fact, as in Barbara's "landing-place moral dilemmas," is not to be outdone. "Not that Tipp was blind to the deadness of things . . . in his beloved house, or did not sigh for a return of the old stirring days when South-Sea hopes were young . . . but to a genuine accountant the difference of proceeds is as nothing. The fractional farthing is as dear to his heart as the thousands which stand before it. He is the true actor, who, whether his part be a prince or a peasant, must act it with like intensity."[37] In fact, Lamb may have given Melville this last idea also. Both Ishmael and the "Bartleby" narrator make a point of telling us that although they have received puny parts in the grand program of Providence, they insist on playing them well.

"Reader, what if I have been playing with thee all this while?" Elia concludes his essay. "Peradventure the very *names,* which I have summoned up before thee, are fantastic—insubstantial."[38] Melville too says, "These may seem names, the like of which are not usually found in the Directory" (B 18). The important thing, however, is that Elia is telling us here that he has made the whole thing up, and that at this point, then, we may fairly ask, made up what? What has he given us? Some homage to a hoax, and a string of portraits of pathetic old cronies? A hoax upon a hoax?

True, he says, "Be satisfied that something answering to them has had a being," but the moral lies more with the incidental fact which Elia happens on in reference to Plumer, who "besides his family pretensions . . . was an engaging fellow and sang gloriously." The word sing takes hold. "Not so sweetly sang Plumer as thou sangest, mild childlike, pastoral M," Elia goes on, and finally: "Much remains to sing. Many fantastic shapes rise up, but they must be mine in private: already I have fooled the reader to the top of his bent . . . . "[39] The essay in Lamb's hands is thoroughly literary, subtle and quiet, half of hoax, half a song. It is this tone, this sort of play, which was so suggestive to Melville. For, in addition to his focusing on the economics of man's vulnerability, and his dropping the whole game of the wife as target in order to broaden the hoax, Melville was aiming at a tone, somewhere between—or beyond—that of either Irving, who was out to give us entertainment, or Hawthorne, who, as if to make up for Irving's frivolousness, was intent on giving us "food for thought." R. W. B. Lewis, finding much similar between "Wakefield" and "Bartleby" in the self-impelled isolatoes of the two stories, notes this difference: "Hawthorne's capital letters point to a fixed type of human situation that he is, primarily, trying to illustrate; while much of the odd charm of *Bartleby* is its tantalizing escape from fixity."[40] If this is the case, Lamb may have helped guide Melville toward this elusive charm, to his own "rare humor."[41]

Melville may well have tried to work exclusively from

Irving's Rip and Hawthorne's Wakefield. Hawthorne, as we said, had invited other versions of his story. Melville may have wanted to try his own version, but been nervous about merely imitating his friend. Such nervousness could even have spurred the whole strange group of "Agatha letters." In these, just one month after having written Hawthorne about how the latter had "most admirably employed materials which are richer than I had fancied them," Melville wrote Hawthorne not just to suggest material, but to tell Hawthorne at length how to use it.[42] The material specifically was a Nantucket story of a husband, Wakefield-like, as Melville noted, abandoning his wife Agatha Hatch. It is speculation of course, but Melville may have written up the whole Agatha story in his letters, in order to have Hawthorne suggest he do the story himself, and to show he had a new angle on it. Melville also, looking on enviously at the "ubiquity" of Hawthorne's fame, may have taunted himself that he too, like Hawthorne, should be able to encompass women in his fiction; for the aim of the Agatha story as Melville described it was in good part to emphasize the suffering endurance of the wife.

Then, when Melville had Hawthorne's permission, and apparently tried a novel in the Rip and Wakefield vein—about a man attacking necessity through his wife—the wife very likely got in the way because Melville was pulled too hard between sympathy for the husband and for the wife, whereas both Irving and Hawthorne in these stories confined themselves primarily to the husband's point of view. How much purer and simpler to deal then directly with necessity, in the form of economic ambition and economic vulnerability, to bring in Wall Street and attorneys as Lamb did, leaving out women entirely to bring in the London financial district and its accountants and clerks. Melville later would make several attempts to bring in women—with Hunilla, with Marianna in "The Piazza" watching the clouds for company—but these portraits all occur in merely interesting pieces, rather than in confident artistic works like "Bartleby." When Melville heard the Agatha story, it seems from his letters that what he wanted to write from it was a *Mayor of Casterbridge,* just as he would have understood how to make his Marianna or one of the factory girls into a Tess; but he was not ready for this, nor would the American bent for sexual polarities suggest it.

"Bartleby" was a peak for Melville. The problem of this story for Melville would only be where to go from there, how to surpass it, how to achieve the same level of artistic mastery in some other area in his next piece.

The structure which allowed for the consummate artistry of both *Moby-Dick* and "Bartleby" would be, I believe, his cue. What Melville had learned in the course of writing *Mardi* was to separate out polarities, clearly and from the beginning, and to send the reader shuttling between the two. In *Moby-Dick,* he gave us both Ishmael and Queequeg—and Ahab and Moby Dick. "Bartleby" achieves this same sort of impasse on a smaller scale but with a sterling evenness, the scrivener and attorney face to face, each with his own absurd response to the absurd situation, and the story's whole momentum building from the energy the two spend fighting their way out of their simple but inextricable entanglement.

After "Bartleby," it was with the diptychs, plus *Israel Potter,* and *The Confidence-Man,* that Melville continued with his development of a strong balanced structure on which to build his "rare humor." Indeed it seems that it was in the short two-part pieces which he apparently wrote while working on *Israel Potter* that he was deliberately pushing himself forward from the achievement of the anonymous "Bartleby." In the diptychs, Melville could increase both the emphasis on economic reality and the severity of the glare upon our illusions of rationality. He could also increase the visibility of the two-part structure, aligning the two parts with the twin cultures of England and America at a time when this sort of comparison was both a fashionable and a fascinating game. It was helpful, too, that he had his London journal handy for recalling impressions and details and setting fantasies in motion.[43]

With all this maneuvering, however, the diptychs turned out mechanical. In order for the balanced structure to be as strong as Melville could make it in a "Bartleby," it helped a great deal that one of the main partners in the hug was somewhat inconspicuous even if only by being the narrator. In "Bartleby," in fact, this important person is never even named, so that the shuttling one has to do between the lawyer's and Bartleby's solutions to things is something which the reader must realize he is doing, rather than be told he is doing by a didactic author. The very form of the diptych, however, announces the opposition too clearly to the reader. Melville's determination to try satire instead of humor does not help either; the diptychs are flat pieces disparaging what Melville even tells us directly are the "preposterous assumptions" (Poor Man's 177). In "The Two Temples," the preposterous assumption is that a religious title infers holiness; in "Poor Man's Pudding and Rich Man's Crumbs," the assumption is that nature and charity are boons to the poor. We could not argue with Melville for disparaging these notions, but the choppy form of the diptych cuts him off just as he is getting into his subject. Even the satire is shortchanged, for these pieces do not go to the other extreme of being witty, or biting. Certainly it was clever to throw England and America at each other with their competitive pride in piety, religiosity, and good fellowship. Certainly, too, it was helpful that his portraits were not just modish, but rooted in his own experiences in London in 1849.

Resonances, however, are what the pieces want. It would be inappropriate to expect humor in sketches clearly offered as satire, but resonances we must have. We do get a few—memorable touches that take us beyond the confines of mere flat statement. The image of the desolate-looking, suddenly unemployed physician in the second of the "Two Temples" has a Dickensian wryness to it. All the watery words leaking into the cold, damp sketch of the Coulter cottage have a characteristic Melvillian power in illustrating that water, so-called poor man's wine, is no boon but a curse. Finally, the Hogarthian barbarity of the royal European charity in "Rich Man's Crumbs" is memorable.

It is in "The Paradise of Bachelors and the Tartarus of Maids" alone, however, where the resonances transcend the form, where the tone transcends thin satire, and where, by the way, we get insight into why Melville remained with the male frontier humor tradition in most of his fiction. As in "The Two Temples," Melville adds to the two polarities of rich-and-poor and English-and-

American, a third, and this time not the hackneyed pious-and-impious, but male-and-female. Here his subject is challenging enough to elicit his power; it involves not only human usage, but the human lot. The contact with economic reality is imposed now upon another rough texture, biological reality. Here, in fact, Melville has found a way to tap the possibilities of the Agatha story; his desire there to express sympathy for both male and female points of view may have been, as we said, an insoluble problem because he was writing in a tradition limiting itself to the perspective of the self-aggrandizing male. In this piece, however, Melville tries something new. In the first sketch, he even directly confronts the humor tradition, insinuating into his portrait of the men a certain criticism he has never leveled at his bachelor parties before.[44] Melville suggests these men are not merely lovable, laughable, and melancholy, but effete; not just subject to criticism for their easy wealth and complacency, but warped, their urbanity tainted with the charges brought against the earlier, also supposedly celibate, Templars.

The economic angle of this diptych is brought out immediately in the first sketch, on our way to the wealthy bachelor party when we are given a glimpse of the sickening din and mud of Fleet Street. The full irony of juxtaposing the two sketches of bachelor men and women, however, does not emerge until near the end of "The Tartarus of Maids." After the description of the factory as unremitting economic exploitation, as well as the evocation of the human body as slave to its biological machinery, the narrator learns, paling, that all these women are "girls." To be an unmarried man in England somehow translates to all the ease of wealth; to be a virgin girl in America means that you have all that biological machinery within you, and must submit yourself as well to the machinery of exploitation and poverty. This awareness transcends the usual slapdash question of Melville's narrators, "Who aint a slave?" For, as Melville lets his narrator feel, if all men are slaves to the machinery, women are *taught* an "unvarying docility to the autocratic cunning of the machine" (Tartarus 209), and thus are even less than slaves. "The girls," Melville says in "Tartarus," "did not so much seem accessory wheels to the general machinery as

121

mere cogs to the wheels" (Tartarus 202). The shock here is at females' being so near and so subject to biological as well as economic machinery. All this is beyond the main tradition in which Melville worked, however. Indeed there is no humor in this diptych, which leaves satire behind also to approach something much more emotionally dense, such as Thomas Hardy would deal with in his novels.

Melville, however, was not Hardy, and he was either not equipped or not sufficiently interested to begin what would have amounted to a new career in another tradition of literary prose. Beginning a new career in poetry would be quite different; for one thing, after all his ambition, Melville might suffer himself to be an amateur poet, but surely could not force upon himself a whole new apprenticeship in prose. At any rate, he did not; instead he wrote one more diptych, directly and securely back in the male humor tradition. The diptych this time, however, did not consist of two sketches back to back, but two novels. Admittedly, to say this is to stretch the term, but Melville's final and masterful diptych, as I see it, is *Israel Potter: His Fifty Years of Exile* and *The Confidence-Man: His Masquerade.*

Put the two novels back to back and it is clear that they are both about faith in an ideal: one book is about what kind of sensation it is to have faith, and the other about what kind it is to have none. Both books are so extreme as to be problems in the Melville canon, the former for being so genial and expansive, the latter for being so relentlessly wry. Critics for a long time ignored *Israel Potter* as too unmetaphysical, too sunny and easy in its humor. Then, too, for a long time they were put off by the metaphysics with a vengeance of *The Confidence-Man,* and by the bleakness of its humor. It is unlikely that Melville consciously thought of the two novels as the two parts of a diptych. Rather, what seems to have happened is that his pattern of separating out the polarities of perspective had with a certain inevitability produced the greatest separation possible, along with the fullest resonances—a consciously sunny, expansive book, and then a consciously wry, contracted book.

Both are picaresque novels, with a clearly linear emphasis on narrative, one episode following another in the life of an adventuring loner. Israel, the eternal victim, goes from one master to the next, among whom are interspersed the famous ones: Ben Franklin, John Paul Jones, Ticonderoga Allen. The Confidence-man, eternal victimizer, goes from one subject to the next, among whom may very well be the famous ones: Ralph Waldo Emerson and Henry Thoreau. In *Israel Potter* these episodes span a whole lifetime; in *The Confidence-Man* they span one day. Israel's story was subtitled "A Fourth of July Story," and was published in July. The Confidence-man's, of course, is focused brilliantly upon the first of April—and was published on that day. Along, then, with the mirroring effect of Israel and the Confidence-man, we have that of the two holidays—one a celebration of Americans' ability to defend themselves, the other a celebration of their ability to con others; and both celebrating Yankee ingenuity and spirit. What is more, as in the shorter, unsuccessful diptychs, one story keeps largely to England, and the other to America, but neither allows the blind pride of preposterous assumptions, either of chauvinism or of Tory nostalgia.

Finally, although one moves very fast and the other very slowly, they are both hinged upon the business of seeing through disguises. Indeed, the original inconsequential autobiography which Melville picked up in 1849 or earlier may have sparked the whole two-sided issue of a con man, for in that book one Israel Potter, like either a street beggar or a parlor con man, was petitioning his readers for a pension. He was working on their emotions in order to win their sympathy and support for his claim, and sliding over touchy questions like why it took him fifty years to try to get back to America.[45] In Melville's *Israel Potter,* the speaker is given the benefit of the doubt; the disguises Melville's Potter concocts are rambunctiously, happily inventive—and innocent. He dresses as a ghost at one moment, a scarecrow at another, and he fast-talks the part of a feverish, amiable Peter Perkins at a third; but it is always clear that we may, in fact, *trust* him. The Confidence-man's disguises, on the other hand, take up the other possibility raised by the original Israel Potter's story. The Confidence-man's disguises are coldy and soberly manipulative. Their cold brilliance is, in fact, the jewel of the book.

At the same time, however, through all their eternal changes both men remain the same. As appropriate to the picaresque form, the rogue characters are at once static and immensely energetic. They are continually, repetitiously in a position to involve themselves directly in the sheer hammering of experience that makes up one aspect of human life. It is true that with the exception of Babbalanja, all Melville's characters, as humors characters, are static figures deflecting and reflecting the predicament of man alone in the universe, either in the inflation of his desires or in the deflation of his actualities. In the picaresque *Israel Potter* and *The Confidence-Man,* however, this staticness elongates to linear episodic narrative. The two novels proceed in parallel lines, like Melville's characteristic men-of-war which proceed companionably side by side, firing broadsides into each other as they go.

The two central figures also have a certain stylization that we do not find in Melville's other humors characters, and that lies in part in the biblical resonance of their characterization. It is not that Israel is the Tribe of Israel because he wanders for fifty years and ends up in the Egyptian brickyards. Nor is it that he is Christ because in "Requiescat in Pace," looking back, we hear of "that slit upon the chest . . . which afterwards, in the affair with the Serapis, being traversed by a cutlass wound, made him now the bescarred bearer of a cross" (*IP* 219). Nor is the Confidence-man either Christ because in his first disguise he is lamblike, humble, meek—or the devil because he deceives men or is continually compared to a snake.

Israel Potter and the Confidence-man are neither angel nor devil, but neither are they merely rogues, the footloose mainstays of the traditional picaresque narrative. They partake of the human as they do of the godly. They are mental projections—not so much of any concept as of a state of mind, free of the trappings of actuality. This is not to say, we should emphasize, that they are allegorical embodiments in the tradition of Spenser, Bunyan, and Hawthorne.[46] If, in fact, Israel Potter, after his fifty years of exile, sitting on Bunker Hill marveling at the changes, and pinching

himself to see if he is the same person, reminds us of Rip Van
Winkle awaking at the Hudson River canyon, his beard long and
white, his rifle rusty at his side, we should not be surprised. Nor
should we be at the final chapter of *The Confidence-Man*. This shows
us the central figure amongst the sleeping bunkers, leading the
Israel Potter/Rip Van Winkle old man, who is clinging to his Bible
and chamber pot (a nineteenth-century version of the certainties of
death and taxes) into the darkness, one dream figure leading
another, and the Confidence-man leaving us in darkness and sleep.
Melville has taken Irving's dream mechanism and all his napping
and smoking—and his humor. Melville, however, simply lets it all
happen on a deeper level. The sleeps are deeper. The dreams are
deeper. The humor is deeper.

Looking more closely at the two books, *Israel Potter,* to begin
with, is a *jeu*. Its humor is large and expansive. Its assumption is that
nature is generous; the discovery of the New World a wonderful
adventure; and man, the solitary discoverer, a figure of strength,
independence, and vitality. The opening chapter, "The Birthplace
of Israel," immediately establishes the basic principle of generosity
in the universe, and of wealth in man's sense of infinite possibility:

> The traveller who at the present day is content to travel
> in the good old Asiatic style, neither rushed along by a
> locomotive, nor dragged by a stage-coach; who is willing
> to enjoy hospitalities at far scattered farmhouses, instead
> of paying his bill at an inn; who is not frightened by any
> amount of loneliness, or to be deterred by the roughest
> roads or the highest hills; such a traveller in the eastern
> part of Berkshire, Massachusetts, will find ample food
> for poetic reflection in the singular scenery of a country,
> which, owing to the ruggedness of the soil and its lying
> out of the track of all public conveyances, remains almost
> as unknown to the general tourist as the interior of
> Bohemia. [*IP* 17]

True, the road is rugged, and the loneliness is a challenge. The
emphasis here, however, as in the novel as a whole, is on the
principle of adventure and generosity. We are carried over the

rugged, solitary hills by images of a traveller "who is content," one who will "enjoy hospitalities" and find "ample food." The whole first chapter continues in this quietly celebrative air, the prose easy and straight, letting us admire the "crests or slopes of pastoral mountains," the "lazy columns of smoke" from campfires in the forest, the early spring "curls of vapor from the maple sugar-boilers at work," "the bloom of these mountains in fine clear June days beyond expression delightful" (*IP* 18, 19). Indeed, if these opening pages surprise us with their exhilaration, Melville seems consciously to have pitched us into the joy of discovery: "Travelling northward from the township of Otis, the road leads for twenty or thirty miles towards Windsor, lengthwise upon that long broken spur of heights which the Green Mountains of Vermont send into Massachusetts. For nearly the whole of the distance, you have the continual sensation of being upon some terrace in the moon" (*IP* 17). Indeed Melville's *Israel Potter* immediately has that élan and open excitement of Cyrano de Bergerac's *Voyage to the Moon.*

It is not, in other words, just that nature is bounty, but that man himself is a prodigy. Of the walls, Melville says "the very Titans seemed to have been at work." Israel's people are a "tall, athletic and hardy race," "patient as Sisyphus, powerful as Samson," "herculean" (*IP* 19) in their undertakings. The whole novel is built upon that mood of unerring confidence and rugged ability in the creation of a new country. The very name Israel, particularly in the context of the American Puritan dream, connotes "The Chosen People," and all the pride of that title—pride in suffering as much as in achievement and belief. The character Israel spells out that pride and spirit. He ploughs his land with energy, serves his country with his whole being, and bespeaks his country's ideals simply and eloquently—even to King George himself. In fact, in every episode Israel can be depended upon to be steadfast, almost by instinct, to the ideals of dignity and equality, to the belief that no man should pay homage to another, and yet that all should to the notions of the free man and the free country. In pluck and adaptability, Israel is simply unmatchable.

The adventures of these rugged New World men do not leave

out war. The American independent spirit proves itself in battle, and Israel Potter turns out to be no mere participant but *the* behind-the-scenes hero of the American Revolution. The important thing to recognize is how different this is from Melville's other books. In *Typee, Mardi,* and *White-Jacket,* war of one kind or another is terrible and inevitable. Here, however, the expansiveness of the humor makes war something to enjoy. Finally God's creatures fighting becomes a happy episode, because the ideal they are fighting for— independence—is clearly universally benign, so much so that we never hear of even one Englishman who believes America should remain a colony. Even King George, thoroughly charmed by Israel's straightforwardness, appreciates the American desire for freedom. Indeed, England is given the benefit of the doubt here as having gone to war mistakenly, halfheartedly at most. While England and America are supposed enemies, Melville is careful to remind us that it is the Hessians who are really fighting for England. Here, finally in fact, we have the self-righteous sermon from *Mardi*'s Vivenza sung out with good cheer. The ideals of liberty and trust seem as English here as American, although the Americans like many another young generation have to reteach them to their elders. The love between enemies or opponents, however, suffuses not only the international question; between John Paul Jones and Israel we get a replay of the Queequeg-Ishmael marriage. Complete with confidential chats and bed sharing, it is another relationship of savage and civilized man, the two wooing each other in scene after scene.

Indeed the climax of this book is a battle, which is the book's most explicit bear hug of fellowship. It is also the moment when Jones and Potter work best together: during the famous battle between the *Bon Homme Richard* and the *Serapis.* The two ships, equally brave and vigorous, Melville describes with reference to charms and apothecaries, "rapid compliments of shuttlecocks," "consorts," and a moon "bedded" in vapors, the two ships "like partners in a cotillion, all the time indulging in rapid repartee." Finally,

> The wind now acting on the sails of the Serapis forced her, heel and point her entire length, cheek by jowl,

alongside the Richard. The projecting cannon scraped; the yards interlocked; but the hulls did not touch. A long lane of darkling water lay wedged between, like that narrow canal in Venice which dozes between two shadowy piles, and high in air is secretly crossed by the Bridge of Sighs. But where the six yard-arms reciprocally arched overhead, three bridges of sighs were both seen and heard, as the moon and wind kept rising. [*IP* 163-5]

Melville is nowhere more suggestive. As usual, however, the expanse of the orgasmic settles down to domesticity and finance; the two ships were also a copartnership and a joint-stock company, "as two houses, through whose party-wall doors have been cut; one family (the Guelphs) occupying the whole lower story; another family (the Ghibellines) the whole upper story" (*IP* 167).

For all *Israel Potter*'s expansiveness, for all its celebration of the New World and its possibilities, the humor of this novel does not come across as saccharine, nor the comedy of Israel's survival as mechanical. The trust that is implicit in this book is never to be taken for granted. When three Englishmen introduce themselves as friends of America and ask Israel to accept a mission to help his country,

"Tell me how I may do it," demanded Israel, not completely at ease. "At that in good time," smiled the Squire. "The point is now—do you repose confidence in my statements?" Israel glanced inquiringly upon the Squire, then upon his companions; and meeting the expressive, enthusiastic, candid countenance of Horne Tooke—then in the first honest ardor of his political career—turned to the Squire and said, "Sir, I believe what you have said. Tell me now what I am to do." [*IP* 54]

If this trust seems too easily given, Melville tempers it carefully with a realistic caution, this scene the reversed image of the boon companions scene in *The Confidence-Man*, with its hesitancy to drink.

But after his second glass, Israel declined to drink more, mild as the beverage was. For he noticed, that not only did the three gentlemen listen with the utmost interest to this story, but likewise interrupted him with questions and crossquestions in the most pertinacious manner. So this led him to be on his guard, not being absolutely certain yet, as to who they might really be, or what was their real design. [*IP* 55]

It turns out that "Squire Woodcock and his friends only sought to satisfy themselves thoroughly, before making their final disclosures, that the exile was one in whom implicit confidence might be placed" (*IP* 55). The resolution, as it is fundamentally in this book, is that there is something to trust in. Israel is trustworthy because he trusts himself and his commitment to a trustworthy ideal, independence. It does not matter, then, that he engages in one deception after another to evade his pursuers, or adopts one ingenious disguise after another—that even the heels he walks on are false, with secret papers stashed within. His gamble is based upon trust in the ideal of a young society of brave new men.

Still the grandness of the New World men would cloy but for Israel's freewheeling skepticism. It is not just the Tories whose pomp Israel pokes fun at; it is the great revolutionaries themselves. It is typical, for instance, the way Israel regards the great John Paul Jones on their first encounter—when the imperious naval giant is in Paris to confer with Franklin and only after several hours notices and addresses Israel who has been standing quietly at the side: "'Did your shipmates talk much of me?' demanded Paul, with a look as of a parading Sioux demanding homage to his gewgaws; 'What did they say of Paul Jones?' 'I never heard the name before this evening,' said Israel" (*IP* 83). Regarding the great statesman Benjamin Franklin, Israel's teasing is more sustained—expanding over several chapters—and more important. In a book celebrating the men of the New World, the sons of those Renaissance giants who pledged their all to exploration, discovery, knowledge, and the vast potentials of man, it is typical that Israel pokes fun at the very prototype of the New World humanists, Benjamin Franklin.

The portrait of Franklin is famous as satire; some even go so far as to call it savage satire. It is not, really. It is just amiable affectionate ribbing of a New World Trismegistus decked out with all his astronomical charts and pedantic pamphlets, very much as Walter Shandy was in Sterne's book, and for exactly the same reason. Indeed, if Walter Shandy as he so desired had had his Trismegistus instead of his poor Tristram, Ben Franklin could have been it. In Franklin the Renaissance extravagance gives way to Enlightenment pragmatics, but with the same underlying insistence upon being the complete jack-of-all-trades man of learning, wisdom, and glory for the male potential. For what else was at the root of the American jack-of-all-trades but the much-glorified Renaissance man?

There is one final way that Melville keeps the adventure of trust under tight rein. The final fact is that Israel has placed his confidence in American ideals and gets no reward for having done so. He cannot get a pension, nor even his name upon a plaque. Israel had continually pledged himself, his energy, and his perseverance to serving the ideals of integrity and independence to the greatest extent possible. It is thoroughly in character that he marries the Agatha Hatch type of woman who cares for him when he has a serious accident in London; and then unlike the infamous unstoried Robinson does *not* abandon her, although staying by her in England leaves him no greater reward for his goodness than destitute poverty. He becomes a chair mender, a ragpicker, within a few pages quietly evoking the painful history of the forty years of his want that are his only reward for devotion.

However, Israel, as we have said, for all his suffering is no Christ, just as for all his shrewdness he is no sage. Nor does Melville's expansive humor suddenly go bitter at the end. Israel is simply a type of male endurance. Like Bartleby, he is another projection of the Agatha Hatch steadfastness. Ultimately, it does not matter that America has violated the confidence that Israel has placed in it, for the issue of the pension in the end is presented as a small, final, incidental matter; the lifelong cause of Israel's poverty was really his marrying an Englishwoman, not the denial of a pension when he is seventy-eight. Also, Israel's suffering is passed over quickly, not because, as Matthiessen wrote, Melville was too anguished to dwell on it,[47] but because the suffering is only presented as the rein of reality upon the male song of ambitiousness and ideals; and because Israel has in fact had what he would consider the most important reward, the satisfaction of having lived a life vigorously and adventurously devoted to his own ideals. The point is, finally, as Alfred Kazin has said, *Israel Potter* is Melville's "book about American men in the old, slashing style of romantic war."[48] It is another song of triumph, another male humorous song of itself. And here again, if the New World does not totally pan out as trustworthy, and if Israel is not recognized, still his steadfast confidence in the principle of egalitarian democracy—which the New World is only of all worlds trying hardest to embody—stays true.

Israel Potter is half-humorous, half-lyrical—a song of the potential of man. It is an original novel, too. For all its derivativeness, taking a few chapters for instance from the actual autobiography of Israel Potter, using the picaresque for a form, and getting something too from the humble, pathetic male humorist for the main character's potter's field anonymity, it is strikingly independent. It swings through on the principle that there is something to trust in all our best hopes, even if we cannot name it, even though we know we should know better. The novel is broad and brightly inventive; and it touches on our pain.

In *The Confidence-Man*, we get the other side of the coin. The texture of the book and the experience of reading it immediately tell us so. Here the pace is slow. It is not tedious; from the first sentence when "at sunrise on a first of April" a man in "cream-colors" appears as "suddenly as Manco Capac at the lake Titicaca" (*TCM* 1), a certain theatricality winks at us and carries us along. Nonetheless, the prose in its density puts us under immediate constraint. The reader from the first must be asking questions and be on his guard. Who is the cream-colored man, who the black cripple, are only the first of many questions. Soon we are reading closely for clues, picking them up as deftly as Black Guinea does an inadvertently dropped business card which he will use for his next con. After acquiring the habit of recognizing the trickster each time he appears, we learn also the slow necessity to read everything he says in reverse, until by the end of the book, it is as if whole dialogues were held up to the mirror and we had to decipher them there. The habit of reversing, however, does not quite answer either. Something continually eludes us, something paradoxical having to do with the implications of the moral we seem to be in the process of being taught: that we must trust no one, trust nothing. Seeking reprieve from the paradoxes, all we have is the story, and this is a continual harping, an unrelenting turn again and again on money as coin of the realm. Every friendship resounds to the same question. Ah! we are friends! Now lend me a hundred dollars.

In *The Confidence-Man,* the New World illusion of man has evaporated. Like the South Sea Bubble, the whole of America is a hoax. None of its ideals is to be trusted, all talk of its ideals is mere talk. In episode after episode, our rogue quietly gulls his victims, and in so doing does not merely show them as gullible, but lost, with no portion of the truth to guide them, with no viable faith beneath their nervous improvisational pieties. The story is set on the great artery of America, on the Mississippi, as the Confidence-man himself is an imposter from the East, a true Yankee descended from those great performers Constance Rourke describes so well.[49] All that is grand and impressive here, however, is what we cannot trust. "'After seeing my invention duly catalogued and placed, I gave myself up to pondering the scene about me,'" the Confidence-man characteristically begins at one point, quietly winding himself up to full American pragmatic evangelism. "'Let some world-wide good to the world-wide cause be now done . . . inspired by the scene, on the fourth day I issued at the World's Fair my prospectus of the World's Charity'" (*TCM* 200). The plan is, of course, just another sham. Indeed every one of man's great New World schemes is a sham. The expansiveness of faith is repeatedly shown to be a trick, and the book is a harping on wry humor and tart reversals. We are left with no brave new ideals to hold onto, no triumph to sing about, no male spirit to apotheosize.

Indeed here we get Babbalanja's, Ishmael's, and the "Bartleby" lawyer's expansive, rhapsodic talk turned inside out. Talk here is compulsive hollowness. "'Ah,'" says the wonderfully recalcitrant Missouri bachelor to the man with the brass breast-plate,

> "You are a talking man—what I call a wordy man. You talk, talk." "And with Submission, sir, what is the greatest judge, bishop or prophet, but a talking man? He talks, talks. It is the peculiar vocation of a teacher to talk. What's wisdom itself but table-talk? The best wisdom in this world, and the last spoken by its teacher, did it not literally and truly come in the form of table-talk?" [*TCM* 108]

Indeed the Confidence-man is irrepressible in his talk, a sort of P. T. Barnum spectacle of talk, a sensational performer, different from Melville's other talkers only in that instead of gulling himself with his talk, he is gulling others. The expansiveness is turned inside out to contraction.

In this reversal, Melville is not without precedent in the history of the novel of sensibility. The other side of Henry Mackenzie's mawkish novel of sensibility, *The Man of Feeling,* is his lesser known *Man of the World,* about a character named Sindall, every bit as cruelly insensible to feelings as Harley in the first novel was tearfully sensible to them. Contained within the germ of the sensibility novel is a vision which looks two ways. Sensibility is a great and continual yawing, a promiscuous yearning after feeling. The flip-flopping of extremes is implicit in it; either an artist makes himself ridiculous by catering to this sort of thing, or he gets the joke and makes the most of it.

The Confidence-Man, like *Moby-Dick,* is another novel of exasperated sensibility; except that here the game is, instead of encouraging the sensibilities, numbing them or finding them numb and attempting to jerk them to life.

> "As to that," said the little dried up man [about a poem he has picked up off the floor], "I think it a kind of queer thing altogether, and yet I am almost ashamed to add, it really has set me to thinking; yes and to feeling. . . . I am naturally numb in my sensibilities; but this ode, in its

way, works on my numbness not unlike a sermon, which,
by lamenting over my lying dead in trespasses and sins,
thereby stirs me up to be all alive in well-doing." [*TCM*
45]

When the Confidence-man preaches to the soldier of fortune,
"'Charity marvels not that you should be somewhat hard of
conviction, my friend, since you, doubtless, believe yourself hardly
dealt by; but forget not that those who are loved are chastened,'"
the soldier replies, "'Mustn't chasten them too much, though, and
too long, because their skin and heart get hard, and feel neither pain
nor tickle'" (*TCM* 85). To the Missouri bachelor we hear the
Confidence-man, with the P.I.O. brass plate, "his patience now
more or less tasked," exclaiming, "'Yes, sir, permit me to remark
that you do not sufficiently consider that, though a small man, I
may have my small share of feelings.' 'Well, well,'" the bachelor
replies, "'I didn't mean to wound your feelings at all. And that they
are small, very small, I take your word for it. Sorry, sorry. But
truth is like a thrashing-machine; tender sensibilities must keep out
of the way. Hope you understand me. Don't want to hurt you. All I
say is, what I said in the first place, only now I swear it, that all boys
are rascals'" (*TCM* 103-4). When Charlie Noble and the cosmopolitan are discussing Moredock, the cosmopolitan says in all his
earnestness, "'As for this Indian-hating in general, I can only say of
it what Dr. Johnson said of the alleged Lisbon earthquake: "Sir, I
don't believe it."'' 'Didn't believe it? Why not? Clashed with any
little prejudice of his?' 'Doctor Johnson had no prejudice; but, like a
certain other person,' with an ingenuous smile, 'he had sensibilities,
and those were pained'" (*TCM* 136). And finally Charlie Noble is
pushed to the essential question: "'"What sort of a sensation is
misanthropy?"'" so the cosmopolitan may reply, "'Might as well
ask me what sort of sensation is hydrophobia. Don't know; never
had it. But I have often wondered what it can be like. Can a
misanthrope feel warm, I ask myself; take ease? . . . Has the
misanthrope such a thing as an appetite? Shall a peach refresh
him?'" (*TCM* 137).

Here is the same basic question asked in *Mardi*—what sort of a
sensation is life?—only here Melville is making sport with the

earnestness of sensibility: "'Don't know. Never had it.'" The dropping of pronouns is the cosmopolitan's bid to be at once utterly familiar and direct in his communication, as if, after all his talk, he were going for emphasis to not wasting a word. The wording alone is not the point, however; it is just one more little game. The point is that Melville in *The Confidence-Man* is precisely answering Charlie Noble's question and telling what kind of sensation misanthropy is. Melville is not, we should make clear, *being* misanthropic or even veiling misanthropy under the reversals and word play. Rather, he is toying with the flip side of the sensibility coin, and asking, what does it feel like to be without feelings?

If this question is deliberately self-contradictory, the answer is not, for the misanthropes of the book are giants of sensibility who in turn keep the book from being either allegory or satire. The Missouri bachelor, Pitch, for example, in all his cantankerousness, is actually a mass of hope and feelings. It is not just that after thirty rascally boys, he can actually be talked into one more. It is not only that he explains to us that he must be cantankerous just to cover up his great vulnerability, his heart. These two factors are very important, but they are secondary. The primary thing is that he talks. He expresses his feelings. He engages in colloquy. He is a Yankee talker.[50]

In fact, he talks so much that he is the one character in the book whom the Confidence-man may approach three times, in three different disguises, even while he is the one who notices the Confidence-man's own astounding concatenation of talk. This is because the Missouri bachelor, more than anyone else in the book, is still curious about the human condition and is really listening. He is no fool either; he calls the cosmopolitan "Jeremy Diddler No. 3" (*TCM* 118). Yet, as if unnerved by his dastardly inescapable conclusion about boys, he must air it, he must hear himself say what he feels; while certainly a cynic would have been coldly polite, and uninterested in any conversation. A reviewer of a book on Dostoyevsky has said in passing of Dostoyevsky's characters that they are compulsive talkers, that the oppression they feel puts them in continual need of talking.[51] They talk not just in the usual sense with the people in their circle of family, friends, and acquaintances, but talk also to strangers, telling stories to strangers in bars. Melville in an entirely different realm has caught at this same germ. Talk, talk to strangers, stems from need, and in its resonances are vast emotions. That the reader must constantly turn inside out everything the Confidence-man says, is only Melville's way, with his typically heretical insight, of revealing human need. For the other side of the great desire to *commune* with someone by the sacrament of talk is, at the least, selfish manipulation. This is why, by the way, the narrator of *Notes from Underground,* in a fine stroke, and in only one of this book's interesting parallels to Melville's *Confidence-Man,* interrupts his own moving confession to the compassionate prostitute, interrupts his own genuine sobbing fit, to abuse the whore, hand her a five-ruble note, and push her out the door.

Melville, of course, is working the theme in a very different vein. He gives us the English and American veins of sensibility and monologue rather than the Russian one of spiritual melodrama. Nonetheless, the dynamics are the same. The Missouri bachelor boy-hater needs to talk, just as his apotheosis, the Indian-hater, needs to kill. Both Pitch and Moredock are lone males love-hating the solitary male principle. Both in the extreme of sensibility grab their opponents in Melville's typical bear hug of fellowship. That Melville himself was deliberately and consciously playing this love-hate hug here to its fullest is clear. The judge

> "would relate instances where, after some months' lonely scoutings, the Indian-hater is suddenly seized with a sort of calenture; hurries openly towards the first smoke, though he knows it is an Indian's, announces himself as a lost hunter, gives the savage his rifle, throws himself upon his charity, embraces him with much affection, imploring the privilege of living a while in his sweet companionship."

If a certain acidity of reality disturbs the embrace here—"'What is too often the sequel of so distempered a procedure may be best known by those who best know the Indian'" (*TCM* 131)—later there is no acid. The judge informs us that "'Moredock was an example of something apparently self-contradicting, certainly curious, but, at the same time, undeniable: namely, that nearly all Indian-haters have at bottom loving hearts; at any rate, hearts, if anything, more generous than the average'" (*TCM* 134).

Of course, earnest Frank Goodman, the Caledonian, will quarrel with any such paradox being possible, but this is all the more reason to know Melville means it to be true. Nonetheless, Melville sports with Moredock finally, as a man of impeccable sensibility. The sentences that are Melville's finest addition to the original James Hall source[52] tell us that Moredock, because of the widespread fame of his benevolence, was invited finally to become candidate for governor, "'but begged to be excused. And, though he declined to give his reasons for declining, yet by those who best knew him the cause was not wholly unsurmised. In his official capacity, he might be called upon to enter into friendly treaties with Indian tribes, a thing not to be thought of.'" Then finally, "'And even did no such contingency arise, yet he felt there would be an impropriety in the Governor of Illinois stealing out now and then, during a recess of the legislative bodies, for a few days' shooting at human beings, within the limits of his paternal chief-magistracy'" (*TCM* 135).

If Moredock's history is invoked to be moving, and then to be gently spoofed; if Moredock is first made an impressive passionate old loner, and then edged into being a self-deluding fool, the story and portrait of the other supposed misanthrope in the book, the Confidence-man, is quite otherwise. Like Pitch, the Missouri boy-hater, but more so, the Confidence-man is unassailable in his dignity. He is also consummate in his skill and abolutely steadfast in his purpose. The critical question has always been what his purpose was, and many critics have worried over the problem of whether he is the devil incarnate, mocking the gospel and teaching men to hate by his insidious inside-out preaching.[53] This is not at all the case. As R. W. B. Lewis says, "The Confidence Man is not the bringer of darkness; he is the one who reveals the darkness in ourselves."[54] In fact, in case the reader had missed that the Confidence-man is a revealer of truth and therefore a blessed creature, Melville has the Missouri bachelor muse, after having been gulled of a few dollars by the P.I.O. man, "'Was the man a trickster, it must be more for the love than the lucre. Two or three dirty dollars the motive to so many nice wiles?'" (*TCM* 113). The Yankee pedlar's "practical" jokes were not practical, either.

The Confidence-man, like his Yankee forebears, loves his sport and his victims. With absolute reliability he talks nonsense to test our ability to recognize nonsense. By showing us how easy we are to fool, he shows us how tentative our grasp of things is. In fact there are no certainties to hold on to. That the con man may trick person after person into the delusion that there are certainties, and benign certainties at that, reveals precisely and starkly how few certainties there are. But the steadfast Confidence-man, with all his planning, shrewdness, and loyalty to his work, should not be called a devil for his pains. If we insist upon the word devil, let us at least recognize in him actually not a devil, but a devil's advocate, the critic who picks flaws to bring out the whole truth of a situation. Indeed in the framework of Catholicism, the devil's advocate is called "a promoter of the faith," his job being to show the flaws in candidates for canonization. Here the item for faith is not religion, but the New World vision of man. The Confidence-man reveals the poverty of man's ideals in an era of man's extravagant claims for himself and his newly expanding universe. *The Confidence-Man* is thus the reversal of *Israel Potter*. In *Israel Potter,* the essential expansiveness of the faith is allowed to be sung out because of an underlying contracted sense of the flaws. In *The Confidence-Man,* the essential awareness of the flaws gets its power from an underlying expansiveness. The Confidence-man throughout his adventures is, after all, the true boon companion, in a bear hug with all his victims, gulling them ever in an act of love.

We might at this moment hear it said that Milton's Satan performed a service for mankind, and that Milton's purpose in writing *Paradise Lost* was to justify God's creation of Satan. It might be said then that God gave us Satan in an act of love, and thus Melville is after all also writing about the devil. The difference, aside from a vast difference in tone, is simply that Melville is not writing about God and about why God did whatever he did. Melville is writing about man, and why man does what he does—

even if Melville is this interested in man because Melville is haunted by the belief that there is no God. This same haunting is finally what makes up put aside Milton and his Satan here, and perhaps everyone knows this. It is just as important, however, that we put aside John Bunyan's *Pilgrim's Progress* and Hawthorne's "Celestial Railroad." As Melville's work is not devotional, neither is it allegorical nor allegorically satirical.[55] It is more paradoxical than Bunyan's and, to begin with, feistier than Hawthorne's; it leans over into pathos, then leans back the other way. It is full of an underlying expansiveness although its main mode is contraction. Bunyan's and Hawthorne's works are neat and nicely rounded. The artistic mastery is total here, and Melville is controlling something vastly suggestive, but we have no neat moral, and we would not want one.

Indeed, if we are looking for prototypes for *The Confidence-Man*,[56] we should look to *Lazarillo de Tormes* and Ben Jonson's *Every Man Out of His Humor*. In both of those works we get the string of repetitious practical joke episodes—actually more grim than Melville's—hacking away at the same emptiness. In *Lazarillo,* the rogue is without ideals, is obsessed with survival, and goes from one master to the next, seeing if he can find it with them. His terrible fights with his cruel masters give way in one episode to the fine repartee between him and the squire, between the poor beggar boy and the poor rich man, between lone male and lone male, each outperforming the other in a mutual gulling exercise (described in chapter 2) which rings with all the humor of the pathetic. The unspoken sympathy between the two only underscores the basic situation, however, which the author of the picaresque tale is continually harping upon, that God's house, like the squire's, is empty. Not a stick of furniture, not a crumb of food, not the shred of an ideal—just talk.

In *Every Man Out of His Humor,* we come even closer. Melville must have read this play with care; he marked it up a great deal and in general he liked Jonson very much.[57] It seems what must have appealed here is the very undramaticness of the piece; its linear repetitiousness was an impossible burden for a play, but was a reasonable challenge for a novel. Melville must have been interested, too, in the character who holds that long stringing play together, Asper, that "rough spirit" whose job it is to bring all the other characters back to their senses. It very likely interested him too that in the end, Asper, so roughly critical a joker throughout, takes off *his* mask to reveal his true underlying amiability; his critical spirit was, after all, only a mask, not that different, in other words, from the masks and affectations that all the other characters put on.

This final twist may call our attention to one final central touch in *The Confidence-Man.* Jonson's central joke in his play is that a humor is not just an imbalance, but an affectation of some imbalance. This is a subtle distinction. The joke is not just that we are all off balance and hence ridiculous, but that despite the great and inevitable danger of making great fools of ourselves, we all deliberately create foibles, *create* imbalances for ourselves. Jonson does not worry about why we do this. Perhaps it is to make ourselves interesting; or perhaps to convince ourselves that we exist. Whatever the reason, to recognize the human *instinct* for theatricality is to latch onto what finally renders *The Confidence-Man* not just an interesting and well-crafted book, but a brilliant one. It is generally agreed that the central coup of the book is in its central character's clever pranks. The reader cannot help but be impressed at the series of ploys the Confidence-man has invented, at their great variety, and at his improvisational adaptability. But finally what is impressive about him is more subtle. The brilliance of this character's acting is not just in the broad strokes; it is in the continual minutiae involved in his appropriation of a personality as he moves inconspicuously from one con to the next.

"The merchant having withdrawn," for instance, we hear in chapter 15, "the other remained seated alone for a time, with the air of one who, after having conversed with some excellent man, carefully ponders what fell from him, however intellectually inferior it may be, that none of the profit may be lost; happy if from any honest word he has heard he can derive some hint, which, besides confirming him in the theory of virtue, may, likewise, serve for a finger-post to virtuous action" (*TCM* 60). The convolutions are thought out and real, the mask is interwovenly complex. There is more, however. At another moment: "Sobering down now, the herb-doctor addressed the stranger in a manly, business-like way— a transition which, though it might seem a little abrupt, did not appear constrained, and, indeed, served to show that his recent levity was less the habit of a frivolous nature, than the frolic condescension of a kindly heart" (*TCM* 73). It is not just the subtle convolutions of his acting, or even the way one act is imposed upon another without a moment's thought or hesitation. What holds us is that there is something oddly familiar about the naturalness of this extremely complex theatricality.

Let us look at one last moment, in the cabin. "In short, left to himself . . . he insensibly resumes his original air, a quiescent one, blended of sad humility and demureness. Ere long he goes laggingly into the ladies' saloon, as in spiritless quest of somebody; but, after some disappointed glances about him, seats himself upon a sofa with an air of melancholy exhaustion and depression." Of course, he has in fact sighted his next target and noted instantly "from her twilight dress, neither dawn nor dark, apparently she is a widow just breaking the chrysalis of her mourning" (*TCM* 37); but how thoroughly in a second he adopts a personality. With the lady beside him, we can figure out the familiarity, however. We see immediately that the Confidence-man's acting is only what everyone is doing all the time. It is not just the pun on mourning, that the lady is acting quietly bereaved but is actually just as quietly brimming with the subtle excitement of being about to break out and find her wings. It is not just the subtle evocation of sympathy for her sense of dawning possibility even before our friend opens a conversation with her. It is not, in short, just the sense of humans as creatures incorrigibly on the brink of some expectation. It is the acting. It is the effortlessly natural artificiality, the continually consummate complexity of the acting, as human beings go from one act to another in their endless attempts to assert themselves over the pupal bind of nothingness.

In the end, then, all are confidence men, and not for money, but to assert ourselves above the blandness of existence, a certain absurdity upon which we valiantly if pathetically seek to impose a sense of ourselves. Of course we do not admit that this is going on.

"Help? To say nothing of the friend, there is something wrong about the man who wants help. There is somewhere a defect, a want, in brief, a need, a crying need, somewhere about that man" (*TCM* 177). Charlie Noble is not being unusually cold in this statement. He is expressing the way human beings support their dignity, by saying it is the other guy who is needy. Meanwhile, like the *Fidèle*'s poor sprawling emigrants, each man rocks in the hard, single-planked Procrustean cradle of his own individuality. Or, Volpone-like, heads down the corridor to rob his neighbor who, also Volpone-like, is coughing "Ugh! Ugh! Ugh!" As we go down the hall, however, we do as our best confidence-man of all does, in all good spirits and with all good cheer for our immersion in the pleasure of the moment, in the joy of our simplest theatricality, we go humming "an opera snatch."

"Benito Cereno" does not belong in a chapter on Melville's great works of humor. It is not humorous; it is stark and grim. True, written between *Israel Potter* and *The Confidence-Man,* it resembles one book in working from an actual autobiographical narrative, and both books in focusing immediately and throughout upon the issue of trust. Still it is quite different. It is no Fourth of July song of triumph, nor April Fools' Day joke upon the New World. We have a con man here, Babo, but instead of a string of adventuring improvisations, he is given only one disguise and that is dead serious. If nothing else, Captain Cereno's utterly immovable fixation upon the horror of the blood feud[58] gives the story a steady somberness; and a leaden calm makes it unlike any other work of Melville.

From another angle, however, this novella gives us further insight into Melville's fiction and Melville's humor. "Benito Cereno" shows us Melville's characteristic achievement, the dimension which makes his novels and stories striking and memorable. In most of Melville's fiction, humor provides this dimension. Here, as if Melville has simply tightened the screw one turn, the dimension is irony.

The key to Melville's artistry in "Benito Cereno" is the way the story is presented. The reader has to "get" it. It is easy enough not to, to read the story flat. The prose does not help. From the beginning, the reader has to see his way through the double negatives and heavy interweavings of habitually equivocating sentences. It is satisfying finally to see that all the confusion hinges on two simple questions—what is happening on board the *San Dominick,* and what should Delano do—and to recognize finally Delano's one error; he has not considered the possibility of a Negro rebellion. Once one has the gist, however, the temptation is to read the story simply also, as some critics have done, as a flat reminder to the Delano in us all that evil does exist and that the good men must be more on the alert for the bad than they ever imagined necessary.[59]

At best, something is lacking in this reading. At worst, this reading makes the gross error of assuming that Delano's point of view is Melville's and that the black men are intended to symbolize evil.[60] Delano is not Melville, however. "Getting" it is seeing that the whole story is written from inside Amasa Delano's mind and is an ironic commentary on that mind. Melville does not tell us this. He even writes the book in the third person as if to make it sound as if it is written from the point of view of an omniscient, fair-minded if wordy author. Once we realize what is going on, we see that what we have here is the stream of Delano's thinking. The difficulties of the style, the inveterate tendency toward circumlocution and arch elaborateness, are not quirks of Melville's writing but the habits of Delano's mind. Finally "getting" it is perceiving that the dynamics of the novella consist of Delano modestly congratulating himself upon the intricate, complex, infinitely interesting workings of his own mind.

Indeed the story from beginning to end gives us Delano charting and logging his every thought from the moment the strange ship appears on the horizon. He never lets us miss an intricacy in all the possibilities he prides himself on being attuned to. He likes articulating his thoughts to himself in neatly turned phrases. He likes being a good judge of character, keeping a realistic perspective, and generally knowing his way around the nautical world as well as, through education and his own life, the vast panorama of human experience. It is "no small satisfaction"

(BC 61), also, that he has the tool of a foreign language. Finally in the midst of all his sophistication, he likes his ability to appreciate "nature." If it may very well be that the presence of the "raw" Africans is what has prompted Delano to enjoy fully his vigorously sophisticated, shrewd, yet simply sensible mind, it is also the sight of the Negroes—a Negress sleeping beneath the rigging, for example, like a "doe in the shade of a woodland rock"—which allows him to enjoy "naked nature" (BC 87).

But Delano simply does not know what is going on. Babo is running this show. Babo has devised his own role as well as Cereno's and Atufal's. Babo directs the whole ship in a convincing and colorful drama that plays right into all Delano's delusions. The black even gets Delano working for him. He puts on such a good act of being the attentive body servant that Delano will ask to buy him, so that Babo in turn can murmur, "'Master wouldn't part with Babo for a thousand doubloons'" (BC 84). He gets Delano so into the spirit that in the shaving scene, seeing the Spanish flag used as a neck cloth, it is Delano who says to Babo, "'It's all one, I suppose, so the colors be gay,' which playful remark did not fail somewhat to tickle the negro" (BC 102).

The irony is that Delano goes through the whole experience priding himself on his civilized white mind, yet the great mind here is Babo's, the black man's, the supposed primitive's. Once we see this, it is as if the story may be read again, from Babo's point of view. It is no coincidence that when Babo is slain, and his body dragged through the streets by mules, his tormentors contrive to put his head upon a stake and let those very much open eyes stare out across the plaza, nor that his head is described as "that hive of subtlety" (BC 140). Delano's head deposed, Babo's head stares out at us, in all its concentration.

Although Delano is a fool, however, the story is not a satire on him. Melville uses sympathy to create as delicate a balance as that in any of his best humor. Melville has drawn Delano with singular restraint and impartiality. It is not surprising that readers have liked him. He is neither wise, nor truly idealistic, nor genuinely humane. He seems charitable but we know we cannot trust him. Nonetheless, there is something, and it has to do with his perceptions. It is his willingness to gamble his belief that he is a good charitable fellow against his ability to perceive whether he is actually in danger that makes him sympathetic. Not good. Delano is not good, but there is something appealing about the pleasure he takes in running this risk.

Indeed, it is Melville's evenhanded sympathy which leaves some readers unaware that Delano is an evasive fool. Finally Melville is sympathetic not because of the perceptivity which Delano misses by such a long shot, but because Delano is a type of us all. Delano's problem finally is no more that he is stupid than that he is boorishly complacent. Delano is not stupid, he is simply, like Prufrock, after all, afraid. At the core of "Benito Cereno" is Amasa Delano's fear that God does not exist, and that all that does exist is nothingness. "I to be murdered here at the ends of the earth, on board a haunted pirate-ship by a horrible Spaniard?" Delano typically banters himself. "Too nonsensical to think of! Who would murder Amasa Delano? His conscience is clean. There is someone above. Fie, fie, Jack of the Beach! you are a child indeed" (BC 92). No wonder throughout the story Delano titillates himself with the images and paraphernalia of monks, cloisters, and anchorites; no wonder to say "please" he likes the word "pray." His whole interior monologue is a frightened scatterbrained prayer. There is someone above, isn't there? There is something besides this awful impartiality?

In fact, Delano's fantasy of the Negro is a projection of his own great desire for himself, to trust in the universe as he dreams the Negro does. Noting to himself that Negroes are born servants, Delano waxes rhapsodic:

There is, too, a smooth tact about them in this employment, with a marvelous, noiseless, gliding briskness, not ungraceful in its way, singularly pleasing to behold, and still more so to be the manipulated subject of. And above all is the great gift of good-humor. Not the mere grin or laugh is here meant. Those were unsuitable. But a certain easy cheerfulness, harmonious in every glance and gesture; as though God had set the whole negro to some pleasant tune. [BC 100]

Delano admires the Negroes for exactly what he holds to be his own forte, his unfailing good humor. Poor little Jack of the Beach, trudging along with his schoolbag, is still trudging along, his humor tucked under his arm, as he chats companionably with himself and everyone else, even in the midst of his great sympathy for Cereno making small tentative jests at the Spanish captain.

Delano *is* a fool. It is a fine touch that he *yearns* to be a Negro's "manipulated subject." Babo is not the only one with his head upon a stake in this story. In all Delano's vast ignorance, wishful fantasies, and schoolboy perseverance to do the best he can by a given situation, Delano also has his head upon a stake. Finally, it seems a central point of "Benito Cereno" that to be human is to have your head upon a stake, your eyes staring out—even if you insist, as Delano does, upon seeing nothing, but making a great deal of noise about having done so. Whether one is willing to face it or not, the threat remains of a godless universe with no pleasant tunes, with nothing but some residual horror and a mystifying ability to fascinate.

Melville then does not make Delano better than Babo, or Babo better than Delano, or Cereno best of all. Melville is writing about what it is like to be human. If in the end he pities human beings our self-deluding, self-congratulating minds, he also cannot repress his admiration for the subtlety of which these same minds are capable. Even Delano, insistent as he is that "someone above" solves all mysteries, cannot keep his mind from the intricacies of the Gordian knot. If Melville is asking here what sort of a sensation it is to have a head, one answer is that it is painful. Another, however, is that it is miraculous. The mind in "Benito Cereno" is pitied for its self-important bustle, for the horror it must see if the eyes are truly open. But it is also worshipped for its magic, for the extent of our fascination.

It is for this same reason that Melville never tells a story flat. The author writes in confidence that the reader can take leaps too. Melville tests and teases and toys with the reader. He throws a game at the reader. Through humor—or irony—he demands that the reader give up his conscientious, literal-minded plodding, and take certain leaps, certain risks.

Also, as Delano has conscientiously distinguished between mere grins and true cheerfulness, here once again Melville distinguishes between humor as evasion and humor as revelation. Delano is one of Melville's many evasive humorists, all foils to Melville as author. For there is nothing evasive about the games that Melville throws into his stories and novels. Melville's humor—and his irony—shield him and his reader from nothing. Instead they uncover the worst to us; but, and here is what has gone unrecognized, without Melville ever presenting himself as moral teacher or philosophical preacher. In the framework of true humor and irony, there are no teachings to be taught. It is only that we are in on this together, that together we must all "get" it. We must figure out not just what is going on, but how to take it; and at the moment that we do, author and reader have shared our only consolation in the nothingness. The sociability of the fictional form is rounded out as author and reader are in on the joke together.

V
Agatha

In terms of what has been said above about "Benito Cereno," *Pierre*
would seem to be a success. It does have an extra dimension: it is a
satire.[1] Indeed, without this recognition, the reader is lost. Melville
the satirist in *Pierre* undercuts all his characters until, shorn of their
shallow pretenses—their sentimental piety and false culture—they
push the reader to demand what every satirist wants his public to
demand, the ideals of simplicity and honesty. Melville satirizes the
romantic idyllic setting, the smug sentimental rich, the circus of the
art world. Most of all he satirizes the "Young Enthusiasts" who, in
trying to be "horologes" instead of "chronometers," are trying in
short to be God. Pierre is of course the prime fool, but the ascetic
Apostles are Melville's target too, as well as their guru Plimlim-
mon.

It would seem to speak well for *Pierre* also that it encompasses
one of Melville's favorite motifs, the preposterous hug. In Pierre
and Isabel's hug we have the perfect subject for Melville's wry
humor—or here, satire. Their hug is thoroughly impossible. At the
same time it is thoroughly sentimental. Untrammeled by the
mundane realities of either sibling or sexual bond, this relationship
like many another in Melville's fiction is allowed full rein to soar

preposterously, as Melville writes, out "of the realms of mortal-ness."[2] In addition, it is surrounded by other such hugs, the boyhood friendship of Pierre and Glen before and after it sours, and—best of all—the tenacious attraction of Lucy Tartan to the "newlyweds," Pierre and Isabel. Indeed the scene in which Lucy, the third member in Pierre's harem, arrives at The Apostles, and in which Pierre locks all three of them in a room to protect them, is near farce.

Nonetheless, something is wrong with *Pierre*. Melville is not in control. The book is not stinging satire. It is bizarre. The satire fails because in his main character Melville was writing too close to home. In Pierre, Melville seems at once to be attacking and vindicating himself. The satire comes back too baldly upon Melville himself, the young man who wrote *Typee* and *Mardi,* and who in a fit of heroics wrote that he wished his books to fail.[3] As Edward Rosenberry writes, "The final effect is self-mockery, a spectacle that must embarrass any but the most morbid reader."[4] At the same time a special pleading for the writer impinges upon the book. In the midst of satirizing "enthusiast" Pierre, Melville is still drawn to characterizing him quite positively, as a man of tragic hubris, a quester. Melville is trying at once, in fact, to be satiric and tragic. One book cannot sustain the wrenching between two so disparate artistic purposes.

The hug fails also. The problem is that it involves a female. It was probably Hawthorne's influence that led Melville to attempt a plot with a woman at the center. But also, Melville had always been profoundly attuned to the condition of slavery implicit in the human condition; it was only a matter of time before he noticed that women as well as men were slaves. Indeed, in *Pierre,* written before the "Agatha" attempt, "The Tartarus of Maids," or "The Piazza," it is as if Melville had suddenly noticed women in their own right. Part of the intensity of the book is in this discovery, Melville's simultaneous with Pierre's: "She is my sister—my own father's daughter. . . . The other day I had not so much as heard the remotest rumor of her existence; and what has since occurred to change me?" (*P* 139). Melville's sympathy was the more profound because of women's anonymity, so far-reaching as to embrace themselves. Not only had the men not heard of them but the women themselves, Yillah and Isabel, for example, did not know their own pasts.

Melville's sympathy was too profound, however. Melville did not know how to give women both sympathy and ridicule, the staples for his male figures. It did not help that women were sacred sentimental objects in his world; he had no models of how to knock their sacredness wryly and deftly. Although Hawthorne used humorous highlights, he never exposed his female characters to the full indignity of humor's free play the way Melville might have wanted to, had he known how. The only conventional way to tease women was to portray them as shrews and termagants. Melville had tried this sort of playfulness with Annatoo in *Mardi* and had found it grotesque and unwieldy.

Had Melville felt more confident about his understanding of women, he might have invented his own humor; but as the dreamy stories of his women suggest, he was vague on how women viewed themselves. Women were not quite real to him; yet in a sense they were too real, too large to him. As Isabel becomes Pierre's copyist, her anonymity shifting from the ethereal to the mundane, we should recall that Herman Melville had his copyists, too. Certainly it would have been tasteless to joke in his fiction about his wife Elizabeth and sister Augusta being his copyists. It was a strange twist, for all his anguish, that Melville was the boss in his particular copying office. No wonder he would have as much understanding of the narrator's point of view as of the copyist's in "Bartleby." It only must have compounded the problem that there were so many women in Melville's household.

In short, women were at once too far from his understanding and too near him for Melville to write about them with the control necessary for consummate artistry. You could tease God more easily than a woman, not just because God had a certain familiar maleness about him, but because God did not live right there in your own house with you, flying up to set your room to rights every morning,[5] raising your children, depending upon you to make the family living. It is true that in *Pierre* Melville made some progress in writing about women. He knocks Lucy's idyllic maidenliness. He tries to provide perspective on women working in the "real world," when Pierre explains to Isabel why she should not give music lessons.[6] Eventually, too, he has Lucy Tartan rise to a certain sexual boldness, a stature that entails her coming to get her man and becoming something of a true artist as well.

But this new stature, very Hawthornesque, has no suppleness about it, none of the free play that characterizes Melville's best portraits, best monologues, best treatments of how the human mind sees itself. Rather the portrait of Lucy, like the young woman herself, has a certain stiffness, a certain impregnability. Melville couldn't really find a use for this new stature in the tradition in which he was working. To Melville new stature, like the New World itself, simply meant new illusion. It seemed unfair, however, for a man to have to be the one to have to say this to women. At any rate, saying so would defeat the purpose of having made women taller in the first place. In *Pierre,* Melville made the error of thinking that women too were part of his province, but thereafter he would move with great restraint regarding female characters.

Pierre was not, then, as has been suggested, one of Melville's great quest novels. In *Pierre* Melville was writing satire. At the same time he saw other possibilities in his material—writing a tragedy and writing about women—and found these alternatives hard to resist, although harder still to implement. But most of all, after the exhilarating experience of writing *Moby-Dick,* he was writing too hard and too fast, and he was tired.[7] *Pierre* is a highly interesting book because of its autobiographical material about Melville. It has that documentary appeal of many books, about the chronometrical travails of being a writer. Whatever we may think, however, of a novel about being a writer, Melville seems to have been embarrassed about it. He says of Pierre, whose writing has become more and more strained and sterile, "he seems to have directly plagiarized from his own experiences to fill out the mood of his apparent author-hero" (P 302). We should recall that in *White-Jacket,* Lemsford the poet is made a sympathetic and likable man, but Melville reflecting upon the condition of being a man and opening the channels of his energy and humor made White-Jacket and Jack Chase his two great characters in that novel.

Pierre is a tired book in which Melville is repeatedly telling us what to think, in which Melville's own writing becomes more and more strained. Perhaps if satire and tragedy could complement each other the way humor and melodrama do in Melville's great works, his energy would not have run down so in this book. In any event, it does run down.

Neither did Melville have the energy or confidence for "The Encantadas," or for a batch of short pieces that followed. In these he dabbles with ideas having to do with humor and with the issues that humor addresses. In "The Happy Failure" and "Jimmy Rose," we are told what humor is, and even given some raw materials, but the pieces are thin philosophical gruel indeed. In "I and My Chimney" and the "Apple-Tree Table," the reader cannot help being interested in what is going on, but the claptrap of uninspired domestic comedy gets in the way. In these pieces Melville provides no real embodiment or enactment. They are outlines or story ideas. As Leon Howard says, Melville was writing some of his magazine fiction "without much inspiration. As the Spenserian quotations used in 'The Encantadas' show, he had been attempting to stimulate his flagging invention . . . with allegory."[8]

Indeed paper-thin allegory was the stuff of such stories as that of Hunilla the enduring and Oberlus the hateful. These uncomplicated, utterly unambiguous pieces are in the sketch style of Irving, with the allegorical tendency of Hawthorne and the geographical expertise of Melville; they were written as if Melville were toying with what he was saying rather than, as in his great work, immersing himself in it. The worst of the platitudes of "The Encantadas," because it has proved most tenacious, is Melville's preaching about the two sides of the tortoise: "Enjoy the bright, keep it turned up perpetually if you can, but be honest, and don't deny the black" (E 154). This is decent enough advice, but it is also flat preaching. Who is speaking here? We are given no insight into the narrator, no commentary upon him. He is a dull presence, with no irony, no twist of self-recognition or self-ridicule. He is merely a sailor turned magazinist, earning some money by writing travel sketches touched up with pathos and platitudes, even if at moments rendered with charm. When in the sixth sketch Melville turns to quote a "sentimental voyager," it is not to indulge in a tone he has prohibited himself, but rather to give us more of the same. In these short pieces, Melville fails to find his own level of engagement with what he is saying; his energy never sparks; the humor is thin.

These last pages have concentrated on works of Melville that failed, and in chapter 4 we have spoken of his works of humor that succeeded. It would seem unnecessary and out of place to say anything in conclusion about "Billy Budd." Besides the fact that thirty years intervened between *The Confidence-Man* and "Billy Budd," the latter is simply not a work of humor—nor of irony nor of satire. While in this, his final novella, Melville is working in his familiar territory, with men at sea, it might be said that his method here is entirely different from what it was in his work of the forties and fifties, and thus the novella is outside the scope of this study.

Indeed the implication has been that finally here we have a true Melville without the distraction or diversion of humor; that because there is no humor here, we actually have Melville at his best, his purest. It is because of this implication that some remarks about "Billy Budd" are germane here. The point of this study has been that Melville's humor is central to his greatness. If this is so, then "Billy Budd," being without humor, either partakes of a very different sort of greatness, establishing a whole other area of achievement for its author than I have been discussing—or actually, contrary to the usual view, is less vigorous, less bold, less controlled than Melville was at his best. I believe the latter is true.

It is tempting to believe the former, however: to read "Billy Budd" as a consummate work of art, one in the thoroughly serious vein. Haunting and noble, it seems to impose upon us a tragic recognition of the limits of mortality. Vere in this view is neither to be blamed nor venerated. He is an agent of mortality in a postlapsarian world where mortality means not just death, but the death of innocence. He is a naval captain in an era when naval captains had to protect themselves against mutiny as much as one country had to protect itself against the attacks of another—England, for instance, against the attacks of Napoleonic France. Indeed, England and France here are a modern Greece and Troy, calling up all the heroism of Greek tragedy.

While this reading suggests the starkness at the core of the novella, it does not account for the actual method of the story. Instead of dialogue and enactment, we are given discourse and description; Melville's narrative style here is actually inappropriate to tragedy. If this is so, William York Tindall suggests a cogent alternative, which is that "Billy Budd" is about the numbness of weighing life and death variables. In this interpretation, the method of discourse is central to the story's meaning and impact. "Neither as loose, nor as tight as it once seemed, the strange sequence of precise discourse and indefinite suggestiveness corresponds to our experience of life itself . . . of facing, of choosing, of being uneasy about one's choice, of trying to know."[9] In this sense, surprising as it may be, we might find ourselves adding "Billy Budd" to the sensibility tradition of Melville's main body of writing, which begins with Babbalanja's asking what sort of a sensation life is.

The problem with both of these interpretations is that while they hint at our sense of the nobility behind the story, neither of them takes into account one major aspect of it, the characterization of Billy. If the story has a starkness to it, at the same time it has a rhapsodic quality antithetical to starkness. Indeed, it is the rhapsodic absorption with Billy which has drawn so many readers to the novella. He is a focus for emotion in the story where all else seems numb with mature deliberation and confrontation. Finally Warner Berthoff seems most in tune with Melville's intentions when he reads the story as a paean to "certain phenomenal men."[10] No starkness is intended actually, just a hush so that we may better hear the praise for the lamblike Billy.

Who is Billy, however? If we are to sing his praises, something seems awry. The character evoked with all the imagery and sanctity of Christ does not turn the other cheek, but kills a man. Do natural barbarian and beatified saint actually fit into one character? Is there not something gratuitous and forced about Melville raising up Billy from first Adam to second, from Adam to Christ? Then, too, is Billy Budd realized here or just awkwardly evoked?

My point, finally, is that "Billy Budd" is actually written very much in the same method of all Melville's prose of thirty and forty years before. It is not just that we have the typical Melville arena, the instability of being at sea in the nothingness of the universe, and within that arena God's creatures fighting, the French terrorizing the English, the sailors terrorizing their superiors and two individuals, Billy Budd and John Claggart, locked in the typical Melville embrace of love-hate. The method of character portrait is familiar, too. The narrator, speaking in the first person, takes on the bulk of the story in an unwieldy, convoluted discourse. The other characters growing out of this discourse are, as in Melville's other work, largely evocations rather than fully embodied characters fully responsible for themselves. They are like humors figures, set a-humming, set into motion by things bigger than themselves.

But it is a problem that Melville uses the method of humors characterization, yet removes the humor. We can almost see the humor evaporating out of the story. We are told at first that the old sailor, the Dansker, has a dry humor. His humor gives way quickly, however, to a querying speculation as to what will happen to Billy; then his speculation to silence, a "bitter prudence" (BB 86) which finally dominates the relationship between the old man and the young. The Dansker could have told Billy how to survive. Certainly part of the humor of Melville's earlier books grew out of a very song of survival, from White-Jacket teaching himself not to speak of whales in front of Jack Chase to Ishmael saving himself upon his good friend Queequeg's coffin. Here, however, we are deliberately being given something else, with no wryness, perhaps finally how not to survive.

Nor are we allowed any humor in Billy. The novella opens with the Aldebaran, the black handsome sailor, a hearty bold man who conjures up everything that Jack Chase embodied in *White-Jacket*. From a hearty bold humor, however, we move quickly in the portrait of Billy to a certain anxiety, a certain hermaphroditic submissiveness. Billy is enshrined as the "Happy Failure," as "Jimmy Rose." Ultimately he is too much enshrined, too precious a flower, too slight.

In one other way, "Billy Budd" is very much the same as the books Melville wrote before: the exasperation. It is not just that Claggart is dominated by exasperation. Claggart can so little bear the knowledge of his helplessness that he is wasted into pure exasperation. This might be all right. But Billy Budd is also a figure of exasperation. Here is the irony that is outside the story, that is not controlled by Melville.

One wants to say that Melville's aim in this story was very different from what it was in his earlier work. To understand it, we should think not just of the New Testament, but of secular stories such as "A Simple Heart" and *The Idiot*. The essential problem remains, however. Felicité and Myshkin are both figures of profound and saintly meekness. Neither of them could strike a man dead. To understand Billy, it is better to call up Melville's own past fiction. White-Jacket, we should recall, worried that he would strike dead the officer who tried to flog him; we may also remember Tommo with the boat hook, and of course Taji and Ahab. Billy is far less the cousin to Christ, Felicité, and Myshkin than the child of all Melville's own figures of exasperation suddenly transfixed by the feeling of helplessness—and striking out at the bearer of that bad news.

Finally, something is out of kilter in "Billy Budd." Melville is working in much the same way that he had in the past in his prose fiction, with the same subject and approach. Billy Budd is just another of Melville's young men who suddenly feel their helplessness and swing out at the nothingness to protest it. The problem is how Melville has wanted us to feel about this young man. In his earlier work, Melville had always incorporated a love song. He loved that Typee paradise, those magnificent whales, the sea itself. Ishmael loves Queequeg and even loved Ahab. In removing the humor from "Billy Budd," Melville has left out the tempering of his lyricism, left the rhapsody by itself. The lyricism is not unencumbered here, however; it is unmoored. Without humor, Melville veers off into unconvincing beatitude, Billy dying with "God bless Captain Vere" (BB 123) on his lips, the sailors' chorus echoing with their love for Billy.

Richard Chase speaks of this problem of Billy. Chase offers a helpful explanation, one which we may add to. He suggests that Melville was possibly swayed in this novella by the thought of his twenty-year-old son Malcolm who had killed himself.[11] The shooting incident occurred, we should recall for a further insight, the morning after Melville played the part of the "very strict parent,"[12] to use a relative's phrase. Melville's concern with whether he should have locked out his son that night and with whether he had been a good parent in general may have raised insoluble questions. These seemed to have disturbed his artistic control; and pushed him, in the impossibility of deciding upon either self-approval or self-condemnation, to express, finally, what haunted him most and what at least was incontestable—that he loved his son, and that his son was dead.

It cannot be gainsaid, "Billy Budd" is haunting. The story is strong, the form is also. We must admit to the stardom of Billy here, however, and in that see that something has gone wrong. Melville has used his old methods, but as with treating a wife or a sister, evoking a dead son placed a serious strain on his artistic control. Omitting the humor would have been no problem had Melville really had a new tradition, a different tradition, in which to work. As in *Pierre,* he seeks a model in Hawthorne's fiction; he tells us that Billy with his one blemish—his stammer—was like the beautiful woman "in one of Hawthorne's minor tales" (BB 53). Finally, however, Melville knew his story was headed in a direction where Hawthorne's approach would not be right either; so he clung to his own ways. But working in the same framework gave him no room for the beatitude he was intent upon. One feels Melville reaching here, as he did in his treatment of women, for a new type of prose fiction, but I do not feel him finding it.

We need to leave behind us the notion that "Billy Budd" is Melville's "purest" or most "elevated" work. Let us continue to admire "Billy Budd" for what Melville was reaching for, and for his ability to draw us in to what he is haunted and moved by. Let us not, however, tell students that we have in "Billy Budd" a noble tragedy, and then pretend that the critical problem it presents is merely incidental. With the brilliantly conceived and executed "Bartleby" and "Benito Cereno," one should not attempt to use "Billy Budd" to prove something misleading about a sugary nobility of American literature.

Actually the quiet steady grim humor of "Bartleby" makes

for a purer martyrdom, a more absolute beatitude than that which Melville was straining for in "Billy Budd." Melville's work was most pure when he was writing in full confidence of Adam, not of Christ; when he was in full excitement about the roundness of man's perception of himself; when his humor put him above a forced piety.

What has been said about Melville's problem in encompassing the youth, Billy, and the women, Yillah and Isabel, is not to say that working in the humor tradition was a handicap. Melville chose it because it gave him an outlet, a form, a model. The tradition also gave Melville a broad sociality, a community, so that as much as he struggled as an artist, his art was not in turn anguished. Writing in the humor tradition not only demonstrated his commitment to America, but expressed his feeling of belonging to central Western ambitions—and central Western family jokes. To say that the forms and approach Melville adopted implied certain limitations simply is to say that he would have needed a whole other career to have handled a whole other prose tradition—and why should we require it?

What Melville did was momentous enough: taking that tradition, apprenticing himself to it, until he saw what his humor was and how to make it work for him at its greatest depth. Melville always rode out to the edges of the possible in his humor. His range of effectiveness was determined on the one hand by the extent to which he was able to relax his fears that his humor would be misread—and on the other that he was able to come as close as possible to the brink of what humor could achieve. Humor thrives on the humorist knowing he is a humorist—finding his tone, his format, his audience. That was the learning involved in Melville's first five books. Then it thrives on the humorist being willing to take as many risks as he can with his humor, never falling into stale assertion or untempered lyricism, or corn. Melville, it seems, had often worried that his good humor would be taken for bad. In *White-Jacket* he daubed onto the story some Christian allegorizing to show he was not bad humored, only finely attuned to the absurdity in the universe. And sometimes Melville worried that his humor would be taken for rote good cheer, Stubb's sort of unthinking merriment which cloys in its blissful evasiveness; he worried that his humor would be read as mere subliterary entertainment. Melville often talked about humor in his novels; he thought at lot about what he wanted from it, and how precisely he was to get it.

Melville's career, in short, was the discovery and mapping out of what it was to achieve the greatness possible of a humorist. Part of the tension in speaking in a foreign language is that you have trouble getting your humor across, and without it your meaning is flat and lifeless. This is something of the tension of Melville's writing career, for the public was a sort of foreign country to Melville where he had somehow to overcome barriers to present himself fully. In this connection, however, we have Melville not just satisfied with any joke to relieve the strain of communication—but set on finding precisely the joke he most needed to tell and his public most needed to hear. This is what is most impressive about Melville's humor. He was able to build upon models which since the Renaissance were developing a tradition of the male monologue of freewheeling bravado on the frontier. In addition, however, he was like any great performer able to experiment with those forms, to express his own humor, to make the tradition his.

Why did he stop? Why did he never really try another mode of prose fiction? Why did he persist for twelve years before stopping? Perhaps Heinrich Böll's Clown (in the book of that title) provides a fitting analogy. The truly brilliant clown can only go on as long as he continues to amuse himself with his own antics. Böll's clown becomes a beggar singer—so did Melville, a lyricist, a poet. Poetry was not, however, Melville's métier. Alfred Kazin reminds us that as great as Melville's poetry was in certain respects, he was surely an amateur as a poet.[13] As a humorist, Melville was no amateur; he was a consummate artist, once he had the trick. And perhaps, like Böll's clown, once he had it all too well, he did not need it because he had done it to its limits, and it no longer amused him.

Then, too, a humorist needs not only to be amused by his antics—and perhaps he goes on being so when he has taken the greatest risks possible—he needs a steady interaction with an

audience, to egg on his teasing of them. The risks, the teasing, the
interaction all combine to keep up the performer's energy. After
all, perhaps the problem with "Billy Budd" is that by the time he
wrote that novella, Melville had lost the flirtation with the
audience.

It is difficult not to wish that Melville had had a career more
like Henry James's, longer, more sustained; to be sorry that
Melville could not afford like James to carry on his writing over
many years, but instead had to go to work in a customshouse. We
should keep in mind, however, that Melville was not merely a
victim of circumstances. He chose to keep his vulnerability, just as,
unlike James, he chose to have a family. He never actively sought
the kind of economic security that would have put him in an
entirely different position from the bulk of the human race.[14]
Finally the genius of his humor was that it was the outlet of this
same absolutely fundamental egalitarian democratic vision. Who
else besides Melville, 130 years before our time, conveys what it is
like to ride Manhattan's Seventh Avenue subway at eleven o'clock
on a week night when it is packed with people of every possible
color, costume, and hold on reality? Melville's humor was the
outlet for a far-ranging democratic vision. Perhaps the point is that
democracy is no glory, no salvation. That is why here, too, we need
the humor, or need it most of all. Democracy is only a place where
man's generous notions grow to abundance side by side with the
absurd, and with a stubborn ineluctable pain of existence.
Melville's humor releases the tension of man's predicament in an
ideal, democratic culture.

In a letter to a young poet, in 1903, Rainer Maria Rilke wrote:

> With nothing can one approach a work of art so little as
> with critical words; they always come down to more or
> less happy misunderstandings. Things are not all so
> comprehensible and expressible as one would mostly
> have us believe; most events are inexpressible, taking
> place in a realm which no word has ever entered, and
> more inexpressible than all else are works of art, myste-
> rious existences, the life of which, while ours passes
> away, endures.[15]

If there could be any final word on Melville, we would not need to continue to read his work. If his art did not finally elude our grasp in some way, we would lose interest in it. Without attempting to say a last word, the point of this study has been simply to add a recognition of what his humor is to our reading of Melville. In the watery world to which Melville takes us, and in which he rides out with us, humor is the human fluidity, the quickening moisture, with which we meet halfway the continual ambiguity and difficulty of existence.

Notes

I. Introduction

1 The *Oxford English Dictionary,* for the first use of *humor* in this sense, cites the 1682 translation of Glanius, *Voyage to Bengala,* p. 142: "The cup was so closed, that 'twas a difficult matter for us to open it, and therefore the general gave it us on purpose, to divert himself with the humor of it." The Glanius work is little known now, but the number of English editions listed in the *British Museum Catalogue* and *National Union Catalogue* suggest that in its time it was a popular work.

In *The Amiable Humorist, A Study in the Comic Theory and Criticism of the 18th and Early 19th Centuries* (1960), Stuart Tave traces a further development of the word *humor.* The "amiable humorist" viewed his imbalanced humors or foibles with affection, rather than with ridicule. I suggest that the affection for the humor—like its antecedent, the praise of folly—was a complex phenomenon, a way of studying man's mind. At its best, amiable humor was part of the tradition of prose humor from the Renaissance to our own time, which gave Melville his models. At its worst, amiable humor suggested to Melville what he wanted to steer clear of, a smug, superficial cheerfulness.

For a key statement on the humanist complexity of the praise of folly, useful for an understanding of the affection for the humor, see Erwin Panofsky, "Renaissance and Renascences," *Kenyon Review* 6 (1944): 234–35.

2 See, for example, Henry Clay Lukens, "American Literary Comedians," *Harper's New Monthly Magazine* 80 (1890): 783–97, which, when Melville was virtually forgotten, recalled him as one

of the humorists who had been active in the middle decades of the century.

3 In the extreme case, Melville's humor is given lip service in anomalous contexts. For instance, in the midst of a discussion of Melville's subversiveness, Lawrance Thompson in *Melville's Quarrel with God* (1952) mentions Melville's "excellent sense of humor" (p. 18). Ultimately, it seems, Thompson acknowledges Melville's humor only to find it satanic.

Most critics, however, simply give Melville's humor a secondary position, as if it were an accompaniment for his tragic or symbolist achievement. See, for example, Milton R. Stern, *The Fine-Hammered Steel of Herman Melville* (1957); Merlin Bowen, *The Long Encounter* (1960); Tyrus Hillway, *Herman Melville* (1963); D. E. S. Maxwell, *Herman Melville* (1968); and Ray B. Browne, *Melville's Drive to Humanism* (1971).

Three key studies of Melville's humor will be referred to in this work: Constance Rourke, *American Humor* (1931), pp. 191-200; Richard Chase, *Herman Melville* (1949; reprint ed., 1971), pp. 64-102, 176-202; and Edward H. Rosenberry, *Melville and the Comic Spirit* (1955; reprint ed., 1969).

4 Nathaniel Hawthorne, *Journal,* 20 November 1856, referring to Melville's visit to Southport, 11-13 November 1856, reprinted in Jay Leyda, *The Melville Log,* (1951; reprint ed. with supplement, 1969) 2:528-29: "He can neither believe, nor be comfortable in his unbelief."

5 Herbert Ross Brown, *The Sentimental Novel in America, 1789-1860* (1940), and Richard Chase, *The American Novel and Its Tradition* (1957), hint at this idea which Leslie A. Fiedler spells out in *Love and Death in the American Novel* (1966; reprint ed., 1970). See also Ann Douglas, *The Feminization of American Culture* (1977), in which Melville is portrayed as an artist in rebellion against a sentimental society.

6 Chase, *The American Novel, e.g. pp. 37-41.*

II. Extracts and Etymologies

1 Merton W. Sealts, Jr., "The Records of Melville's Reading," in his *Melville's Reading* (1966), pp. 3-26, provides a good overall introduction to Melville's reading.

2 Ben Jonson, *Every Man Out of His Humor,* in *Ben Jonson's Plays,* 2 vols. (London: Dent, 1910), 1:69; Huntington Brown, *Rabelais in English Literature* (1933; reprint ed., 1967), pp. 86-87, has suggested Rabelais as the source here.

3 François Rabelais, *The Lives, Heroic Deeds and Sayings of Gargantua and His Son Pantagruel,* trans. Sir Thomas Urquhart and Peter Le Motteux (1928), pp. 21-24. The exact edition Melville read is not known, but critics have long assumed that whichever edition, it was the Urquhart-Le Motteux translation.

4 Ibid., p. 2.

5 Erich Auerbach, *Mimesis,* trans. Willard R. Trask (1953), p. 269. Referring to the discovery of the New World, he continues, "This is one of the great motifs of the Renaissance and of the two following centuries." Auerbach devotes much of his Rabelais chapter to the characteristic Rabelaisian humor of the "everything just as at home" theme, developed in the passage describing the exploration of the new world in Pantagruel's mouth. See also his conclusions. "So much for the everyday. But the seriousness lies in the joy of discovery—pregnant with all possibilities, ready to try every experiment, whether in the realm of reality or super-reality—which was characteristic of his time, the first half of the century of the Renaissance, and which no one has so well translated into terms of the senses as Rabelais with the language which he created for his book [p. 284]."

6 Auerbach, *Mimesis,* p. 271, on Rabelais's debt to late medieval preaching. For example, "much as he hated the mendicant orders, their flavorful and earthy style, graphic to the point of ludicrousness, was exactly suited to his temperament and his purpose, and no one ever got so much out of it as he." Rabelais's debt to the mendicants may be compared with Melville's to the Yankee pedlars; although Melville himself was also playing off the sermon tradition.

See also Mikhail Bakhtin, *Rabelais and His World,* trans. Helene Iswolsky (1963), for a fascinating if muddled discussion of Rabelais's noncanonical carnival folk humor. (Bakhtin is so drawn to folk elements in Rabelais that he ignores Rabelais's equally strong aristocratic elements.)

7 Sealts, *Melville's Reading,* pp. 87–88, no. 417. All subsequent references to dates of Melville's reading, unless otherwise indicated, are based on Sealts's alphabetical listings.

8 Cyrano de Bergerac, *The Comical History of the States and Empires of the Worlds of the Moon and Sun . . . Newly Englished by A. Lovell* (1687), p. 2. When Melville borrowed this book from Duyckinck, he signed it out as *Voyage to the Moon,* the title on the binding of Duyckinck's copy of the Lovell Cyrano preserved in the New York Public Library. For a useful introduction, see Richard Aldington's to his translation, *Voyages to the Moon and the Sun* (1923; reprint ed., 1962), pp. 3–29.

9 Cyrano, *The Comical History,* p. 205.

10 Richard Popkin, introduction to *Historical and Critical Dictionary, Selections,* by Pierre Bayle (1965), pp. xii, xiii.

11 Ibid., pp. xxiv, xxv, xxxii.

12 Pierre Bayle, *The Dictionary Historical and Critical of Mr. Peter Bayle, 2nd Ed. Carefully Colated, with many passages restored and the whole greatly augmented with translations of quotations and the Life of the Author, revised by Mr. Des Maizeaux,* 5 vols. (1734–38), 1:40. Sealts, *Melville's Reading,* p. 39, indicates the edition was either this one, a four-volume 1710 edition, or a ten-volume 1734–41 edition. For purposes of comparison, I have, like Millicent Bell (see n. 13) used the five-volume edition. This was also the edition owned by Evert Duyckinck.

13 Millicent Bell, "Pierre Bayle and *Moby-Dick,*" *PMLA* 66 (1951): 626–48.

14 Popkin, introduction, p. xxvii.

15 Melville to Hawthorne, 17(?) November 1851, in *The Letters of Herman Melville,* ed. Merrell R. Davis and William H. Gilman (1960), p. 142.

16 John T. Frederick, "Melville's Early Acquaintance with Bayle," *American Literature* 39 (1968): 545–57. Melville, 5 April 1849, *Letters,* pp. 82–84.

17 See Melville's marginalia in his edition of Jonson's *Works,* transcribed in Wilson Walker Cowen, "Melville's Marginalia" (Ph.D. diss., Harvard University 1965), section 302: Ben Jonson.

18 Ben Jonson, *Volpone,* in *Ben Jonson's Plays,* 1:456.

19 Huntington Brown, *Rabelais in English Literature,* pp. 81–94.

20 Robert Burton, *The Anatomy of Melancholy,* ed. Floyd Dell and Paul Jordan-Smith (1927), pp. 98–99.

21 Rabelais was only one of many authors whose influence may be seen in Burton's vastly eclectic *Anatomy.* But certainly Burton saw important parallels between himself and the Frenchman. Both men were trained in the church, and one was an actual physician, the other a physician by virtue of the *Anatomy.* After his catalogue of madmen, and his reference to Rabelais as a good physician, Burton's Democritus, Jr. says, "I can but wish myself and them a good Physician, and all of us a better mind" (p. 101). Also certainly to both men, as to the whole tradition, Erasmus's *Praise of Folly* was a key source.

22 For instance, Robert G. Hallwachs's unpublished thesis, "The Vogue of Burton: 1798-1832," cited in Lawrence Babb, *Sanity in Bedlam, A Study of Robert Burton's Anatomy of Melancholy* (1959), p. 12, shows that John Ferriar's 1798 *Illustrations of Sterne* revealed Sterne's unacknowledged borrowings from the *Anatomy* and was the immediate impetus for the Burton revival in the Romantic period. Charles Lamb, we should note, wrote an imitation of Burton's style: *Curious Fragments, Extracted from a Common-place Book Which Belonged to Robert Burton.*

Stuart Tave confines his study to the eighteenth and nineteenth centuries and thus says little about sources of amiable humor. On amiable humor, see also chapter 1, n. 1.

23 Herman Melville, "Fragments From a Writing-Desk, Clipping from the 'Democratic Press and Lansingburgh Advertiser,' No. 1," reprinted in *Billy Budd and other Prose Pieces by Herman Melville,* ed. Raymond W. Weaver (1924), pp. 382–90.

24 Samuel Johnson, *Rasselas,* in *Rasselas, Poems, and Selected Prose,* ed. Bertrand Bronson (New York: Holt, Rinehart, 1958), p. 515.

25 Ibid., p. 514.

26 Ibid., p. 528.

27 See C. R. Tracy, "Democritus Arise! A Study of Dr. Johnson's Humor," *Yale Review* 39 (1950): 294–310.

28 F. O. Matthiessen, *American Renaissance* (1941), p. 272. "For a

young American growing up in the early nineteenth century, the adventures of the Abyssinian prince were likely to be still as much a part of his household as whale-oil lamps." Margaret Fuller was one contemporary who took for granted the appropriateness of comparing Melville's first novel with *Rasselas:* "The Happy Valley of the gentle cannibals compares very well with the best contrivances of the learned Dr. Johnson to produce similar impressions" ("Review of *Typee,*" New York *Tribune,* 4 April 1846, reprinted in Hershel Parker, ed., in *The Recognition of Herman Melville* [1967] p. 3). In *Typee,* Melville himself compares the Typee Valley to the Happy Valley.

For a study of the form of *Rasselas,* the "philosophical tale," or *conte philosophe,* see Martha Pike Conant, *The Oriental Tale in England in the Eighteenth Century* (1908; reprint ed., 1966), pp. 110-54.

29 Laurence Sterne, *The Life and Opinions of Tristram Shandy, Gentleman* (New York: Holt, Rinehart, 1950), p. 73.

30 Ibid., p. 250.

31 Ibid., p. 56.

32 Thomas De Quincey, *Confessions of an English Opium-Eater and Other Writings,* ed. Aileen Ward (New York: NAL, 1966), pp. 80, 81.

33 Ibid., pp. 81-82.

34 Ibid., p. 66.

35 Ibid., p. 83.

36 Aileen Ward, foreword to De Quincey, *Confessions,* pp. vii-xvii.

37 Herman Melville, *Journal of a Visit to London and the Continent, 1849-1850,* ed. Eleanor Melville Metcalf (1948), pp. 80-81.

38 As an aside, see Melville's own experience with country living evoked by Jay Leyda in "White Elephant vs. White Whale: How, in the Berkshire Festival country, Melville wrote *Moby-Dick* with a 160-acre Incubus round his neck," *Town and Country* 101, no. 4299 (August 1947): 68, 69, 114d, 116-18.

39 Charles Lamb to William Wordsworth, 22 January 1830, in *The Portable Charles Lamb, Letters and Essays,* ed. John Mason Brown (1948), p. 188.

40 Lamb, "Imperfect Sympathies," in *The Portable Charles*

Lamb, pp. 279–80. De Quincey's "Confessions" were published in *London Magazine* in October and November 1821; Lamb's "Imperfect Sympathies" appeared in the same periodical in August of that year.

41 Ibid., p. 284.

42 Ibid., p. 279.

43 Melville to R. H. Dana, 1 May 1850, *Letters,* pp. 106–8.

44 Washington Irving, *The Sketch Book of Geoffrey Crayon, Gent.* (New York: NAL, 1961), p. 83.

45 Our only recorded date of Melville's reading of Irving is his likely reading of *A History of New York* in 1847; see Sealts, *Melville's Reading,* p. 70, no. 292. With Irving's 1819–20 serial publication of the essays which made up *The Sketch Book,* however, Irving had become the outstanding figure in American literature. As with Burton and Johnson, Irving was a household name in the years in which Melville was growing up.

46 In short, it is important to recognize the balance between foreign and indigenous elements in American humor. See the lively quarrel between J. De Lancey Ferguson and Constance Rourke on the notion of American humor as spontaneous generation or parthenogenesis ("The Roots of American Humor" and "Examining the Roots of American Humor" in *American Scholar* 4 [1935]: 41–49 and 249–53). See also Brander Matthews, "American Humor," in his *America of The Future and Other Essays* (1909), pp. 161–76, on roots in seventeenth-century English literature; Walter Blair in his introduction to *Native American Humor* (1937; reprint ed., 1960), on the influence of Sir Walter Scott and others; and Walter Blair and Hamlin Hill, *America's Humor, from Poor Richard to Doonesbury* (1978), on many influences—the book seems devoted in part to correcting an overly nativist view of American "jokelore."

47 Richard Dorson, *Jonathan Draws The Long Bow: New England Popular Tales and Legends* (1946), p. 11.

48 George Lyman Kittredge, *The Old Farmer and His Almanack, Being Some Observations on Life and Manners in New England A Hundred Years Ago Suggested by Reading the Earlier Numbers of Mr. Robert B. Thomas's Farmer's Almanack, Together with Extracts Curious, Intrusive and Entertaining, As Well As a Variety of Miscellaneous Matter* (1920; reprint ed., 1967), pp. 19–22.

49 Ibid., p. 48.

50 Dorson, *Jonathan Draws The Long Bow,* pp. 134–35.

51 See, for example, Rourke, *American Humor,* pp. 58–59; Chase, *Herman Melville,* pp. 94–95; Matthiessen, *American Renaissance,* pp. 639–40; Kenneth S. Lynn, ed. *The Comic Tradition in America* (1968), pp. 153–54.

52 In many anthologies, including Blair, *Native American Humor,* pp. 337–48.

III. Embarkations

1 Melville to Hawthorne, 1 (?) June 1851, *Letters,* p. 128.

2 George Stewart, "The Two *Moby-Dicks,*" *American Literature* 25 (1954): 417–48. Stewart's compositional analysis, of course, has been updated (for instance, by James Barbour, "The Composition of *Moby-Dick,*" *American Literature* 47 [1975]: 343–60). But the ultimate point of interest here is not in how many stages Melville composed a book, but in how many ways he conceived of prose in a given book.

3 Lamb to Thomas Manning, 15 February 1802, *The Portable Charles Lamb,* p. 94.

4 Most critics to be sure recognize similarities between *Typee* and Melville's later work, but they emphasize the differences and a change in Melville's outlook and approach. See, for example, Matthiessen, *American Renaissance,* p. 377; Bowen, *The Long Encounter,* pp. 16, 55; W. E. Sedgwick, *Herman Melville* (1944), pp. 27–59; and Rosenberry, *Melville and the Comic Spirit,* pp. 5, 9–48. Two exceptions, although not with reference to humor, are James Miller, *A Reader's Guide to Herman Melville* (1962), p. 20, who finds it "difficult to believe that so deep a mind as Melville's could so readily and completely shift its orientation"; and Leon Howard, historical note to Herman Melville, *Typee* (1968), pp. 277–301, especially p. 301 (Hershel Parker's "Evidences for 'Late Insertions' in Melville's Works," *Studies in the Novel* 7 [1975]: 409–13, notwithstanding).

We should not be surprised that, as my analysis will suggest,

Melville from the start wrote as he wished, that he was ambitious and daring at the outset. His father died a bankrupt when Herman was twelve, but his family was upper middle class and distinguished.

5 Melville to John Murray, 15 July 1846, *Letters,* p. 39. The context should be noted; in this letter Melville seems to be trying to justify his acceptance of the expurgation of *Typee.*

6 Roland Barthes, "The World as Object," in *Critical Essays,* trans. Richard Howard (1972), pp. 3-12.

7 Charles Feidelson, Jr., *Symbolism and American Literature* (1953), p. 165.

8 Melville is referring to the anonymous *Young Man's Own Book: a manual of politeness, intellectual improvement and moral deportment, calculated to form the character on a solid basis and to insure respectability and success in life* (1832). The phrase Melville quotes (*T* 132) is a paraphrase of this book's frontispiece quotation. The book is an example of a genre popular at the time.

9 On Melville's plodding rendition of Rabelais, see for example, Charles Gordon Greene, "Review of Mardi," Boston *Post,* 18 April 1849; reprinted in Parker, *The Recognition of Herman Melville,* pp. 14-16: "After the arrival at "Mardi," the book becomes mere *hodge-podge,* reminding us of the *talk* in Rabelais, divested of all its coarseness, and, it may be added, of all its wit and humor. . . . In a word, "Mardi" greatly resembles Rabelais emasculated of everything but prosiness and puerility."

It was a French critic, Philarete Chasles, in the *Revue des Deux Mondes,* who called Melville "an American Rabelais," in his article "Voyages reels et fantastiques d'Herman Melville," reprinted in rough translation in *The Literary World,* 4 and 11 August 1849, quoted in Perry Miller, *The Raven and the Whale* (1956), pp. 251, 260. Miller, Rosenberry, and Merrell R. Davis, *Melville's Mardi* (1952; reprint ed., 1967) document and provide helpful discussion of *Mardi's* borrowing from Rabelais.

10 Babb, *Sanity in Bedlam,* p. 35.

11 Howard Vincent, *The Tailoring of White-Jacket* (1970), p. 12. This book provides a helpful introduction to Melville's use of nonliterary sources.

12 Ibid., pp. 201-2.

13 Willard Thorp, historical note to Herman Melville, *White-Jacket* (1970), p. 415.

14 Keith Huntress, "Melville's Use of a Source for *White-Jacket*," *American Literature* 17 (1945): 66-74; Vincent, *The Tailoring*, pp. 9, 108.

15 Newton Arvin, *Herman Melville* (1950; reprint ed., 1972), p. 111.

16 William Gilman, *Melville's Early Life and Redburn* (1951).

17 Luther Mansfield, bringing their existence to light in "Melville's Comic Articles on Zachary Taylor"(*American Literature* 9 [1938]: 411-18), evidently thought reprinting only one of the ten articles was sufficient for a series in which he saw such meager literary merit. Rosenberry, *Melville and the Comic Spirit,* p. 188, n. 1, as if worried that knowledge of them would prejudice readers against Melville's comedy, chided Mansfield for "uncharitably" exhuming them. Chase, *Herman Melville,* p. 77n., and Davis, *Melville's Mardi,* pp. 38-39, are more interested and dispassionate.

18 Herman Melville, "Authentic Anecdotes of 'Old Zack,' Anecdote, No. III," *Yankee Doodle* 2 (31 July 1847): 167.

19 Herman Melville, "Authentic Anecdotes of 'Old Zack,' Anecdote, No. I," *Yankee Doodle* 2 (24 July 1847): 152.

20 Melville to Evert Duyckinck, 14 December 1849, *Letters,* p. 96.

21 "He has no violent predilection for his regimentals and seldom appears in them, which in fact, is the case with most of his officers, of whom it is even observed that '*they seldom appear in externals on duty.*'" Herman Melville, "'Gen. Taylor's Personal Appearance,' or Old Zack Physiologically and otherwise considered," *Yankee Doodle* 2 (7 August 1847): 172. See also Zack's request for jackets "large over the back and free in the arms," "Anecdote IX," *Yankee Doodle* 2 (11 September 1847): 229.

IV.   Whales and Confidence

1 10 April 1847; see Sealts, *Melville's Reading,* p. 45.

2 Melville does not mention Montaigne by name, but Montaigne's famous essay seems a likely source here.

3 Donald Yannella, "'Seeing the Elephant' in *Mardi*," in *Artful Thunder: Versions of the Romantic Tradition in American Literature in Honor of Howard P. Vincent,* ed. Robert DeMott and Sanford Marovitz (1975), pp. 105-17. Yannella, p. 107, quotes J. R. Bartlett, *Dictionary of Americanisms* (New York: 1848): "To see the Elephant, is a South-western phrase, and means, generally, to undergo any disappointment of high-raised expectations. It is . . . quite synonymous with the ancient 'go out for wool and come back shorn.'"

4 Chase, *Herman Melville,* pp. 64-102.

5 Whitney Hastings Wells, "*Moby-Dick* and Rabelais," *Modern Language Notes* 38 (1923): 123. Wells notes the borrowing but makes no comment on it. The chapter in Rabelais is book 1, chapter 10, "Of That Which Is Signified by the Colours White and Blew."

6 Rabelais, *The Lives, Heroic Deeds and Sayings,* pp. 30-31.

7 Northrup Frye's "Theory of Genres," in *Anatomy of Criticism* (1957), pp. 243-341, especially pp. 312-14, helpfully classifies *Moby-Dick* as a romance-anatomy, pointing out that the usual critical approach to the form of such works as *Moby-Dick* "resembles that of the doctors in Brobdingnag, who after great wrangling finally pronounced Gulliver a *lusus naturae.* It is the anatomy in particular that has baffled critics, and there is hardly any fiction writer deeply influenced by it who has not been accused of disorderly conduct." It is odd that few critics have referred to Frye's useful concept; and yet at the same time we must note that it is important to distinguish, as Frye does not, between Menippean satire and the melancholy anatomy.

8 Burton, *Anatomy of Melancholy,* p. 16.

9 Ibid., pp. 11, 425.

10 Ibid, pp. 11, 529, 24, 103, 530.

11 Ibid., p. 411.

12 Ibid., p. 64.

13 We are not certain what Melville had read of *Tristram Shandy* before writing *Moby-Dick.* We know that in 1849 he first read and enjoyed immensely a few chapters of that novel, and by the time he wrote "Cock-A-Doodle-Doo!" he felt familiar enough with it to speak of it as a remedy for melancholy, in much the way Burton before or Irving after would traditionally speak of their

beloved books as cures for hypos. We know also that America was saturated with Shandyisms—that, like Samuel Johnson, Sterne was in the air. Luther Mansfield even suggests that Melville may have gotten many of his stunts from an intermediary, Southey's *Doctor,* a popular romantic rehashing of Sterne which contains prefatory matter labeled "History and Romance Ransacked for Resemblances and Non-Resemblances to the Horse of Dr. Daniel Dove." (Although Sealts does not list Southey, see Richard Moore, "A New Review by Melville," *American Literature* 47 (1975): 265–70, which suggests Melville reviewed Southey's *Commonplace Book* in *The Literary World.*) Mansfield sets us in the wrong direction by suggesting that Melville took up these stunts only to change them into serious mood-setting devices. Mansfield is closer in his linking of Ishmael and Queequeg's bedtime chats with Mr. and Mrs. Shandy's "beds of justice"; Luther Mansfield and Howard Vincent, explanatory notes to Herman Melville, *Moby-Dick* (1962), pp. 570, 579–80, 624 et al.).

14 Sterne, *Tristram Shandy,* p. 265.

15 Mansfield and Vincent, explanatory notes, pp. 593–94, n. line 16: "Melville seems to have perversely misinterpreted the classic Roman as *l'homme fatal* of romantic literature. . . . Perhaps here too, Melville experienced a skeptical failure to understand such virtuous faith and courage as the classical tradition attributed to Cato."

16 Henri Bergson, "Laughter," in *Comedy,* with an introduction by Wylie Sypher (1956), pp. 59–190.

17 Jean-Jacques Mayoux, "De Quincey: Humor and the Drugs," in *Veins of Humor,* ed. Harry Levin (1972), p. 123. This, incidentally, is one of the best essays written on the subject of humor.

18 Lamb to Wordsworth, 20 March 1822, *The Portable Charles Lamb,* p. 156.

19 Lamb, "Imperfect Sympathies," pp. 279–80.

20 Evert (and George?) Duyckinck, "Melville's Moby Dick; or, The Whale," New York *Literary World* 9 (15 November 1851): 381–83 and (22 November 1851): 403–4, reprinted in Parker, *The Recognition of Herman Melville,* p. 41.

21 Mansfield and Vincent, explanatory notes, p. 773. See also p. 681.

22 Harrison Hayford and Hershel Parker, eds., *Moby-Dick* (1967), p. 12, n. 3.

23 Chase, *Herman Melville*, pp. 64-102.

24 Ibid., p. 100: "As patriots we may enjoy with Melville his excursions into American folklore. It was for him, a healthy impulse. Like Ahab, he was gifted with the high perception; without it *Moby-Dick* would lack the over-all structure of its universal-historical allegory. Yet underneath the high perception, supporting and nourishing it, Melville knew there must be a low enjoying power. This he sought and found in the folk spirit of his country."

25 Ibid., p. 91.

26 Chase, *The American Novel*, pp. 93-113. "The essential voice of Melville is to be heard in the half humorous, subtly erotic lyric tone which is peculiar to *Moby-Dick* [p. 111]."

27 See Eric Partridge, *Dictionary of Slang and Unconventional English*, 7th ed. (1970), p. 218; and John S. Farmer and W. E. Henley, *Dictionary of Slang and Its Analogues* (1965). The curious thing is how several slang meanings of the word did seem to surface in print suddenly in 1860: the affidavit or declaration, the dictionary or overly fine language, and the male sexual organ. (It seems fair to assume that the slang existed in speech before it was documented in print.)

28 Charles Lamb, "Barbara S————," *London Magazine*, April 1825, reprinted in *The Portable Charles Lamb*, pp. 375-81.

29 Irving, *The Sketch Book*, p. 41.

30 Ibid., p. 39.

31 Nathaniel Hawthorne, "Wakefield," in *Twice-Told Tales* (Columbus: Ohio State University Press, 1974), pp. 139-40.

32 Ibid., p. 131.

33 In his lecture, "The South Seas," Melville comments, "Who that has read it can forget that quaint sketch, the introductory essay of Elia, where he speaks of the Balclutha-like desolation of those haunted old offices of the once famous South Sea Company—the old oaken wainscots hung with the dusty maps of

Mexico and soundings of the Bay of Panama—the vast cellarages
under the whole pile where Mexican dollars and doubloons once
lay heaped in huge bins for Mammon to solace his solitary heart
withal?" (Herman Melville, _The Portable Melville,_ ed. Jay Leyda
[1952], p. 576). See also Joel O. Conarroe, "Melville's 'Bartleby'
and Charles Lamb," _Studies in Short Fiction_ 6 (1968): 113‑18. Conarroe
points out several borrowings, such as Evans and Turkey, and the
names not being in the directory. He is probably correct in
suggesting that Melville gets the name Bartleby from Bartlemy in
"Oxford Vacation," that is, the Lamb sketch following "The
South-Sea House." To Conarroe's observations, however, we
must add an emphasis on what Lamb helped liberate in Melville, the
humorous vision. Lamb had not written piously of the martyred
Bartholomew, but with an affectionate wry teasing and unor-
thodoxy. "There hung Peter in his uneasy posture—holy Bartlemy
in the troublesome act of flaying," Lamb had written nostalgically
of the two old schoolbook pictures (p. 421). Who else beside
Lamb—and Melville—would call a martyred saint by an affectionate diminutive and speak of his _uneasy_ posture and the _troublesome_
act of flaying?

34 Lamb, "The South-Sea House," in _The Portable Charles
Lamb,_ p. 323.

35 Melville writes of Turkey, "In the morning, one might say,
his face was a fine florid hue, but after twelve o'clock, meridian—
his dinner hour—it blazed like a grate full of Christmas coals . . .
the face which, gaining its meridian with the sun, seemed to set
with it, to rise, culminate and decline" (B 18).

36 Lamb, "The South-Sea House," p. 321.

37 Ibid., p. 325.

38 Ibid., p. 328.

39 Ibid.

40 R. W. B. Lewis, _Trials of the Word_ (1965), pp. 36-39.

41 Melville to R. H. Dana, 1 May 1850, notes that while en
route to Europe in October 1849, he "found a copy of Lamb in the
ship's library—and not having previously read him much I dived
into him & was delighted—as every one must be with such a rare
humorist & excellent hearted man" (_Letters,_ p. 108).

42 Melville to Hawthorne, _Letters,_ pp. 153‑61.

43 Melville, *Journal.*

44 This is so even though the sketch is based upon the easily happy dining party he had in London on 18 December 1849.

45 Israel Potter, *The Life and Remarkable Adventures of Israel R. Potter,* (1824; reprint ed. 1962); Arnold Rampersad in *Melville's Israel Potter* (1969) has commented on this aspect of the original Israel Potter story.

46 Rampersad, *Melville's Israel Potter,* compares *Israel Potter* with Bunyan's *Pilgrim's Progress.* See n. 55 below on *The Confidence-Man.*

47 Matthiessen, *American Renaissance,* p. 491.

48 Alfred Kazin, introduction to Herman Melville, *Israel Potter* (1974), p. 8.

49 See Rourke, *American Humor,* pp. 3–32. Rourke failed to see in *The Confidence-Man,* if she knew the book at all, Melville's great descendant of the Yankee pedlar. She concludes her brief discussion of Melville, on p. 200: "With the writing of his one great book [*Moby-Dick*] Melville's work was finished." Chase, however, brings to our attention the important connection between the prototype Rourke describes, and both Israel Potter and the Confidence-Man (*Herman Melville,* pp. 185–202).

50 Rourke, *American Humor,* p. 30: "A deep relish for talk had grown up throughout the country." See also pp. 7–8, on prolonging the talk, and p. 23 on the Yankee as oracle, all of which should be applied to the Confidence-man as well as to Pitch.

51 V. S. Pritchett, review of *Dostoyevsky: Reminiscences, New York Review of Books* 22 (30 October 1975): 8ff.

52 James Hall, "Indian-hating.—Some of the sources of this animosity.—Brief Account of Col. Moredock," in his *Sketches of History, Life, and Manners, in the West* (Philadelphia: Harrison Hall, 1835), 2:74–82, reprinted in Herman Melville, *The Confidence-Man,* ed. Hershel Parker (1971), pp. 249–54. See also Herman Melville, *The Confidence-Man,* ed. Elizabeth S. Foster (New York: Hendricks House, 1954), pp. 334–41.

53 For example, John Shroeder, "Sources and Symbols for Melville's *Confidence-Man,*" *PMLA* 66 (1951): 364–80.

54 R. W. B. Lewis, afterword to Herman Melville, *The Confidence-Man* (1964), p. 276.

55 Willard Thorp in *Herman Melville* (1938), pp. xi–cxxix, sees *The Confidence-Man* as "an allegory . . . like *Pilgrim's Progress* or Hawthorne's 'Celestial Railroad.'" See also Parker's edition of *The Confidence-Man,* pp. ix–xi; and Rosenberry, *Melville and the Comic Spirit,* pp. 161–66. In "Melville's Ship of Fools," *PMLA* 75 (1960): 604–8, Rosenberry continues to conceive of *The Confidence-Man* as allegory but rejects "The Celestial Railroad" as a key source or analogue in order to emphasize the "ship of fools" tradition. Regarding this tradition, see Panofsky's distinction between the medieval Brantian attitude toward folly, and the Renaissance Erasmian attitude toward folly.

56 Foster says of *The Confidence-Man*'s sources, "the Bible, *Pilgrim's Progress,* Shakespeare, and *Paradise Lost* mingle with all varieties of picaresque fiction, from coney-catching anecdotes to Don Quixote; Hawthorne's fine-wrought allegorical stories intermix with the raw histories of frontier settlement, Indian massacre, river bandits, steamboat con men; the wisdom of the ancients, Lucian's irony and Tacitus' pessimism, flow beside the brash confidence of the new Western world" (pp. xciv–xcv). Rosenberry, *Melville and the Comic Spirit,* also mentions *Tristram Shandy,* but advisedly drops it in "Melville's Ship of Fools." For comments on *The Confidence-Man* in relation to Jonson's *Volpone* and *Bartholomew Fair,* see Sedgwick, *Herman Melville,* p. 188; Rosenberry, "Melville's Ship of Fools," p. 607; and Jay H. Hartmann, "*Volpone* as a Possible Source for Melville's *The Confidence-Man,*" *Susquehanna University Studies* 7 (1965): 247–60, which includes useful background material and draws important parallels. See also, for historical context and analogue, Jay Robert Nash, *An Anecdotal History of the Confidence Man and His Game* (1975).

57 Cowen, "Melville's Marginalia," section 302: Ben Jonson. See also Melville, *Journal,* pp. 31, 84–85.

58 Harry Levin, *The Power of Blackness* (1958), p. 190: "Melville, the exponent of brotherhood among races, seems ready to concede that life is a blood-feud."

59 This reading is responsible, in fact, for Arvin's dismissal of the novella: "As a parable of innocence in the toils of pure evil, however, all this is singularly unremarkable, and we are forced to

feel that Don Benito has gone very little beyond the rudiments when, at the end, he enforces the lesson his terrible experiences have taught him: 'To such a degree may malign machinations and deceptions impose. So far may even the best man err in judging the conduct of one with the recesses of whose conditions he is not acquainted.' To be sure!" (*Herman Melville*, p. 240).

60 Matthiessen, *American Renaissance*, p. 508. It is of course Delano, not Melville, who has failed to reckon with the key fact Matthiessen describes; and Delano, not Melville, who is superficial.

V. Agatha

1 For early discussions of *Pierre* as satire, see William Braswell, "The Satirical Temper of Melville's *Pierre*," *American Literature* 7 (1936): 424-38; and "The Early Love Scenes in Melville's *Pierre*," *American Literature* 22 (1950): 283-89.

2 "Sisters shrink not from their brother's kisses. And Pierre felt that never, never would he be able to embrace Isabel with the mere brotherly embrace; while the thought of any other caress, which took hold of any domesticness, was entirely vacant from his uncontaminated soul, for it had never consciously intruded there. Therefore, forever unsistered for him by the stroke of Fate, and apparently forever, and twice removed from the remotest possibility of that love which had drawn him to his Lucy; yet still the object of the ardentest and deepest emotions of his soul; therefore, to him, Isabel wholly soared out of the realms of mortalness, and for him became transfigured in the highest heaven of uncorrupted Love" (*P* 142).

3 Melville to Lemuel Shaw, 6 October 1849, *Letters*, p. 92.

4 Rosenberry, *Melville and the Comic Spirit*, p. 149 and p. 196, n. 16. See also p. 151: "Years later Melville wrote his own remorseful commentary on the unwholesome humor of *Pierre* . . . 'In elf-caprice of bitter tone/I too would pelt the pelted one:/At my shadow I cast a stone.'—'Shelley's Vision,' *Timoleon*."

5 Elizabeth Shaw Melville to Mrs. Lemuel Shaw, 23 December 1847 in Leyda, *The Melville Log*, 1:266.

6 "'My poor, poor, Isabel!' cried Pierre; 'Thou art the mistress of the natural sweetness of the guitar, not of its invented regulated artifices and these are all that the silly pupil will pay for learning'" (*P* 334).

7 Melville wrote *Pierre* in three months, from late November 1851 to 20 February 1852; see Hershel Parker, "Why *Pierre* Went Wrong," *Studies in the Novel* 8 (1976): 7–23 (although Parker's reading of *Pierre* differs from the one in this study).

8 Leon Howard, *Herman Melville, A Biography* (1967), p. 212.

9 William York Tindall, "The Form of *Billy Budd*," in *Billy Budd and the Critics,* ed. William T. Stafford, 2nd ed. (1968), pp. 186–93.

10 Warner Berthoff, "'Certain Phenomenal Men': The Example of Billy Budd," in his *The Example of Melville* (1962), pp. 183–203.

11 Richard Chase, "*Billy Budd,* Antigone and *The Winter's Tale,*" in *Billy Budd and the Critics,* pp. 203–6. "In some ways at least Billy Budd strikes us as not quite believable. There are contradictory elements in his character; he is, for example, 'innocent,' yet he has had 'experience'... I would suggest that the relative failure of Billy Budd as a fictional character can be accounted for in a very simple manner. Melville was too personally involved with Billy Budd. Whether he was picturing his own son Malcolm (who shot and killed himself at the age of twenty) or speaking of his own youth or of Christ or making a general statement of the perpetual sacrifice of innocence to law and society, the idea of Billy Budd appeared so overwhelmingly moving to the aged Melville that he was not able to express it in artistically cogent language [p. 203]."

12 Catherine Gansevoort to Henry Gansevoort, 16 September 1867, in Leyda, *The Melville Log,* 2:691: "Cousin Herman is I think a very strict parent & Cousin Lizzie thoroughly good but inefficient. She feels so thankful she did not scold him or remonstrate as she intended so she cannot blame herself for having induced him from despair at her fault-finding to put an end to his life."

13 Alfred Kazin, "The Poetry of Herman Melville," seminar at City University of New York, the University Center, 1 May 1975.

14 For example, see Howard, *Herman Melville,* p. 205: "How much Herman really knew about the campaign in his behalf [to get him a job] is uncertain. It seems highly improbable that his uncle Peter . . . would have confined his efforts to the two days following Maria's first appeal if his favorite nephew had really 'earnestly wished for' the office; and it is inconceivable that Judge Shaw should have been so casual and uninformed in his efforts at assistance if either Herman or Elizabeth had been actively interested."

15 Rainer Maria Rilke, 17 February 1903, in *Letters to a Young Poet,* trans. M. D. Herter Norton, rev. ed. (1954), p. 17.

Bibliography

ALDINGTON, RICHARD. Introduction to his translation of *Voyages to the Moon and the Sun,* by Cyrano de Bergerac. 1923. Reprint. New York: Orion, 1962.

ARVIN, NEWTON. *Herman Melville.* 1950. Reprint. Westport, Conn.: Greenwood, 1972.

AUERBACH, ERICH. *Mimesis.* Translated by Willard R. Trask. Princeton: Princeton University Press, 1953.

BABB, LAWRENCE. *Sanity in Bedlam, A Study of Robert Burton's Anatomy of Melancholy.* East Lansing: Michigan State University Press, 1959.

BAKHTIN, MIKHAIL. *Rabelais and His World.* Translated by Helene Iswolsky. Cambridge: M.I.T. Press, 1963.

BARBOUR, JAMES. "The Composition of *Moby-Dick.*" *American Literature* 47 (1975): 343-60.

BARISH, JONAS. *Ben Jonson: A Collection of Critical Essays.* Englewood Cliffs: Prentice-Hall, 1963.

BARRY, ELAINE. "Herman Melville: The Changing Face of Comedy." *American Studies International* 16 (1978): 19-33.

BARTHES, ROLAND. "The World as Object." In *Critical Essays.* Translated by Richard Howard. Evanston: Northwestern University Press, 1972.

BAYLE, PIERRE. *The Dictionary Historical and Critical.* 2d ed., rev. 5 vols. London: Knapton, 1734-38.

―――. *An Historical and Critical Dictionary.* Translated by Jacob Tonson. 4 vols. London: Harper, 1710.

BELL, MILLICENT. "Pierre Bayle and *Moby-Dick.*" *PMLA* 66 (1951): 626-48.

BERCOVITCH, SACVAN. *The Puritan Origins of the American Self.* New Haven: Yale University Press, 1975.

BERGSON, HENRI. "Laughter." In *Comedy.* Garden City: Doubleday, 1956.

BERTHOFF, WARNER. *The Example of Melville.* Princeton: Princeton University Press, 1962.

BICKLEY, R. BRUCE, JR. "The Triple Thrust of Satire in Melville's Short Stories: Society, the Narrator, and the Reader." *Studies in American Humor* 1 (1975): 172-79.

BLAIR, WALTER. *Native American Humor.* 1937. Reprint. San Francisco: Chandler, 1960.

―――, and HILL, HAMLIN. *America's Humor from Poor Richard to Doonesbury.* New York: Oxford University Press, 1978.

―――, and MEINE, FRANKLIN. *Half Horse Half Alligator: The Growth of the Mike Fink Legend.* Chicago: University of Chicago Press, 1956.

BOWEN, MERLIN. *The Long Encounter.* Chicago: University of Chicago Press, 1960.

BRASWELL, WILLIAM. "The Early Love Scenes in Melville's *Pierre.*" *American Literature* 22 (1950): 283-89.

―――. *Melville's Religious Thought.* 1943. Reprint. New York: Farrar, 1973.

―――. "The Satirical Temper of Melville's *Pierre.*" *American Literature* 7 (1936): 424-38.

BROWN, HERBERT ROSS. *The Sentimental Novel in America, 1789-1860.* Durham: Duke University Press, 1940.

BROWN, HUNTINGTON. *Rabelais in English Literature.* 1933. Reprint. New York: Farrar, 1967.

BROWN, STERLING. *The Negro in American Fiction.* 1937. Reprint. Port Washington: Kennikat, 1968.

BROWNE, J. ROSS. *Etchings of a Whaling Cruise . . . to which is appended a Brief History of the Whale Fishery, Its Past and Present Condition.* New York: Harper, 1846.

BROWNE, RAY. *Melville's Drive to Humanism.* Lafayette, Ind.: Purdue University Studies, 1971.

CHASE, RICHARD. *The American Novel and Its Tradition.* Garden City: Doubleday, 1957.

————. *Herman Melville, A Critical Study.* 1949. Reprint. New York: Hafner, 1971.

————, ed. *Melville, A Collection of Critical Essays.* Englewood Cliffs: Prentice-Hall, 1962.

COHEN, HENNIG. "Wordplay on Personal Names in the Writings of Herman Melville." *Texas Studies in Literature* 4 (1963): 85–97.

COLEMAN, DOROTHY. *Rabelais: A Critical Study in Prose Fiction.* Cambridge: Cambridge University Press, 1971.

COLIE, ROSALIND. *The Resources of Kind, Genre-Theory in the Renaissance.* Berkeley: University of California Press, 1973.

CONANT, MARTHA PIKE. *The Oriental Tale in England in the Eighteenth Century.* 1908. Reprint. New York: Farrar, 1966.

CONARROE, JOEL O. "Melville's 'Bartleby' and Charles Lamb." *Studies in Short Fiction* 6 (1968): 113–18.

CORRIGAN, ROBERT W., ed. *Comedy: Meaning and Form.* San Francisco: Chandler, 1965.

COWEN, WILSON WALKER. "Melville's Marginalia." Ph.D. dissertation, Harvard University, 1965.

CROCKETT, DAVID. *The Autobiography of David Crockett.* 1834–36. Reprint (3 vols. in 1). New York: Scribners, 1923.

CYRANO DE BERGERAC, SAVINIEN. *The Comical History of the States and Empires of the Worlds of the Moon and Sun . . . Newly Englished by A. Lovell.* London: Rhodes, 1687.

DAVIS, MERRELL R. *Melville's Mardi.* 1952. Reprint. Hamden, Conn.: Archon, 1967.

DeMOTT, ROBERT, and MAROVITZ, SANFORD, eds. *Artful Thunder: Versions of the Romantic Tradition in American Literature in Honor of Howard P. Vincent.* Kent: Kent State University Press, 1975.

DENNY, MARGARET, and GILMAN, WILLIAM H., eds. *The American Writer and the European Tradition.* New York: Haskell House, 1968.

DORSON, RICHARD. *Jonathan Draws the Long Bow: New England Popular Tales and Legends.* Cambridge, Mass.: Harvard University Press, 1946.

DOUGLAS, ANN. *The Feminization of American Culture.* New York: Knopf, 1977.

FARMER, JOHN S., and HENLEY, W. E. *Dictionary of Slang and Its Analogues.* New York: University Books, 1965.

FEIDELSON, CHARLES, JR. *Symbolism and American Literature.* Chicago: University of Chicago Press, 1953.

FERGUSON, J. DE LANCEY. "The Roots of American Humor." *American Scholar* 4 (1935): 41-49.

FIEDLER, LESLIE A. *Love and Death in the American Novel.* 1966. Reprint. London: Paladin, 1970.

FIREBAUGH, JOSEPH J. "Humorist as Rebel: The Melville of *Typee.*" *Nineteenth Century Fiction* 9 (1954): 108-20.

FLETCHER, RICHARD. "Melville's Use of Marquesan." *American Speech* 39 (1964): 135-38.

FLIBBERT, JOSEPH. *Melville and the Art of Burlesque.* Amsterdam: Rodopi, 1974.

FOSTER, ELIZABETH S. Introduction and explanatory notes to *The Confidence-Man,* by Herman Melville. New York: Hendricks House, 1954.

FREDERICK, JOHN T. "Melville's Early Acquaintance with Bayle." *American Literature* 39 (1968): 545-57.

FREUD, SIGMUND. *Jokes and Their Relation to the Unconscious.* Translated by James Strachey. New York: Norton, 1963.

FRYE, NORTHRUP. *Anatomy of Criticism.* Princeton: Princeton University Press, 1957.

GILBERT, DOUGLAS. *American Vaudeville: Its Life and Times.* New York: Dover, 1940.

GILMAN, WILLIAM. *Melville's Early Life and Redburn.* New York: New York University Press, 1951.

GREEN, PETER. *Sir Thomas Browne.* London: Longmans, 1959.

GREENE, THOMAS M. *Rabelais: A Study in Comic Courage.* Englewood Cliffs: Prentice-Hall, 1970.

GRIMSTED, DAVID. *Melodrama Unveiled: American Theater and Culture, 1800-1850.* Chicago: University of Chicago Press, 1968.

GROBMAN, NEIL. "Melville's Use of Tall Tale Humor." *Southern Folklore Quarterly* 41 (1977): 183-94.

GROSS, SEYMOUR, and HARDY, JOHN, eds. *Images of the Negro in American Literature.* Chicago: University of Chicago Press, 1966.

HARTMANN, JAY H. "*Volpone* as a Possible Source for Melville's *The Confidence-Man.*" *Susquehanna University Studies* 7 (1965): 247-60.

HAUCK, RICHARD BOYD. *A Cheerful Nihilism: Confidence and "The Absurd" in American Humorous Fiction.* Bloomington: Indiana University Press, 1971.

HERBERT, T. WALTER, JR. *Moby-Dick and Calvinism, A World Dismantled.* New Brunswick: Rutgers University Press, 1977.

HERRERO, JAVIER. "Renaissance Poverty and Lazarillo's Family: The Birth of the Picaresque Genre." *PMLA* 94 (1979): 876-86.

HILLWAY, TYRUS. *Herman Melville.* New York: Twayne, 1963.

HOFFMAN, DANIEL. *Form and Fable in American Fiction.* 1961. Reprint. New York: Norton, 1973.

HOWARD, LEON. *Herman Melville, a Biography.* Berkeley: University of California Press, 1967.

HOWELLS, W. D. "Our National Humorists." *Harper's* 133 (1917): 442-45.

HUIZINGA, JOHAN. *Homo Ludens, A Study of the Play Element in Culture.* 1950. Reprint. Boston: Beacon, 1955.

The Humourist's Own Book: a cabinet of original and selected anecdotes, bons mots, sports of fancy, and traits of character: intended to furnish occasion for reflection as well as mirth. By the author of The Young Man's Own Book. Philadelphia: Desilver, Thomas, 1836.

HUNTRESS, KEITH. "Melville's Use of a Source for *White-Jacket.*" *American Literature* 17 (1945): 66-74.

JONES, BARTLETT. "American Frontier Humor in Melville's *Typee.*" *New York Folklore Quarterly* 15 (1969): 283-88.

JONES, JOSEPH. "Humor in *Moby-Dick.*" *University of Texas Studies in English* 25 (1945): 51-71.

KAZIN, ALFRED. Introduction to *Israel Potter*, by Herman Melville. New York: Warner, 1974.

KITTREDGE, GEORGE LYMAN. *The Old Farmer and His Almanack, Being Some Observations on Life and Manners in New England A Hundred Years Ago Suggested by Reading the Earlier Numbers of Mr. Robert B. Thomas's Farmer's Almanack, Together with Extracts Curious, Intrusive and Entertaining, As Well As a Variety of Miscellaneous Matter.* 1920. Reprint. New York: Benjamin Blom, 1967.

LAMB, CHARLES. *The Portable Charles Lamb, Letters and Essays.* Edited by John Mason Brown. New York: Viking, 1948.

LAUTER, PAUL. *Theories of Comedy.* Garden City: Doubleday, 1964.

LAWRENCE, D. H. *Studies in Classic American Literature.* 1923. Reprint. New York: Viking, 1964.

LEACOCK, STEPHEN. "Two Humorists: Charles Dickens and Mark Twain." *Yale Review* 23 (1934): 118-29.

LEVIN, HARRY. *Contexts of Criticism.* Harvard Studies in Comparative Literature, no. 22. Cambridge, Mass.: Harvard University Press, 1957.

————. *The Power of Blackness.* New York: Random, 1958.

————, ed. *Veins of Humor.* Harvard English Studies 3. Cambridge, Mass.: Harvard University Press, 1972.

LEWIS, R. W. B. Afterword to *The Confidence-Man,* by Herman Melville. New York: NAL, 1964.

————. *Trials of the Word.* New Haven: Yale University Press, 1965.

LEYDA, JAY. *The Melville Log, A Documentary Life Of Herman Melville, 1819-1891.* 2 vols. 1951. Reprint, with supplement. New York: Gordian, 1969.

————. "White Elephant vs. White Whale: How, in the Berkshire Festival Country, Melville wrote *Moby-Dick* with a 160-acre Incubus Round his Neck." *Town and Country* 101 (August 1947): 68, 69, 114d, 116-18.

LUCID, ROBERT. "The Influence of *Two Years Before the Mast* on Herman Melville." *American Literature* 31 (1959): 243-56.

LUKENS, HENRY CLAY. "American Literary Comedians." *Harper's* 80 (1890): 783-97.

LYNN, KENNETH S., ed. *The Comic Tradition in America.* 1958. Reprint. New York: Norton, 1968.

MANSFIELD, LUTHER. "Melville's Comic Articles on Zachary Taylor." *American Literature* 9 (1938): 411-18.

————, and VINCENT, HOWARD P. Explanatory notes to *Moby-Dick,* by Herman Melville. New York: Hendricks House, 1962.

MARX, LEO. *The Machine in the Garden.* London: Oxford University Press, 1964.

MATTHEWS, BRANDER. *The America of the Future and Other Essays.* New York: Scribner's, 1909.

MATTHIESSEN, F. O. *American Renaissance, Art and Expression in the Age of Emerson and Whitman.* New York: Oxford University Press, 1941.

Maxwell, D. E. S. *Herman Melville.* London: Routledge & Kegan Paul, 1968.

Mayoux, Jean-Jacques. *Melville.* Translated by John Ashberry. New York: Grove, 1960.

Meine, Franklin J., ed. *Tall Tales of the Southwest: An Anthology of Southern and Southwestern Humor, 1830–1860.* New York: Knopf, 1930.

Melville, Herman. "Authentic Anecdotes of 'Old Zack.'" *Yankee Doodle* 2 (1847): 152, 167, 172, 188, 199, 202, 229.

———. *Billy Budd and other Prose Pieces.* Edited by Raymond Weaver. London: Constable, 1924.

———. *Clarel, A Poem and Pilgrimage in the Holy Land.* Edited, by Walter E. Bezanson. New York: Hendricks House, 1960.

———. *Collected Poems.* Edited by Howard P. Vincent. Chicago: Packard, 1947.

———. *Journal of a Visit to London and the Continent, 1849–1850.* Edited by Eleanor Melville Metcalf. Cambridge, Mass.: Harvard University Press, 1948.

———. *Journal Up the Straits, October 11, 1856–May 5, 1857.* Edited by Raymond Weaver. 1935. Reprint. New York: Cooper Square, 1971.

———. *The Letters of Herman Melville.* Edited by Merrell R. Davis and William H. Gilman. New Haven: Yale University Press, 1960.

———. *The Portable Melville.* Edited by Jay Leyda. New York: Viking, 1952.

———. Review of *The California and Oregon Trail: Being Sketches of Prairie and Rocky Mountain Life,* by Francis Parkman, Jr. *The Literary World* 4 (1849): 291.

———. Review of *The Red Rover,* by J. Fenimore Cooper. *The Literary World* 6 (1850): 276–77.

———. Review of *The Sea Lions, or The Last Sealers: A Tale of the Antarctic Ocean,* by J. Fenimore Cooper. *The Literary World* 4 (1849): 370.

[Mercier, Henry James, and Gallop, William]. *Life in a Man-of-War, or, Scenes in 'Old Ironsides' During Her Cruise in the Pacific.* Philadelphia: Lydia Bailey, 1841.

MEREDITH, GEORGE. "An Essay on Comedy." In *Comedy*. Garden City: Doubleday, 1956.

MERWIN, W. S., trans. *The Life of Lazarillo de Tormes, His Fortunes and Adversities*. Garden City: Doubleday, 1962.

MILLER, JAMES E., JR. *A Reader's Guide to Herman Melville*. New York: Farrar, 1962.

MILLER, PERRY. *The Raven and the Whale, The War of Words and Wits in the era of Poe and Melville*. New York: Harcourt, 1956.

MONTAIGNE, MICHAEL DE. *The Works of Michael de Montaigne; Comprising His Essays, Letters, and Journey Through Germany and Italy*. Translated by Charles Cotton. Edited by William Hazlitt. 2d ed. London: Templeman, 1845.

MOORE, RICHARD. "A New Review by Melville." *American Literature* 47 (1975): 265-70.

NASH, JAY ROBERT. *An Anecdotal History of the Confidence Man and His Game*. New York: M. Evans, 1975.

NEAL, JOSEPH CLAY. *Charcoal Sketches, or Scenes in a Metropolis*. Philadelphia: Carey and Hart, 1844.

OLIVER, EGBERT S. "'Cock-A-Doodle-Doo!' and Transcendental Hocus-Pocus." *New England Quarterly* 21 (1948): 204-16.

OLSON, CHARLES. *Call Me Ishmael*. San Francisco: City Lights, 1947.

PANOFSKY, ERWIN. "Renaissance and Renascences." *Kenyon Review* 6 (1944): 201-36.

PARKER, HERSHEL. "Evidences for 'Late Insertions' in Melville's Works." *Studies in the Novel* 7 (1975): 407-24.

———, ed. *The Recognition of Herman Melville*. Ann Arbor: University of Michigan Press, 1967.

———. "Why *Pierre* Went Wrong." *Studies in the Novel* 8 (1976): 7-23.

PARTRIDGE, ERIC. *Dictionary of Slang and Unconventional English*. 7th ed. New York: Macmillan, 1970.

PILKINGTON, LAETITIA. *The Celebrated Mrs. Pilkington's Jests: or The Cabinet of Wit and Humour. To Which Is Now First Added, a Great Variety of Bon Mots, Witticisms, and Anecdotes of the Inimitable Dr. Swift*. 2d ed. London: Nicoll, 1764.

POPKIN, RICHARD. Introduction to *Historical and Critical Dictionary, Selections*, by Pierre Bayle. Indianapolis: Bobbs-Merrill, 1965.

POTTER, ISRAEL. *The Life and Remarkable Adventures of Israel R. Potter.* 1824. Reprint. Edited by Leonard Kriegel. New York: Corinth, 1962.

PRITCHETT, V. S. Review of *Dostoyevsky: Reminiscences,* by Anna Dostoyevsky. *New York Review of Books* 22 (30 October 1975): 8ff.

RABELAIS, FRANCOIS. *The Lives, Heroic Deeds and Sayings of Gargantua and His Son Pantagruel.* Translated by Sir Thomas Urquhart and Peter Le Motteux. New York: Simon, 1928.

RAMPERSAD, ARNOLD. *Melville's Israel Potter.* Bowling Green, Ohio: Bowling Green University Popular Press, 1969.

RICHTER, JOHANN PAUL FRIEDRICH. *Flower, Fruit and Thorn Pieces.* Translated by Edward Nobel. 2 vols. Boston: Monroe, 1845.

RILKE, RAINER MARIA. *Letters to a Young Poet.* Translated by M. D. Herter Norton. Rev. ed. New York: Norton, 1954.

ROSENBERRY, EDWARD H. *Melville and the Comic Spirit.* 1955. Reprint. New York: Farrar, 1969.

———. "Melville's Ship of Fools." *PMLA* 75 (1960): 604-8.

ROURKE, CONSTANCE. *American Humor, A Study of the National Character.* New York: Harcourt, 1931.

———. "Examining the Roots of American Humor." *American Scholar* 4 (1935): 249-53.

———. *The Roots of American Culture and Other Essays.* New York: Harcourt, 1942.

ROWLAND, DAVID, trans. *The Excellent History of Lazarillo de Tormes, The Witty Spaniard.* London: Hodgkinson, 1677.

RUBIN, LOUIS D., JR. ed. *The Comic Imagination in American Literature.* New Brunswick: Rutgers University Press, 1973.

SCHULZ, MAX F.; TEMPLEMAN, WILLIAM D.; AND METZGER, CHARLES R., eds. *Essays in American and English Literature Presented to Bruce Robert McElderry, Jr.* Athens: Ohio University Press, 1968.

SEALTS, MERTON W., JR. *Melville's Reading, A Check-list of Books Owned and Borrowed.* Madison: University of Wisconsin Press, 1966.

SEDGWICK, WILLIAM E. *Herman Melville, The Tragedy of Mind.* Cambridge, Mass.: Harvard University Press, 1944.

SEELYE, JOHN. *Melville: The Ironic Diagram.* Evanston: Northwestern University Press, 1970.

SELTZER, LEON F. "Camus's Absurd and the World of Melville's *Confidence-Man.*" *PMLA* 82 (1967): 14-27.

SHROEDER, JOHN. "Sources and Symbols for Melville's *Confidence-Man.*" *PMLA* 66 (1951): 364-80.

SHULMAN, ROBERT. "The Serious Functions of Melville's Phallic Jokes." *American Literature* 33 (1961): 179-94.

SMITH, HENRY NASH. *Virgin Land: The American West as Symbol and Myth.* New York: Random, 1950.

SMITH, JAMES L. *Melodrama.* London: Methuen, 1973.

STAFFORD, WILLIAM T., ed. *Billy Budd and the Critics.* 2d ed. Belmont, Calif.: Wadsworth, 1968.

STERN, MILTON R. *The Fine-Hammered Steel of Herman Melville.* Urbana: University of Illinois Press, 1957.

STEWART, GEORGE. "The Two *Moby-Dicks.*" *American Literature* 25 (1954): 417-48.

STEWART, RANDALL. *American Literature and Christian Doctrine.* Baton Rouge: Louisiana State University Press, 1958.

TAVE, STUART. *The Amiable Humorist, A Study in the Comic Theory and Criticism of the 18th and Early 19th Centuries.* Chicago: University of Chicago Press, 1960.

THOMPSON, HAROLD W. *Body, Boots and Britches.* Philadelphia: Lippincott, 1940.

THOMPSON, LAWRANCE. *Melville's Quarrel with God.* Princeton: Princeton University Press, 1952.

THORP, WILLARD. Introduction to *Herman Melville: Representative Selections.* New York: American Book, 1938.

TRACY, C. R. "Democritus Arise! A Study of Dr. Johnson's Humor." *Yale Review* 39 (1950): 294-310.

VINCENT, HOWARD P. *The Tailoring of White-Jacket.* Evanston: Northwestern University Press, 1970.

———. *The Trying-Out of Moby-Dick.* Boston: Houghton Mifflin, 1949.

W., H. Review of seven books of American humor, by Titterwell, Samuel Slick, David Crockett, and Jack Downing. *Westminster Review* 32 (1838): 136-45.

WARD, AILEEN. Foreword to *Confessions of an English Opium Eater and Other Writings,* by Thomas De Quincey. New York: NAL, 1966.

WELLS, WHITNEY HASTINGS. *"Moby-Dick* and Rabelais." *Modern Language Notes* 38 (1923): 123.

WELSFORD, ENID. *The Fool—His Social and Literary History.* New York: Farrar and Rinehart, 1935.

WILLIAMS, STANLEY T. *The Spanish Background of American Literature.* 2 vols. Hamden, Conn.: Archon, 1968.

The Young Lady's Book of Elegant Poetry: comprising selections from the works of British and American Poets. By the author of The Young Man's Own Book. Philadelphia: Key & Biddle, 1835.

The Young Man's Book of Classical Letters or, The Classical Letter-Writer, consisting of epistolary selections; designed to improve young ladies and gentlemen in the art of letter-writing . . . By the author of The Young Man's Own Book. Philadelphia: Key & Biddle, 1835.

The Young Man's Own Book: a manual of politeness, intellectual improvement and moral deportment, calculated to form the character on a solid basis and to insure respectability and success in life. Philadelphia: Key, Meikle & Biddle, 1832.

Index

If a character is not listed, a reference may be found by checking the pages indicated for the work in which he or she appears. Works are listed under the author's name.

Abimelech, 12, 13
acatalepsy, 12, 95, 106
Adam, 46, 154, 158
Africans, 34, 144
Ahab, 56, 82, 83, 86–88, 96–97, 104, 110, 119, 156, 174
Alcofrybas, 8, 90, 105
Aldington, Richard, 165
allegory, 13, 105, 124, 135, 139, 152, 158, 174, 177
Allen, Ethan, 123
almanac, 6, 32–35, 108–109
America, 30, 48, 58, 65, 72, 79, 106–108, 119–32, 158, 167, 173
American culture, 54, 84, 89, 90, 94, 104, 163, 174
American humor, 2, 30–36, 54, 75–78, 103–110, 113–14, 150, 168
American language, 34, 108, 172
American literature, 3, 5, 7, 35, 55, 95, 136, 157, 168, 170
American Revolution, 127
amiable humor, 2, 17, 20, 31–32, 162, 166
anatomy, 2, 57–59, 82, 90, 92–95, 100, 107, 172
Antigone, 96
Apollo, 18
Arabia, 63
Ariosto, Lodovico, 18
aristocrat, 10, 55, 164
Aristophanes, 94
Arriaga, Roderic De, 13
Artemus Ward, 24

Arvin, Newton, 68, 177
astronomy, 11, 21, 26, 34, 130
atheism, 84, 92, 106
Atlantic Ocean, 41, 110
Auerbach, Erich, 10, 164

Babb, Lawrence, 166
Babbalanja, 49, 51–52, 54–61, 80, 124, 132, 154
Babo, 74, 142–46
Bakhtin, Mikhail, 164
Barbour, James, 169
Barnum, P. T., 77, 104–106, 133
Barthes, Roland, 40, 77
Bartholomew, Saint, 175
Bartleby, 110–20, 130
"Bartleby" lawyer, 74, 110–20, 132
Bayle, Pierre, *Historical and Critical Dictionary,* 2, 7, 11–14, 19, 20, 22, 106–107, 165
Beckett, Samuel, *Waiting for Godot,* 84, 113
Bell, Millicent, 13–14, 165
Bergson, Henri, 97
Berthoff, Warner, 154
beverages, 25, 99, 129; command to drink, 9; *see also* laudanum, milk, tea, water, wine
Bible, 10, 52, 74, 124, 125, 177; Pentateuch, 54, 71; New Testament, 16, 137, 156; *see also* separate books
blacks (Negroes), 29, 102, 104, 106, 143–46

Blair, Walter, 168
blue devils (blues), 59, 96
Böll, Heinrich, *The Clown,* 159
borrowing, 3, 7, 11, 16, 22, 24, 31, 164, 166; *see also* Melville, models
Brant, Sebastian, 177
Braswell, William, 178
Brown, Herbert Ross, 163
Browne, Sir Thomas, 27, 50, 54
Bunker Hill, 124
Bunyan, John, *Pilgrim's Progress,* 50, 124, 139, 177
burlesque, 10-11, 34
Burton, Robert, 168; *Anatomy of Melancholy,* 2, 5-7, 18-21, 24-27, 31-32, 50-52, 55-59, 86, 92-97, 103, 106-108, 166, 172

Caledonians, 28-30, 62, 72, 100, 137
Calvinism, 13-14
cannibalism, 40-43, 48, 53, 61, 71, 79, 84, 100, 102, 103, 167
Cape Horn, 65, 73, 75
Carroll, Lewis, *Alice in Wonderland,* 105
Catholicism, 138; the Index, 15
Cato, Marcus, 92, 96, 173
Cervantes, Miguel de, *Don Quixote,* 31, 177
Chapman, George, 64
characterization, 3, 10, 19, 30; *see also* particular characters, particular character types, and Melville, characterization
Chase, Richard, 3, 89, 104-107, 156, 163, 171, 174, 176, 179
Chasles, Philarète, 170
Chaucer, Geoffrey, 50
Christ, 102, 124, 130, 154-58, 179
Christianity, 14, 27, 45-47, 84, 93, 158
chronicle, 6
Chronicles, 52
cock-and-bull story, 2, 90, 95-97
Coleridge, Samuel Taylor, 50, 92
Columbus, Christopher, 11
comedy, 11, 16-17, 37, 49-51, 82, 102, 113, 128, 152, 171
comic Prometheus, 56, 59, 104-105
Conant, Martha Pike, 167
Conarroe, Joel O., 175

conduct book, 46-47, 170
Confidence-Man, the, 44, 97, 123-25, 131-38, 140-41, 176
Congregationalism, 82
Conrad, Joseph, *Heart of Darkness,* 40
consolatio, 19, 24, 86, 95
conte philosophe, 21, 167
Copernicus, Nicolaus, 19, 93
Crates, 13
Crockett, Davy, 2, 35, 54, 104, 108; *Almanac,* 35; *Autobiography,* 35
Cyrano de Bergerac, Savinien, 11; *Comical History of the States and Empires of the Worlds of the Moon and Sun (Voyage to the Moon),* 2, 7, 10-11, 25, 126, 165

Dana, Richard Henry, 70, 77
Dante Alighieri, 50
Davis, Merrell R., 170, 171
democracy, 4, 55, 58, 62, 65, 79, 83, 91, 131, 160
Democritus, 19, 93
Democritus Junior, 18-20, 24, 55-58, 92-95, 103, 105, 166
De Quincey, Thomas, 26; *Confessions of an English Opium Eater,* 2, 7, 24-27, ·32, 90, 97-102, 107; "Suspira Profundis," 100
Descartes, René, 11, 57, 102
desire, 6-9, 20-21, 44, 48, 57, 62, 105-107, 111-113, 116, 124, 127, 136, 145
Devil, the, and demonic, 47, 51, 124, 137-39, 163
devils, 44, 57, 81, 86; blue devils (blues), 59, 96
Dickens, Charles, 58, 120
dicta, *veni vidi vici,* 9; *I desire, I am (What I desire to be, I am)* 9, 11, 55, 58, 105, 111; *I think therefore I am,* 11, 58; *I feel and that's all I know,* 58
dictionary, 6, 12, 22, 174
Diedrich Knickerbocker, 30-31, 114
Diogenes Laërtius, *Lives and Opinions of Eminent Philosophers,* 21-22
diptych, 119-25
discourse, 6, 21, 29-30, 37, 59, 154
Dorson, Richard, 33

Dostoyevsky, Fëdor, 135–36; *Crime and Punishment,* 40; *The Idiot,* 156; *Notes from Underground,* 136
Douglas, Ann, 163
drink, *see* beverages
Dutch, the, 30, 64
Duyckinck, Evert, 14, 75, 100, 165

Ecclesiastes, 52
Eden, 14, 46
Egyptian pyramids, 18, 102
Elia, 24, 27–30, 70, 100–103, 105, 115–17, 174
Eliot, T.S., "The Love Song of J. Alfred Prufrock," 145
Emerson, Ralph Waldo, 123
encyclopedia, 6, 7, 12, 19, 22, 26, 33, 47, 61, 107
England, 2, 18, 20, 33, 71, 84, 95, 119–23, 127–28, 153–55
English language, 34, 162
English literature, 2, 7, 16–30, 136, 168
Enlightenment, 12, 130
Erasmus, Desiderius, *Praise of Folly,* 162, 166, 177
erudition, *see* knowledge
essay, 38, 54, 70, 90, 100–103, 107–108, 115–17; *see also* Irving, Lamb, and Montaigne
Europe, 30–32, 34, 104, 106, 116, 120
European literature, 5, 36, 105, 109
evangelism, 1, 132
evil, 14, 40–43, 64, 143, 177
exploration, *see* travel
extravagance, 4, 6, 10–11, 15, 23, 49–52, 62, 79, 130, 138
extravaganza, 2, 7, 19, 86, 90–95, 103, 106

farce, 149
Farmer's Almanack, 7, 33
Feidelson, Charles, Jr., 41
female and femininity, *see* women
Ferguson, J. De Lancey, 168
Ferriar, John, *Illustrations of Sterne,* 166
Fiedler, Leslie A., 163
Fielding, Henry, 31
Flask, 83, 84

Flaubert, Gustave, "A Simple Heart," 156
Fleece, 82, 105
foible, 17, 100, 140, 162
folk and folklore, 5, 10, 32–36, 89–90, 104–110, 114, 164, 174
folk humor (periodical humor), *see* American humor
folly, 7, 162, 166, 177
forms, 2–6, 21–22, 33–38, 89–107, 124, 157, 167, *see* particular forms
Foster, Elizabeth, 177
France, 33, 43, 153–55
Franklin, Benjamin, 123, 129–30; *Poor Richard's Almanac,* 91
French literature, 7–14
frontier, 1–7, 10–11, 21, 31–32, 72, 89–90, 104, 107, 120, 159, 177
frontier humor, *see* prose humor
Frye, Northrup, 172
Fuller, Margaret, 167

Gansevoort, Catherine, 179
Gansevoort, Henry, 179
Gansevoort, Peter, 180
Genesis, 11, 27, 46–47, 52
genres, 10, 22, 170, *see* forms
Geoffrey Crayon, 24, 31, 103, 105
George, Saint, 84
George III (of England), 126–27
German romantic, 51
giant, 6–10, 19, 22–23, 34, 90–93, 105, 129, 135
Gilman, William, 73
Glanius, *Voyage to Bengala,* 162
God, 3, 8, 10, 14–16, 35, 45–47, 53, 59, 61, 66, 74, 83, 88, 127, 138–39, 145, 148, 150, 155, 156, 163
gods and godly, 9, 21, 45, 54–55, 59, 61, 83–84, 104, 124, 146
Goethe, Johann von, 50
Goldsmith, Oliver, *History of the Earth and Animated Nature,* 47
gothic, 26
Greece, 153

Hall, James, 137
Hallwachs, Robert G., 166

Hanway, Jonas, 25
Happy Valley, 20–21, 23, 26–27, 32, 47–48, 98, 167
Hardy, Thomas, 122; *Mayor of Casterbridge,* 118; *Tess of the Durbervilles,* 119
Harry Bolton, 73–74, 110
Hartmann, Jay H., 177
Hatch, Agatha, 118, 121, 130, 149
Hawthorne, Nathaniel, 3, 13, 124, 149–52, 157, 163, 177; "The Birthmark," 157; "The Celestial Railroad," 139, 177; "Wakefield," 113–18
Hazlitt, William, 101
head and heart, 23
Heraclitus, 19
Hercules, 9, 18–19, 84, 126
heresy, 1, 4, 14, 15, 20, 29, 91, 93, 136
Herodotus, 50
Hill, Hamlin, 168
Hinduism, 84
Hipparchia, 13
hoax, 1, 30, 89, 105–106, 116–17
Hogarth, William, 120
Homer, 50, 51, 64
Howard, Leon, 152, 169, 180
hubris, 96
Hudson River, 125
humanism, 129, 162, 163
humor, 3, 17, 21, 140, 162; *see also* American humor, amiable humor, and prose humor
humors, 3, 16–17, 46, 61, 89, 162
humors character, 16, 39, 58–59, 70, 114–15, 124, 155
hypo, 92, 95–97, 173

Indians, 33, 85, 101, 107, 134–37, 177; Neversink Indians, 103; Pequod Indians, 103; Sioux Indians, 129
irony, 15, 16, 19, 30, 88, 121, 142–47, 152, 153, 156
Irving, Washington, 2, 30–32, 90, 101, 103, 107, 125, 152, 168, 172; *History of New York,* 30, 168; *Sketch Book,* 7, 31–32, 103, 107 113–18, 125, 168
Isaac, 12

Isabel, 148–51, 158, 178
Ishmael, 24, 56, 77, 80–94, 97–110, 116, 119, 127, 132, 155, 156, 173
Islam, 84, 93
isolatoes, 82, 87, 100, 117

Jack Chase, *see* "jacks"
"jacks," 68; Jack Chase, 1, 62–64, 68–69, 80, 151, 155; Happy Jack, 68; White-Jacket, 58, 60–69, 151, 156; Mad Jack, 65, 68
Jackson, Andrew, 1
Jael, 29
James, Henry, 70, 160
jeu d'esprit, 2, 11, 125
Jews, *see* Judaism
Johnson, Samuel, 5, 25–26, 29, 54, 97, 134, 168, 173; *Rasselas,* 7, 20–21, 47–49, 167, *see* Happy Valley
Jonah, 84
Jonathan Jaw-Stretcher's Yankee Story All-My-Nack, 7, 34; "The Very Latest Glimpse O' the Great Sea-Serpent," 34, 108
Jones, John Paul, 123, 127, 129
Jonson, Ben, 16–18, 139; *Bartholomew Fair,* 177; *Every Man in His Humor,* 16; *Every Man Out of His Humor,* 7, 16–18, 139–40; *Volpone,* 17, 142, 177
Josh Billings, 24
Judaism and Jews, 14, 29, 33, 46, 84, 124, 126
Jupiter, 18

Kazin, Alfred, 131, 159
Kepler, Johannes, 11
Kerouac, Jack, *Dharma Bums,* 71
Kings, 52
knowledge and learning, 9, 11, 19, 22–27, 32–34, 45, 47, 89–90, 95, 102, 106–108, 129–30

Lamb, Charles, 2, 27–30, 38, 90, 100–101, 107, 117, 175; "Barbara S——," 112, 116; *Curious Fragments, Extracted from a Common-place Book Which Belonged to Robert Burton,* 166; "Imperfect Sympathies," 7, 28–30;

"The Old Margate Hoy," 28; "Oxford Vacation," 175; "South-Sea House," 30, 113-19, 175
Lamb, Mary, 27
Latin, 13
laudanum, 25-26
Laurel and Hardy, 82
Lazarillo de Tormes, 7, 14-18, 26, 106, 139
Lazarus, 16
learning, *see* knowledge
Lemsford, 38, 68, 151
letter, 38, 77
Levin, Harry, 177
Lewis, R.W.B., 117, 137
Leyda, Jay, 167
libertine, 11, 105
Literary World, The, 170, 173
Liverpool, 73
London, 27, 30, 74, 116, 119-20, 130, 176
Lucian, 177

machinery, 21, 30, 58, 63, 97, 104, 121, 134
Mackenzie, Henry, *Man of Feeling* and *Man of the World,* 133
Maimonides, Moses, *Guide to the Perplexed,* 12
male, *see* men
Manhattan, 103, 160
Manicheanism, 14
Manifest Destiny, 104
Mansfield, Luther, 96, 171, 173
Mapple, Father, 80, 82
Mars (god of war), 18, 59
Massachusetts, 125
Matthews, Brander, 168
Matthiessen, F.O., 131, 166, 178
Mayoux, Jean-Jacques, 99, 173
medieval, 6, 9, 164, 177
melancholy, 18-20, 26, 31-32, 59, 90-100, 106-109, 121, 141, 166, 172
melodrama, 3, 32, 40, 51, 57, 62, 96, 136, 152
Melvill, Allan, 20, 170
Melvill[e], Maria Gansevoort (Mrs. Allan Melvill), 180
Melville, Augusta, 150
Melville, Elizabeth Shaw (Mrs. Herman Melville), 51, 150, 179, 180

Melville, Herman, his era, 1-3, 21, 32-34, 48, 60, 72-79, 104-109, 162-63, 167, 168; family, 20, 51, 150, 156-57, 170, 179, 180; development as prose writer, 2, 5, 7, 37-40, 49-61, 64, 68-80, 91, 95, 119-22, 127, 148-61, 169-70; narrative stance, 17, 38, 60, 61, 70, 80, 82, 92-93, 109, 119, 152-53, 155; characterization, 39, 49-51, 56-61, 68, 71, 73-74, 87, 118-22, 124, 149-51, 154-58, 179; style, 2, 39, 42, 47, 50, 53, 61-62, 64, 131, 143, 152, 154; models, 2-37, 40, 46, 52, 54-60, 67-71, 75-78, 86, 89-110, 113-19, 123, 131, 139-42, 149, 157-59, 162-64, 170, 174-75; chronology of reading, 5, 10, 11, 14, 16, 18, 20, 21, 24, 27, 30, 32, 40, 50, 163, 165, 172; religious views, 3, 13-14, 45, 84, 92, 163, *see* God and religion; ideas in his novels, 11, 60, 101; the Agatha story, 118-19, 121, 130, 149; Agatha as representative of what he could not encompass in his prose, 148-61; poetry, 5, 122, 159, 178; prose: "The Apple-Tree Table," 152; "Authentic Anecdotes of 'Old Zack,'" 69, 75-78, 171; "Bartleby," 2, 74, 103, 110-20, 130, 132, 157-58, 175; "Benito Cereno," 74, 142-48, 157, 178; "Billy Budd," 153-58, 160, 179; "Cock-A-Doodle-Doo!," 172; *The Confidence-Man,* 2, 76, 119, 122-25, 131-42, 176, 177; "The Encantadas," 118, 152-53; "Fragments from a Writing-Desk," 20; "The Happy Failure," 152-53, 155; "I and My Chimney," 152-53; *Israel Potter,* 2, 119, 122-31, 138, 142, 176; "Jimmy Rose," 152-53, 155; *Journal of a Visit to London and the Continent,* 119; *Letters of Herman Melville,* 14, 30, 38, 76-77, 118-19, 170, 175, 178; *Mardi,* 37-39, 41, 49-61, 69, 72, 79, 91, 95, 119, 127, 134, 149, 150, 170; *Moby-Dick,* 2, 5, 14, 37-39, 42, 45, 54, 56, 59, 69, 71, 75, 79-110, 119, 133, 167, 172-74; *Omoo,* 37, 38,

69-73; "The Paradise of Bachelors and Tartarus of Maids," 119-22, 149; "The Piazza," 118, 149; *Pierre*, 74, 75, 148-52, 157, 178, 179; "Poor Man's Pudding and Rich Man's Crumbs," 119-22; *Redburn*, 37-38, 69, 72-75, 110; "The South Seas" (lecture), 174; "The Two Temples," 119-22; *Typee*, 37-53, 61, 64, 68-70, 76, 79, 87, 127, 149, 156, 167, 169, 170; *White-Jacket*, 1, 24, 37-39, 42, 49, 53, 59-69, 71, 75, 77, 79-80, 127, 151, 155, 158
Melville, Malcolm, 156-57, 179
men (males), 2-3, 6-10, 17, 35-36, 39, 49, 53, 79, 87-92, 95, 100, 108, 113-14, 120-22, 126-32, 136-39, 150-51, 153, 159, 174
mendicants, 164
Menippean satire, 172
Mercier, Henry James, and Gallop, William [A Fore-top-man], *Life in a Man-of-War*, 67-68
Mexican War, 75
Midas, King, 107
milk, 90, 92, 107
Miller, James, Jr., 169
Miller, Perry, 170
Milton, John, *Paradise Lost*, 138, 177
mind, 3, 6, 13, 20-23, 28, 60, 90, 151
missionaries, 51, 69-72
Mississippi River, 132
Moby Dick, 14, 82, 86-88, 90, 91, 97, 110, 119
Molière, 11
monologue, 4, 6, 22, 80, 86, 89, 95, 97, 99, 101, 105, 110, 136, 151, 159
Montaigne, Michel de, 14, 171, "Du Repentir," 87
motifs, 2, 41, 53, 89, 104-105, 148-49, 164

Nantucket, 81, 118
Napoleon, 153
Nash, Jay Robert, 177
Negroes, *see* blacks
New Holland, 33
New World, 2, 5, 9-10, 20, 30-33, 107, 116, 125-32, 138, 142, 151, 164, 177
New York, 30, 33

Northwest Passage, 23
novel of sensibility, 2, 90, 95-97, 133

obscenity, 9, 13, 55, 90
Oedipus, 96
opium, 25-26, 97, 99, 106

Pacific Islands, 72
Pacific Ocean, 41, 54
Panofsky, Erwin, 162, 177
parable, 49, 177
paradise, 14, 20-21, 42, 46, 48, 61, 72, 116, 156, *see* Happy Valley
paradox, 19, 47-48, 57, 72, 132, 137, 139
Paris, 129
Parker, Hershel, 169, 179
parody, 1, 34, 42, 70, 77, 87, 95, 100, 107
Parsee, 88
Perseus, 83, 84
persona, 19, 20, 24, 26, 93, 109; *see also* Melville (narrative stance), and pseudonymic humorists
Peru, 91
Peter, Saint, 175
philosophical tale, 21, 167
picaresque novel, 14-16, 18, 26, 37, 71, 106, 123-24, 131, 139, 177
Pip, 82, 91
Plater (Platter), Felix, 94
Plato, 103
Poe, Edgar Allan, 92, 102
Popkin, Richard, 12, 14
Potter, Israel (author), 123
practical jokes, 9, 15, 26, 75, 90, 114-16, 138, 139
Pritchett, V.S., 135
Procrustes, 142
progress, 1, 33-34
Prometheus, 9, 27, 35, 51, 56, 59, 104, 105
prose, 4-10, 17, 37-38, 50, 57-60, 122, 154-59, 169
prose humor, 2-37, 82, 89, 113, 158-62
Protestantism, 13
Psalms, 52
pseudonymic humorists and monologuists, 24, *see* individual humorist-monologuists (under their first names)
pun, 27, 96, 141

Puritans, 32, 42, 126
Pyrrhonism, 14

Queequeg, 80, 82, 84, 87–88, 94, 103, 110, 119, 127, 155, 156, 173
quest, 7, 141, 149, 151, see travel

Rabelais, François, 18, *Gargantua and Pantagruel,* 2, 7–11, 20, 22–25, 31, 50, 55, 57, 90–92, 95, 106–108, 164, 166, 170; *Pantagrueline Prognostications,* 34
Radney, 96
Rampersad, Arnold, 176
Rebecca, 12
Redburn, 24, 70, 72–74, 110
Reform Movement (in pre–Civil War United States), 1
religion, 10–11, 17, 40, 47, 84, 91–95, see particular religions
Renaissance, 2–6, 15–19, 22–25, 32–33, 105–107, 129–30, 159, 162, 164, 177
Rilke, Rainer Maria, 160
rogue, 9, 14–16, 35, 71, 105, 124, 132, 139
romance, 3–4, 37, 48–49, 172
romantic, 63, 89, 131, 148
Romantic period, 2, 51, 56, 59, 108, 166, 173
Rosenberry, Edward, 149, 163, 171, 177, 178
Rosicrucians, 19
Rourke, Constance, 132, 163, 168, 176
Russian literature, 136

Sam Slick, 104
Samson, 18, 126
Satan, see Devil
satire, 11, 16, 27, 47, 73–75, 120, 122, 130, 135, 139, 144, 148–53, 172, 178
scatology, 9, 20
scholasticism, 6, 9, 13
science, 10–11, 19, 22, 26, 33, 54, 93, 104, 106
Scoresby, William, 99
Scotch, the, see Caledonians
Scott, Sir Walter, 168
Sealts, Merton W., Jr., 163
sea serpent, 2, 34–35, 108
Sedgwick, William, 177

Seneca, Lucius, 80, 93
sensibility, 24, 46, 54, 57–59, 68, 69, 90, 96–97, 100, 107, 133–37, 154, see novel of sensibility
sentimentality, 3–4, 34, 47, 50, 72, 148, 150, 153, 163
sentimental novel, 3, 89
sermon, 6, 10, 82, 134, 164
sex, sexuality and eroticism, 1, 4–9, 12–13, 20, 22–23, 35, 41, 43, 48–50, 53–54, 87–91, 95, 119, 148, 151, 174
Shakespeare, William, 32, 50, 84, 91, 101, 177; *King Lear,* 96; *Much Ado About Nothing,* 113
Shaw, Lemuel, 180
Silverstein, Shel, 40
Sisyphus, 126
skepticism, 56, 80, 96, 129
sketch, 38, 107, 120–22, 152; see Irving, *Sketch Book*
Smollett, Tobias, 16, 71
sociability, 38, 43, 57, 61, 147
Southey, Robert, *The Doctor* and *Commonplace Book,* 173
South Sea Bubble, 116, 132
South Sea Islanders, 33
South Seas, 30, 70
Spain, 144–46
Spanish literature, 7, 14–16, 18, see picaresque novel
Spenser, Edmund, 50, 51, 124, 152
spleen, 19, 92, 95–96
Starbuck, 83, 85
Sterne, Laurence, *Tristram Shandy,* 2, 7, 21–25, 70, 90, 95–97, 105, 107, 108, 130, 172–73, 177
Stewart, George, 37, 169
Stoics, 19, 80, 94
Stubb, 82–84, 86, 90, 101, 104, 105, 159
Stuyvesant, Peter, 103
style, 2, 5, 7, 13, 26, 47, 50, 152, 166; see Melville, style
Swift, Jonathan, 11, 31, 50
symbolism, 41

taboo, 45, 48
Tacitus, Cornelius, 177
Tahiti, 70–72

Taji, 51–56, 59, 68, 156
talk, 57, 61, 82–86, 89–91, 132–36, 139, 170, 176
tall tale, 2, 7, 35, 83, 90, 104, 105
Tave, Stuart, 162, 166
Taylor, Zachary, 75–77
tea, 25–26, 99
Templars, 121
theology, 45, 60, *see* religion
Thomas, Robert, "Fifty Years Ago!," 33–34, 108
Thompson, Lawrance, 163
Thoreau, Henry, 123
Thorpe, T.B., "The Big Bear of Arkansas," 36
Tindall, William York, 154
titans, 104, 116, 126
Tom, Dick, and Harry, 108
Tommo, 39, 40–49, 53, 56, 156
Tories, 123, 129
Tracey, C.R., 166
tragedy, 4, 85, 105, 149–54, 157, 163
transcendentalism, 1
travel, 3, 6–12, 15–16, 20–23, 52, 55, 72, 90–94, 129, 152–53, 164
travel narrative, 3, 37, 49, 50, 70, 89, 152
trickster, 104–105, 132, 138
Trismegistus, 22–23, 130
Tristram Shandy, 22–24, 95, 130
Troy, 153

Turks, 33
twister, 2, 90, 95, 107

vagabond, 6, 15–17, 26, 70
vagary, 6, 20, 23
Varmifuge Vampose, 2, 34, 108
Venus, 17
vernacular, 10, 13, 90
Vincent, Howard, 61, 170, 173
Vishnoo, 84

Wall Street, 118
Washington, George, 103–104
water, 20, 25–26, 81–82, 98–99, 120, 161
whites (Caucasians) 40, 46, 51, 60, 79, 85, 106, 144
wine, 20, 25–26, 120
wit, 113
women, 6–9, 13, 29, 39, 43, 49–51, 53, 60, 62, 71, 87, 90–91, 113–22, 149–51, 157–58, 163

Yankee Doodle, 75
Yankees, 30, 34, 71, 104, 110, 123, 135, 138; Yankee pedlars, 104, 138, 164, 176
Yannella, Donald, 172
yarn, 38, 49, 64, 67, 104, 107
Yillah, 51, 150, 158
Young Man's Own Book, 46, 170

The text of this book has been typeset in
Bembo by Autopage Book Composition,
Inc., Oceanside, New York. The book has
been printed on a low-acid, long-lived
paper by Cushing-Malloy, Inc., of Ann
Arbor, Michigan. Riverside Book Bind-
ery, Inc., Rochester, New York has bound
the book.